FAERIE BLOOD

THE CHANGELING CHRONICLES: BOOK 1

EMMA L. ADAMS

When I was sixteen years old, I walked out of hell, thinking I'd finally be free of the faeries.

Ten years later, the joke was on me. Instead of spending my Saturday afternoon lazing around at home, there I was, deep in a troll's lair with a piskie hovering over my shoulder.

"He took my friend's charm," whined the piskie.

"Yes, you said." I continued sorting through the array of junk the troll had gathered, searching for the tell-tale glint of a spell. Charms were notoriously tricky to get right, but given the wad of cash on offer, I'd get a nice bonus if I returned this one to its rightful owner.

In the suburbs, you took whatever work you could get, even skulking around a troll's nest. I'd had to wait until the beast went off hunting before I risked sneaking in. As far as enjoyment went, I'd rank the experience somewhere up there with putting a harness on a kelpie. Though at least kelpies didn't smell like a blocked drain. Grimacing, I shoved a heap of human clothes aside that I hoped had been acquired via theft and not as a bonus from its latest meal. Trying to make faeries obey human laws was tricky at the best of times, but I drew the line at sifting through troll dung to figure out if it had recently consumed a human being or not. Luckily, that job fell to the clean-up squad, who sat one rank below me on the less-than-impressive ladder of poor souls freelancing for Larsen Crawley.

The word "freelancer" sounded like it ought to mean something like "dragon slayer". In my case, that was almost literally true, but there was zero glamour in kneeling in unappealing wetness to sift through contraband. Trolls had magpie-like tendencies for reasons I couldn't fathom, and I found several charms nestled beneath a pile of old computer parts.

"Gotcha." I identified the small, glinting cylindrical charm from among the others. "What kind of spell is this?"

"Beautification," said the piskie.

Figures. I slid the charm into my pocket and headed towards the exit.

A shuffling noise came from ahead and drew me to a halt as the troll's hulking frame filled the entryway. Oh, shit. I'd planned to confront the creature later, sure, but not here in its cramped nest. Trolls were notoriously territorial. Great job there, Ivy.

I reached for the sword I kept sheathed at my waist, waving farewell to my resolution to get through this without unnecessary bloodshed. The troll bellowed, swinging a giant fist at me. I ducked, inwardly cursing the cave's tight walls, and drew the blade from its sheath. Towering over me despite the low ceiling, the troll's body resembled a misshapen boulder and was resilient to virtually anything.

Except—like all faeries, with no exception—iron.

I repositioned myself, raising my sword, hoping it'd have the good sense to move before I had to use it. Unfortunately, expecting good sense from a troll was like expecting manners from a brain-eating boggart, and the blade glanced off the troll's arm. I hadn't put all my weight behind it, but the bright spray of blood made the troll scream in alarm and stomp its huge feet hard enough to shake the whole lair. A second swing of its fist sent me reeling sideways, my feet skidding right into a pile of... *ugh. Troll dung.*

"Take a hint," I snarled, swinging the blade again. Already the iron had left a spiderweb of cracks along the troll's massive arm, and its feet stumbled, driving me further back into the dung heap. "I'm sparing your life, boulder-brain."

Boulder-brain aimed another punch at my head. I ducked, and the troll's fist went straight through the wall of its own lair. The troll roared and tried to pull its hand free, sending bits of crumbling rock over my head, but its fist was well and truly stuck.

As its other hand swiped at me, I dropped to the ground, crawled between its legs and pointed my blade at its spine. The troll flailed its free arm, howling in frustration. I'd have laughed at its predicament if I wasn't doing my absolute best to forget what I'd just crawled through. Naturally, the piskie had disappeared into thin air at the troll's appearance, and not a soul remained in the nest except for the pair of us. Oh, and my sword, of course. Irene had been my faithful companion through ten years of fighting the evil forces of Faerie and laying down the law. The iron gleamed even through the vibrant bluish-red sheen of the troll's blood on its tip.

"You're lucky I only gave you a warning," I told the troll. "I'm confiscating the charm you stole, and representatives from the city's council will be here shortly to question you and to confiscate anything else you might have taken unlawfully." I suspected everything here in its nest was stolen, but the interrogation wasn't my job. I was just the sword-for-hire, the runner of dangers. Someone who played nicer with others would be in charge of trying to get a response from my adversary that didn't consist solely of grunts.

"Well?" I gave the troll one last warning tap on the spine with my sword. Faint red lines fanned outward, the result of faeries' incurable allergy to iron. "Do you understand me?"

"Yes," the troll whimpered. "Yes, Lady Sidhe."

"I'm not Sidhe," I said. "I'm human."

The hilt of my sword struck the back of its head, and the troll crumpled, its hand still wedged in the earthen wall.

Job done. Even Larsen wouldn't let me into the guild in this state, so I resigned myself to heading home first to pick up a cleansing spell from my flatmate, Isabel. Once I'd cleaned up, I'd collect my bounty. Troll dung aside, the faerie blood on my blade would attract all kinds of trouble. The kind worse than a pissed-off troll.

Twenty years on from the faeries' arrival and we were still cleaning up their mess. Summer and Winter Sidhe might have supposedly come to Earth to stop humans destroying one another, but when they'd buggered off home, they'd left us saddled with their monsters squatting under our bridges and nesting in our rafters. There were no Seelie or Unseelie Courts here, and no path back to Faerie, but the fae probably fared better in our realm because there was a marginally lower chance of being flayed alive.

Isabel sometimes remarked that the faeries got the raw end of the deal. I wasn't inclined to agree.

As I was setting up a ward outside the troll's nest in case it woke up, the piskie reappeared at my side. "Thanks for the help," I muttered. "Really appreciate it."

The piskie fluttered its tiny gossamer wings. "I am honoured, human."

I rolled my eyes. Faeries truly were the most literal creatures in existence.

Time to go home. I didn't have far to walk—good job,

because taking the bus in this state was out of the question—but Isabel and I lived on the cusp between witch and shifter territories, and it was still light enough for me to draw revolted stares from both as I made my sorry way home. By the time I'd showered, changed and left my clothes to soak in the bath, it was early evening and I was starved, so I took a detour to grab some takeout Chinese on the way to the guild. I munched on stir-fried noodles as I walked through what had once been an ordinary suburb of south Birmingham before the faeries' invasion had ripped it in two and the exposed supernaturals laid claim to various parts of what remained. Invariably, the influx of magic into the city brought the need for those willing to do the uncomfortable work of making sure the surviving half of the regular human population didn't suffer too much damage as a result.

The squat red-brick construction where Larsen's guild was located had likely been a normal office building once, but now its rooms were full of weapons and storage lockers packed with questionable junk of the sort I'd found in the troll's lair. There was a gym and a target practise hall around the back, but I only used them when nobody else was around, for the most part. Mercs were given to indulging in nonsensical competitive stunts that usually ended with the equipment broken and someone taking a hospital trip.

Larsen accosted me at the doors, wearing his usual scowl. His sloppy T-shirt-and-jeans getup was more suited to a seedy bar than an organised guild of professional mercenaries, but this was hardly an elite establishment. Anyone who couldn't afford to hire a mage to solve their supernatural problems came to Larsen... as a last resort.

"There you are. I was beginning to think I'd need to send someone after you." He looked me up and down with a mixture of suspicion and contempt, along with a not-insignificant level of annoyance that I'd come back in one piece. Why he thought being the head of what amounted to a magical lost property unit was worth lording it over everyone else was a mystery to me.

"I didn't think you wanted me to come in here covered in blood." I'd thoroughly scrubbed myself in the shower, yet I still felt like the stench clung to my skin. Not just the troll dung, but the faint aroma of decaying magic made my skin crawl like it wanted to leap clear of my body.

"Blood?" Larsen raised an eyebrow. "You were supposed to retrieve a stolen object, not start a fight."

"I'm not the one who started it," I said. "I got the charm, knocked out the troll and put a ward around its nest. When clean-up go down there later, there are a bunch of other items I'm pretty sure are stolen."

"And just how did you take down a troll single-handedly?"

"Take a guess." I gestured to the sword at my waist. "Iron."

I was hardly the only human capable of defending herself from supernatural creatures. I'd had more incentive than most, but regularly escaping intact from fights with Faerie's biggest, ugliest denizens tended to make people ask curious questions. Mostly it was a combination of witch charms and a handy skill with a blade, and Larsen wouldn't know I had faerie magic unless I hit him in the face with it. Humans, even witches and shifters, weren't Sighted.

"Fine," he growled. "Come in."

I walked through the grimy glass doors. A gorgeous woman waited in the lobby—the unnatural kind of gorgeous that practically advertised her Summer Faerie heritage with a neon sign. Golden curls flowed to her waist, and though her ears were slightly rounded, she'd never pass as human.

"You found my charm?"

I pulled out the sparkling object. "No problem. This is a beautifying spell, isn't it?"

"Yes. I need that." She snatched it from my hands.

Really? She thought she needed a beautification spell? Her face might have caused a traffic accident despite the frown pulling at her lips. Nobody pulled off melodrama quite like the faeries. She'd inherited that much from her fae side, but I'd seen her attitude a thousand times in half-faeries with parentage from the Summer or Winter Courts. They saw their human side as a curse, and though she was stunning, she couldn't see past her own blood, which would never be good enough for Summer.

She might have sent me crawling into a troll's nest and showed zero gratitude for it, but I knew too well how easily the words of the Sidhe could worm their way into your head. I held her gaze. "Take it from me, though—you really don't need it."

My good deed for the day done, I left the building before Larsen could jump on me again. I needed a stiff drink.

Stopping at my flat to change into something nice—finding a clean, bloodstain-free outfit was unsurprisingly difficult—I headed out to the local pub. The Singing Banshee was a dingy place that catered to supernaturals and humans alike, so I wouldn't get too many stares walking in armed to the teeth. Two knives concealed up my sleeves, two at my ankles. Boots rather than strappy shoes, jeans rather than a short skirt. Long brown hair tied back, just in case. Simple, practical. The owner, Steve, gave me a nod when I perched on a stool against the bar, safely hidden beneath the low lighting that the pub employed alongside an ambient noise machine so that the local shifters' heightened senses weren't overwhelmed upon entering. My own magic was only visible to people with the Sight and most faeries would have more sense than to wander into an establishment like this, but I appreciated the anonymity.

Two shots later and my annoyance faded to a pleasant

buzz. Nobody approached me at the bar. I'd acquired a reputation since a sleazy necromancer tried to grope me a couple of years ago and triggered the stinging spell I kept hidden on me. The story ended up being exaggerated. He'd regained the use of his hands again… eventually.

Being a weekend, the pub was more crowded than usual, with scruffy shifters hanging out near the pool table, witches sipping cocktails in groups, and even the odd necromancer sulking in a corner. I didn't expect to see the mages until a flock of them walked in, all long coats and posh, cultured accents. This wasn't your typical mage hangout, so it came as no surprise when they started whining loudly about the terrible lighting. I liked this old, dingy place precisely *because* mages didn't come inside. Their territory was way over the other side of town, so what the hell they were doing here was anyone's guess.

A couple of them shot cursory glances towards me, but otherwise I was as invisible as anyone not at their societal level. The word 'necromancer' floated my way, and I tuned in to their conversation long enough to gather they'd had a disagreement with the leader of the local Necromancer Guild again. Luckily, the necromancers usually never came in here either, and the ones present didn't seem to have noticed the intrusion. Nothing ruined a night out quite like an oncoming undead horde.

Go away, I thought, sipping my vodka and coke. Luckily, the other patrons reflected my general attitude and the mages soon traipsed off, complaints lingering in their wake.

Steve rolled his eyes after them. "Those mages think they're too good for everywhere."

"About right." I put down my empty glass. "Bet none of them has ever seen the inside of a troll's nest."

"Grim." Steve reached out to refill my glass. "Tell you what, this one's on the house."

"Cheers," I said. Steve had been on my side ever since I'd helped him kick out a piskie infestation a few years ago. "Believe me, troll dung is a fucking nightmare to clean out of denim."

"You ought to ask for hazard pay," he said. "It's exploitation, what Larsen does."

"It's work." I shrugged. "I get the benefits and accept the hazards. If I asked for a raise I'd be out on the streets."

I had no intention of ending up out there again. I'd signed up at the mercenary guild ten years ago when people were desperate enough to hire anyone to help with their supernatural-related issues, even a sixteen-year-old girl, and while I was a tad pickier with new cases than I'd been back then, we'd be far worse off if I gave the guild the middle finger. Yes, Isabel would accuse me of avoiding facing my problems if I told her that, but she'd never been on the receiving end of one of Larsen's beer-soaked rants.

Besides, since most of my problems would happily eat me alive, given the chance, I saw no issue in avoiding them.

A shout rang across the pub. I snapped my head around, the back of my neck prickling. My gaze panned over the crowd until I spied a short, dishevelled man in jeans and jacket, too far away for me to make out his features.

"Not that Trevor Swanson again," said Steve, resting his elbows on the counter.

I turned back to the bar, watching the man out of the corner of my eye. "Who?"

"Swanson. That bloke over there… his kid went missing last night."

A chill raced down my spine. Hearing those words always sent my mind careening in directions I didn't want it to, even though children disappearing was hardly uncommon here in the suburbs where supernaturals and humans mingled and the faeries had left irreversible damage.

Swanson rose upward, the light falling on his face and on the person he spoke to. The man, who'd been hidden in shadow until now, wore a suit entirely too well-tailored for an establishment like this. His strong-boned face, well-combed hair and smart attire would have drawn my attention even if he hadn't pulled out the sword.

It wasn't unheard of to see someone carrying a sword on the street. It was decidedly less common to see someone pull a hand-and-a-half sword out of *thin air*.

I kept stock still, unwilling to draw attention to myself despite my curiosity. The mage held the sword in a loose grip, but from his stance, I could tell he knew how to use it, and that the first guy had picked a fight with the worst possible opponent in the room—including me.

Swanson shrank away, stark terror flitting across his expression. "Shit," he said. "I didn't know you were—"

"Lord Colton, the head of the mages," said Steve from behind the bar. "Oh, boy. He's in trouble."

I felt the blood drain from my own face. That guy was the head of the mages? Rumour said... well, rumour said a lot of things, but everyone agreed that since he'd gained leadership, the mages had begun to implement measures that made it downright difficult for a witch to use magic professionally without being a member of a coven. While my friendship with Isabel had spared me a visit from the authorities thus far, if he happened to glance at me, and if his purportedly sharp senses picked up on the tell-tale glow of faerie magic around me, my cover would be blown.

I ducked my head, gripping the edge of the bar between my fingertips. Few things in this world scared me, but this particular head mage had acquired a reputation and a half in the months he'd held the title. The shifters insisted he kept a bunch of troll heads hanging in his office inside the mages' headquarters and that he could take off someone's head without even touching them.

Yet I didn't give a rat's arse whether *he* knew about my unconventional magic—I cared more about word reaching places I didn't want it to.

"If you'd prefer to have a more civilised conversation, what did you wish to ask me?" The mage's smooth, cultured voice drew my gaze against my will. I was too far away to tell what his magical abilities might be, aside from the trick with the sword, but he didn't give off serial killer vibes. Then again, appearances could be deceptive. Anyone who'd been around faeries knew that.

The man who'd shouted at Lord Colton rocked back on his feet, ducking his head. "My... my kid," said Swanson tremulously. "He went missing a week ago. The police haven't done a thing to help, and we're desperate to have him back."

"I thought that's what you shouted at me," said the Mage Lord. "Missing persons aren't my area, unless you wish to hire one of my mages. We charge reasonable rates."

"Do you, now?" The man appeared to recover some of his confidence. "Your doorman slammed the door in my face."

Oh, man. The mage didn't look angry—that I could tell from this distance, anyway—but there was little doubt he could kill everyone in this room if he wanted to. Missing kid or not, threatening the head of the mages was a good way to end up with your head mounted on the wall.

Lord Colton's voice, however, betrayed nothing. "If you wish to hire one of my mages, please address all correspondence to my receptionist, Wanda. I don't take bribes, and unless magic is involved in this case, it's absolutely none of my business."

Friendly. What a piece of work. I hadn't met the last Mage Lord in person, but it was plain to see that they hadn't improved their manners in the past decade. The other mages hovered in the pub's entryway, half-hidden by the low lighting, and I found myself wondering if the entirety of their ranks consisted of clones of the same Generic Thirty-Something White Man in Suit.

Admittedly, I wouldn't call Lord Colton *generic.* The light of his blade reflected in stormy grey eyes visible even in the low lighting, and the air crackled above his shoulders like a lightning storm about to break out in the middle of the pub. It was rare enough that I set eyes upon a *human* magic user with that much raw power that it was difficult not to stare, but I ducked my head as the Mage Lord's gaze swept the bar one last time.

Then he left in a sweep of his long cloak. I breathed out, the tension in the room easing somewhat. The murmur of conversation resumed, though considerably muted compared to beforehand.

Mages never come in here, I heard someone say. *Creepy as the necromancers, they are.*

"Scary dude," said Steve. "I didn't even see him come in."

"Probably blended into the crowd," I said. Or used a mage trick. Like with the sword. What the hell kind of magic was that? Most mage magic was flashes and sparks, not screwing with the laws of physics. Magic rarely astounded me these days, but that was a hell of a party trick.

"Right, I'm off." I hopped off my stool. I'd had entirely too much excitement for what was supposed to be a quiet night off. Isabel was at a coven meeting, so I'd stay up until she got back, and we'd have a good rant about the mages together.

I walked down the road to the flat, scanning the shadows out of habit. We lived miles from anywhere the fae made their homes, but occasionally, nasties from work followed me to the doorstep. Wards blazed from every corner of the building to protect us from that eventuality, and an unbroken ring of magic-forged iron surrounded the fence around the front garden, too. Isabel didn't want piskies getting into her flowerbeds, where she grew rare herbs to use in spells. The closest I'd come to telling her about Faerie was when I'd explained why I'd prefer not to have plants *inside* the house. The scars all over my body from a bad experience involving a faerie's magical thorns turning me into a human pincushion spoke for themselves, but even Isabel hadn't heard the full story.

Once over the boundary, I relaxed my guard and approached the doorstep. Then I stopped, heart sinking, as a figure stepped from the shadows.

Swanson, the guy who'd been foolish enough to pick a fight with the head of the mages himself in a desperate bid to save his child, waited outside my flat.

2

Trevor Swanson looked at me with desperation in his eyes. I could put two and two together easily enough.

"You want to hire me?" If the wards had let him in, he didn't intend me harm, and he was pure human to boot. "I usually close after five, but you can come inside for a chat."

Sometimes, I wanted to knock myself for being too nice, but after the way that obnoxious mage had treated him, I just didn't have it in me to turn him away. Besides, I needed the money.

Or so I told myself.

Thanks to Isabel's top-notch dirt-repelling wards, no blood or questionable stains remained on the stairs or in the carpeted hallway from when I'd walked in here in my ruined clothes. She'd taken to setting up the spells in the hall after the incident a few years ago when I'd come back from a bad job covered in redcap entrails and had wound up spending hours scrubbing fae innards out of the carpet with an irate landlord threatening to revoke our security deposit.

My bloodstained clothes were still soaking in the bathroom and the flat smelled strongly of spell-disinfectant, but that was a mile better than troll dung. I switched on a couple of lamps before Swanson stumbled over the many obstacles littering our living room, which doubled as Isabel's workshop and was full of so many tripwire spells that if Swanson had meant me any kind of ill intent, he'd have been bodily thrown outside. As it was, he nervously watched the flat door as I pushed the bolt into place and then jumped when a winged piskie flitted overhead.

"Get out." The piskie, who went by the name of Erwin, had been around since before we'd moved in, and no amount of iron would deter the little bugger from flying around like he owned the place. "I'm seeing a client."

The piskie buzzed into Isabel's room, and I closed the door, smothering a sigh. How he managed to continuously fly past our iron wards, I'd probably never know. He had the intelligence and attention span of a gnat.

Swanson looked decidedly uncomfortable when he took in the faint glow of Isabel's candles placed at intervals around the chalk symbols drawn on the carpet and the bottles of glowing liquid on the coffee table, but I didn't have an office, and we didn't entertain a lot of non-magical clients. He'd have to deal with it.

"Sit down," I said. "I'd offer you a drink, but I guess you've had a few already."

He didn't look angry anymore, just tired, his eyes sunken with a despondent look I tried not to look too closely at. This was going to be rough. Maybe I needed another drink after all. "What happened?"

He cleared his throat. "Dustin didn't come home last week after a night out at the park. It's not the first time but... I got a bad feeling. He's been in trouble before, so the police looked the other way when I told them." The rough edge to his voice clawed me somewhere deep inside. Even if I could have afforded to be picky with the jobs I took on, I couldn't quell the instinctive response to every missing children case that crossed my path. My own history aside, any child that went missing in a city teeming with wild fae would be lucky to make it through the night.

"What's your offer?" I asked.

"Ten thousand."

My jaw hung loose for a moment until I schooled my expression back into something resembling professionalism. Ten grand? Seriously? There had to be a catch. As my gaze lingered on him, Swanson averted his eyes and glanced over his shoulder. I'd chalk up the gesture to not wanting to be overheard, except I'd sealed the door, and he'd seen me do it.

"What else?" I gave him my best *no bullshit* stare. "What haven't you told me? There's got to be a reason you picked a fight with the head of the mages. They don't usually deal with missing people."

"No," he said, "but I thought they might deal with changelings."

The word rang through my head. I stood rigid, cold sweat gathering on the back of my neck, cursing my body's instinctive response to the word.

Changeling.

I was getting the hell away from this case. Now.

"Sorry, I can't help you," I said crisply. "I strictly work on human cases, or minor spellwork. Nothing faerie-related."

Swanson's throat bobbed as he swallowed. "Please."

Dammit. No. I couldn't. Searching for missing kids, sure. I took on every case, even the ones with the worst outcome. Changelings, though? They shouldn't exist. Not anymore.

"Twenty thousand."

"Fuck." The curse escaped before I could stop it. "Listen, it's not the money I care about. I don't deal with—them."

"Then why do you have a piskie living in your house?"

"Piskies are harmless household pests. Faerie lords are… not." Replace the word 'not' with your epithet of choice. I wouldn't say 'sadistic dickheads with a penchant for torturing humans for kicks' in front of him, but that was reason enough to turn him down and walk away with my life and sanity intact. Yet if I said no, I knew the guilt would burrow deep inside me, joining the other burdens resting upon my heart.

"I'm sorry," I said, my tone softening. "I don't think I can be much help. If it *is* a faerie… I wouldn't even know where to start looking. You should talk to the mages again. They know more than I do."

A lie. I didn't know every corner of the city like the mages did, but I knew more about the faeries than a lifetime of therapy would erase. And I knew that escaping their realm alive once was no guarantee of a repeat performance.

"Please." His voice cracked on the word.

Dammit. "Tell me what happened. If the faerie who took him isn't in our realm anymore, nobody can follow, including me. How do you know he was taken? Did you see this… changeling?"

"Yes, and he's not acting like Dustin at all. He's thirteen, and usually I know what he's thinking, but recently, he's changed. He… he tried to kill our dog. There was blood everywhere. After I stopped him, he brought—" He swallowed. "He brought rats into the house. I found them dead on his bedroom floor, surrounded by… by spells. I think they were spells. Nasty-looking ones."

I suppressed a shiver. "Have you tried setting up iron wards around the house?"

His blank expression told me he hadn't lied about his lack of knowledge, at least. "Why?"

I took in a breath. "You need a crash course in all things Faerie. I can't promise it'll be pleasant, but for now, put an iron ward around your house." I leaned over to the coffee table, careful not to knock any of the candles or bottles over, and picked up a metallic-coloured band. If activated, it'd cover the immediate area in a faerie-proof ward. Isabel had a whole cupboard full of them, though they varied in strength, and this one wouldn't last more than a week.

He took the band, wearing a sceptical expression. "This will keep the faeries out? Why… why would they come in the first place? Is this like… like the ones that came twenty years ago?"

"No," I said, a little too sharply. "Those were Summer and Winter Sidhe lords, and it's against their laws to steal human children. If Dustin was taken by one of the fae, we're looking at someone who's breaking the laws of both realms."

"But… why'd they pick us? We're not magical."

I opened my mouth then closed it. I never understood how faeries' minds worked. I hadn't been magical, either, when I was taken. It didn't seem to matter. Some people just drew the shitty straw. "I'll drop by tomorrow and have a look around," I evaded. "I can drive off the changeling and find the faerie who took Dustin. If they're still in this realm. If not…"

His eyes went wide. "Dustin's in the faerie realm?"

"Unlikely," I added, though my heart gave a familiar squeeze. "Like I said, there are laws, and most fae can't even cross between realms. Except Sidhe, and they usually don't have any reason to take an interest in humans. It's far more likely to be a faerie from this realm playing a prank."

"I don't understand," he said. "I thought the faeries could cross between our realm and their own. Isn't that what they did?"

"Usually only highly adept Sidhe lords can cross over. The invasion was the only exception that I know of." No lies there. "I can't pretend I understand how it works, but even most faeries living on this side can't go back to their own realm. They're stuck here. That means the faerie's more likely to be in this realm than not."

His bloodshot gaze caught mine, beseeching. "Are you sure?"

No. Maybe. "Ninety-five percent sure. We'll talk more tomorrow."

"I'll come back first thing."

"If you give me your address, I can come to yours and get started right away," I said. "I'll bring my standard contract. Unless you'd like to sign now."

"Yes," he said immediately.

The poor guy was way out of his depth. That much had been obvious even before he'd revealed he'd willingly sign a contract in a witch's living room drenched in magical paraphernalia when he had less magic than your average troll.

I hope I don't regret this. Isabel's spells were the best in the region, and I had no trouble tracking people within *this* realm.

Bring in the faeries, though, and all bets were off.

"Okay." I crossed the room to the desk in the corner and shifted a stack of papers aside to extract a form displaying my signature and my terms. His eyes roved over the page without taking in a word, and then he scribbled his signature at the bottom.

"Call me tomorrow morning," I said, when he'd handed me the signed form. "We'll get started then, but I can't make any promises that I'll be able to help. Faerie magic isn't something most humans understand. I certainly don't."

More of a white lie this time, but I'd rather not get his hopes up any more than I had to. Swanson nodded, mumbling thanks, as I unlocked the door and let him outside.

I took some calming breaths and considered the facts. No Sidhe had entered our realm in over twenty years. No human had crossed between the realms in ten, as far as I knew. The other faeries left behind after the invasion, based on my shaky knowledge, had no way back. That included the kidnapper, but I'd need to see the fake 'child' and ask some choice questions to get to the bottom of how they'd created a changeling in the first place.

I was lugging my ruined clothes from the bathtub when Isabel came into the flat, wearing one of her usual long flowery dresses and more shiny bangles on her slim brown arms than the inside of the troll's nest. Despite her innocent appearance and general mild-mannered nature, she could hold her own in a fight. I'd once seen her kick a half-ogre through a window, and she was five feet tall and probably weighed a hundred pounds, if that.

"Wow," she said. "I take it the case didn't go well?"

"It went." I examined my jeans, wondering how many times I could stitch them back together before they came apart at the seams. Probably one less time than I'd done it. Looked like I was due for another shopping trip, with the money I didn't have.

Yet.

I left my leather jacket in the bath to soak a bit longer and brought my jeans into the living room to show Isabel the damage. "Got a repair spell handy?"

"You know you could use a needle and thread instead."

"Your way is sturdier." Witches might not be into flashy magic, but her spell would last longer than any inexpert sewing attempt I tried. Until I had to crawl into another troll's nest.

Isabel fished a spell from among the pile on the desk next to the stack of forms. A non-witch might assume that she was a stationery fanatic, since most of her spells took the form of rubber bands, while her handmade point-and-shoot explosives resembled pencils or pens. The witches were encouraged to make their spells look like household objects because it reassured clients that the arcane forces they tapped into were relatively harmless. I didn't blame Swanson for his alarmed reaction, though, considering the number of chalk symbols drawn on the carpets and the burn stains on the walls from test-driving new spells. My closest friend was the best I knew at both offensive and defensive witch magic, and her spells had saved my neck more times than I could count.

"Someone was here." She brushed spell-dust off her hands. "A client?"

"New one, yeah." I sank into an armchair. I had to sink, because the second-hand furniture had a tendency to collapse without warning.

"I wouldn't tell the landlord," Isabel said. "You know what he's like about letting 'weirdos' into the flat."

I snorted. "Has he ever met us?"

She grinned and shook her head. "You know what I mean. Weirdos who don't pay rent."

"We don't always," I reminded her. Witches earned a pittance, while my own payments depended on whether Larsen was feeling particularly generous. Jobs had been few and far between lately, and he only suffered me to keep coming into the guild because I kept all the nasty faeries away. Like keeping a bad-tempered cat to get rid of a mouse infestation.

"This new case… what is it?" She watched me hold up my newly repaired jeans, the knees as seamless as the day I'd fished them out of the bargain bin. "Must be urgent, if they came here after dark."

"It's a tricky one," I admitted, not wanting to go into specifics. There was still a chance Swanson had imagined the changeling part. Funny how those legends stuck around, even in this grim new reality where the faeries didn't need to steal humans away to their own realm to inflict a grisly fate upon them.

I'd told Isabel the bare bones of my own story, just enough that she didn't question my eccentricities, but she'd been young enough when her fellow witches came out of hiding in the aftermath of the Sidhe's arrival that she'd never set eyes upon one of *them*. If they'd ever come here since, I didn't know. They hid themselves well... unless they wanted you to see them.

"Tricky how?"

"Missing kid, suspected faerie involvement," I said. "The mages refused to help, and I couldn't say no."

"Missing kid?" She studied me in a shrewd manner. I'd tried not to give too much of my own history away, but there were only so many conclusions she could draw from my interest in those cases. She knew I was an orphan of the invasion, like her, but when it came to my past, the word 'complicated' was an understatement.

"Yeah. I need to visit the Swansons' house first. Just in case he's mistaken his own kid for an evil faerie. It can happen."

Isabel gave me one of her *you're bullshitting me* looks. "I assume you gave him an iron spell?"

"Had to. He doesn't know about faerie wards. The mages left him in the dark." Or one guy in particular. I shoved away the image of the lethal blade appearing from nowhere. Whatever the Mage Lord had been doing in this part of town, I'd probably never see him again. "I'll need a tracking spell, I think."

"I'll get one ready." Isabel cleared a space on the floor, deftly moving candles around.

"You're the best, you know that?" She didn't charge me for spells, claiming they were enough compensation for the holes she occasionally blew in the walls. To which I argued that between the explosions and the monster guts, we both caused equal destruction, but after seven years being flatmates, I'd given up trying to offer her money. Her argument was that she enjoyed what she did.

I wouldn't say I *enjoyed* my job most of the time, but my skill set didn't leave many options open. Since my return, mundane jobs had felt as out of reach as the world before the faeries came. My CV consisted of survival skills and little else, I didn't play nicely in a team, and frankly, it was a wonder I'd even found a flatmate. I'd had multiple failed attempts until I'd put out an online ad with the words: "Requires a high tolerance for blood and entrails. Weapons are fine, but no musical instruments. In fact, no music in general."

Somehow, the ad had drawn in Isabel, who claimed she didn't mind the quiet and that her skill with cleansing spells would more than compensate for the mess I left everywhere. Her own requirements revolved around not reporting her questionable spell experiments to the landlord, but I wasn't a tattletale and I'd lost enough security deposits of my own. Isabel knew some of my demons, but not all of them.

I went to retrieve my jacket from the bathtub. Blood lingered in the water, crimson tinged with the blue from the cleansing spell I'd wrapped around the sleeve. I removed the spell—another rubber-band-shaped device—and watched it crumble into blue fragments as I pulled the plug. A swirling vortex of lines lingered above the water, a remnant of the potent magic present in faerie blood.

Leaving the room, I decided to double up on the wards around my room tonight, even if it meant making that piskie hate me for the next week. I preferred to keep my demons caged.

3

The following morning started with a blissful five minutes of imagining I might get to lie in on a Sunday, before a shrill noise brought me crashing back to reality. Groaning, I rolled over and picked up my phone. It was an old touchscreen model I'd bought second hand and had a jagged cut down the screen, but it worked well enough. "Hello?"

"Ivy Lane? This is Mr Swanson."

Oh crap. God help me, I'd said yes. I swung my legs over the bed and did my absolute best to sound like a professional who hadn't just dragged herself out of bed. "Hi. Did you manage to get the iron ward set up?"

"We did, but the changeling escaped."

Dammit. "I'll be there in five minutes."

Glad I'd showered extensively the day before to wash every taint of faerie blood from my skin, I hurriedly dressed and grabbed my backpack, plus knives, which I shoved into their holsters on my belt. I kept them by my bed for easy access, along with jars of salt, iron filings, and herbs that repelled various other supernatural menaces.

Isabel raised an eyebrow as I ran past, grabbing the spells she'd prepared from the table and shoving them into my backpack. "I take it you don't have time for cookies."

Dammit. Isabel's baking was possibly the best in existence. The world really hated me sometimes.

"Save me some for later," I said. "I've got to talk to this guy first."

"Okay. I'll probably be at the Cavanaughs' upstairs. Their ceiling's leaking, and I said I'd help."

"Cool." I pulled out my phone again to check on Swanson's address, groaning as I realised he lived in the more affluent part of town, which meant I'd have to ride the bus. Most of the local drivers hated me by this point because of all the times I'd walked on covered in blood, but I sucked it up and walked to the bus stop.

The day was crisp and clear for early autumn, ragged leaves blowing through the streets. The picture of mundaneness, at least on the outside. Typically, a half-faerie got onto the bus one stop after me and proceeded to loudly complain to the driver about my not-concealed iron weapons. Far from in the mood for an argument, I jumped off two stops early and ran the rest of the way.

The houses turned from broken-down old blocks of flats to rows of nice suburban houses like a picture straight out of the old, pre-invasion world. The roads had no potholes, the parks were well maintained, and everything seemed to shine like someone had flung a dirt-proof ward over the entire area. Probably true, considering I stood on the brink of mage territory. I stared through the window of a particularly nice house for a moment, watching two kids enthralled by some show playing on the wall-sized TV. Was this how my own childhood had been, minus the magic? This part of town didn't look like a war had hit it. There was nothing left of the place I'd grown up in.

I gave myself a mental shake. *Quit reminiscing and get on with the job, Ivy.*

I turned into the right street and approached the house the Swanson family lived in. Nothing struck me as out of place, though the slight shimmering around the door showed Swanson had managed to set up the iron ward I'd given him. Was the changeling hiding inside the house, or had it run outside to avoid the iron?

One way to find out. I rang the doorbell, shifting my backpack on my shoulder.

Swanson answered, his shadowed eyes suggesting that he hadn't slept a wink since we'd last spoken. His greying hair stuck up at all angles. Several scratch marks on his arms indicated the changeling had revealed its true colours, unless he'd been attacked by something else.

"Hey," I said. "I'm set. Where's... the changeling?" I'd almost said, 'your son', but that was more a desperate attempt at optimism talking. If it turned out his son was into dark magic, it could be dealt with. Faeries, though...

"The changeling's hiding," he said. "It saw the iron and ran."

Luckily, I'd come prepared. Each kind of faerie needed slightly different bait, so I'd stashed a variety in my backpack. Changelings were an oddity, though, and not one I knew enough about to make an educated guess on how to catch it.

"What are you doing?" asked Swanson as I crouched in the hallway and began sifting through the contents of my bag. Isabel colour-coded her spells, and trackers took the form of green rubber bands. I took one in my hand.

"Tracking the changeling." I held the spell for him to see. "This is witch-made. I normally use them on humans, but it ought to work on faeries, too."

Swanson didn't move. "I thought you were going to find my son."

Admittedly, tracking humans was easier than fae. "All right, do you have anything of your son's I can use? Hair works best." Or fingernails, but I distinctly preferred the former.

Every nerve in my body told me this was a bad idea, but I stayed put while Swanson went upstairs and came back with a few golden curls of hair.

"I'll have to do the spell inside the house," I said. "It's warded, so it'll be fine." I couldn't quite cover the lie in my voice this time.

Swanson led the way into the living room. A pale, dark-haired woman sat with her head down and what appeared to be an old T-shirt tightly clenched in her hands. Must belong to their kid. The sofa looked like genuine leather, the TV mounted to the wall was the same size as the one in the house whose window I'd peered through, but none of their money or material possessions had been able to save their son.

Mrs Swanson lifted her head, her pleading eyes meeting mine. "Are you here to help find Dustin?"

"I'm going to use a tracking spell, if that's okay." I held up the band. "I can track your son, but only if he's still in this realm."

Those words had the exact effect I'd dreaded. Two sets of horrified eyes stared at me. "In this realm?"

"If he was taken to Faerie… like I said, I won't be able to follow, and I don't know what effect it'll have on the spell either." It was only fair to warn them. "Do you still want me to try?"

"Yes, of course." Swanson's eyes followed me as I set the spell down on the carpeted floor and tapped the band's side, causing its edges to expand into a larger circle. My heart was already hammering, and I subtly shifted the sword at my waist, ready to grab it if things turned bad.

Then I threw the golden hairs into the centre of the makeshift circle. Green light flared up around the edges, and I leaned forward. The Swansons wouldn't see anything but a meaningless blur of lights, but to anyone with the remotest sensitivity to magic, the spell would reveal the location of the person whose traces I'd placed into the circle.

I held my breath. The lights swirled, forming patterns that dazzled my eyes and made my head spin. Then the spell winked out, the green light turning grey, lifeless.

An icy chill ran down my spine. For the spell not to work meant one of two things: the faerie had put a spell-resistant charm on its captive… or it had left this realm behind.

Mrs Swanson's face fell. "Didn't it work?"

I didn't know what they'd seen, if anything, but the expression on my face had likely been enough. "Are either of you magically sensitive?"

She shook her head. "Why?"

"Just curious." Mostly because I couldn't figure out *why* their kid had been taken, but now the spell had failed, I could no longer cling to any remaining traces of denial about what we were dealing with. "The spell didn't work, but I can track the changeling instead."

"Why didn't it work?" croaked Swanson. "Yesterday… you said most faeries can't cross over from their realm."

"That was true," I said, "but faerie magic works on a different level to what we humans understand. Faerie plays by its own rules."

We might have had to adapt to their arrival, but we were no closer to comprehending our invaders than the day before magic had exploded across the country and brought a flock of dangerous faerie warriors along with it who cared nothing for collateral damage as they razed half our city to the ground.

"Nobody?" Swanson echoed. "But… there are faeries in the city, aren't there? If you spoke to one of them, wouldn't they be able to tell you more?"

I might have laughed if the situation hadn't been so serious. Faeries didn't *talk* to humans, not in the conversational sense. The sole exception in my life was the piskie living in my flat, who had the IQ of a goldfish and had probably been born in the attic we'd found him nesting in.

"Not really," I said. "Most faeries around these days were born in this realm after the invasion or fled when the paths between the realms opened. They don't belong to Summer or Winter. And I doubt they know how magic works regardless. Most faeries on this side don't have much."

After the Sidhe lords had left this realm in ruins, they'd departed, either for the Courts or for the place that lay outside of their boundaries.

A place I hadn't mentioned to the Swansons.

Between Summer and Winter existed a neutral zone of sorts where the Court's rules didn't apply. If the faerie who'd taken Swanson's kid had come from there, no advice I offered would matter a bit, and it would be far kinder to tell them that Dustin had been found dead in an alley. Death was nothing compared to the fate that might befall a human who set foot in *that* part of Faerie.

Swanson considered my words. "You said you can track the changeling, though?"

"If it's still around." I doubted a simple changeling would have the power to cross over between realms, so the creature would likely still be hiding somewhere nearby. I put away the dead spell and pulled a fresh one from my backpack, laying it atop where the faint remnants of the first remained. Luckily for their expensive carpet, trackers didn't leave permanent marks.

"Do you have anything the changeling left behind?" I ought to have thought of that before I set up the circle, but this whole situation had rattled me beyond belief and made me forget the basics.

Swanson walked into the hallway. "Upstairs, but his room... it's a mess."

Oh boy. Gritting my teeth, I followed him into the hallway and up the carpeted stairs. Through the door on the right lay what looked like the inside of a necromancer's lair, or a witch who'd gone bad. Symbols were etched all over the floor, unfamiliar glyphs that made the hairs rise on my arms. Blood soaked into the carpet, and several small furry bodies lay in the centre. Rats. I pressed a hand to my mouth, trying to calm my breathing.

"This... it's what they call dark magic." Most witches objected to magic being pigeonholed into narrow definitions of 'good' and 'evil', but any spells that involved dead animals were invariably designed to cause harm and were strictly forbidden by the Mage Lords. Why the hell would a faerie changeling be messing with these props?

Swanson hesitated by the door, his expression telling me he was as reluctant to go into the room as I was. One of us had to make the first move, so I stepped over the threshold, my gaze averted from the blood. Behind the ghastly scene were the posters of sports teams, comic books and video game collection of an ordinary teenage boy. I concentrated on that image. I was doing this to save an innocent person from the faeries. An innocent person who didn't have magic.

Just like I hadn't.

I crouched down, searching the carpet. Several fine hairs lay there, and when I held them up to the light, they shone silver. The kind of unnaturally bright silvery hair that could only belong to a faerie.

The faint smell of burning caught in my nostrils. I sniffed again, my gaze snagging on one of the candles. Though someone had clearly been in here since and knocked everything askew, the glyphs that had been carved into the carpet with a sharp object formed a circle, encasing the rats dead bodies. At a guess, the candles had been placed at intervals around the edges, too.

"It's a summoning circle." Necromancers used them to summon spirits. Not a branch of magic I was particularly an expert in, but the same went for the faeries. Changelings weren't capable of that level of magic, or so I'd thought.

"What's that?" asked Swanson in a hushed voice. "Summoning what?"

You don't want to know. "I'm going to have to dismantle it. I can't leave this stuff unattended up here even if the changeling's gone."

I might have called the necromancers, but they lived on the other side of town. This was mage territory, and they had as little to do with necromancy as I did. If I didn't scrub the place before the changeling came back, the place might turn into a portal of hell long before the necromancers deigned to send anyone to help.

I signed inwardly. Just for once, I'd have preferred a weekend lie-in like a normal person.

On careful feet, I skirted the blackened spell circle and crouched to examine the fading glyphs. I'd have noticed if any were still active, but I wasn't enough of a fool to touch the circle itself. I reached into my pocket for a salt canister I'd kept on hand since the infamous zombie night a few years ago when a necromancer apprentice had left the doors of the local cemetery unlocked. Didn't do a thing for faeries, but salt would more than suffice for nullifying a necromantic trap. After opening the container, I tipped the contents onto the glyphs.

A high-pitched scream came from downstairs. Swanson's wife.

Oh, shit.

4

I vaulted both circles and ran downstairs without pausing for breath, my sword already in my hand. Swanson shouted out, and I leaped the last two stairs as Mrs Swanson ran from the living room, pursued by something big, black and furred. Sharp teeth snapped on her heels, and I swore, pushing myself between her and the monster. Or rather, hellhound. I hadn't had the pleasure of dealing with one of those for a while.

I slashed with the blade, catching the creature's nose. Blood spurted in a crimson fountain. The dog hissed between its teeth, shaking droplets onto the thick carpet and staining the white wallpaper. I bloody well hoped Isabel's cleansing spells would be strong enough to spare me from having to surrender a huge chunk of my payment towards the cleaning bills, but if any of its acidic drool got onto the carpet, no spell would fix the damage.

I glanced over my shoulder. Swanson had opened the front door, and he and his wife had fled outside, which would normally be the sensible decision, except the wards only covered the house, and the street outside was wide open.

Staying in the house wasn't an option, so I backed away, goading the monster to follow me by moving my blade in a figure-eight motion. I kept walking out of the front door, taking care to keep the beast's eyes on me and not on the two humans cowering behind the garden fence.

"Guys," I said to the Swansons out of the corner of my mouth. "Get behind the iron ward. There might be more than one of them outside."

I didn't see if they did as I asked, because the hellhound chose that moment to try to take a bite out of my face. I stepped to the side and sank my blade into its flank. Blood poured from the wound, thick and reddish blue. Its teeth snapped again, and I ducked, bringing my sword in an arc to sink into its thick neck. Flesh gave way beneath Irene's blade, and the hellhound fell with a pained squeal.

Right as a second one appeared at the side of the house.

Damn. How many were there? Hellhounds were rejects from the Wild Hunt. They sure as hell didn't come from this realm, least of all a magic-free corner of the city like this. Out of the corner of my eye, I glimpsed faces watching me from windows, wide eyes upon the hellhound's body slumped in the middle of the road. When the second saw its fallen companion, it roared, drool splattering the road in sizzling green puddles. Thanking the universe that none of *that* shit had got onto the carpet, I called, "Come and get me."

Waving my sword, I darted down the alley alongside the house. The beast followed, squeezing its bulk into the alley faster than I'd anticipated. I drove my blade at its flank, a superficial cut, but enough to splatter the alley with blood.

I aimed for a killing blow next, but the beast dodged with more agility than I'd have expected from a creature of that size.

Then a third beast appeared behind it, so swiftly that it might as well have popped into existence from nowhere. *Ah, shit.* I'd forgotten the beasts did possess some level of glamour, enough to stay hidden even from my sharp sight. There might be a dozen more hiding nearby, and I'd backed myself into a corner when I'd entered the alleyway.

I swung the blade in an arc that sent the first hellhound rearing back, then I went for its throat. Blood gushed out, and as its body slumped to the ground, its companion took its place. It was noticeably bigger than the first one—had grown bigger in the last few seconds, in fact. Another significant oversight on my part. Hellhounds were originally Winter beasts that gained power from death... and since I'd killed two of them, the death energy swirling in the air would fuel any others hiding from sight.

The beast stalked forward, blue smoke swirling around its feet and around the body of its dead companion. A second hellhound appeared at its back, huge flanks scraping the alley's sides, but it wasn't their size that cowed me. Every muscle in my body locked into place as a wave of icy fear swept over me, potent enough to still my blade in its tracks. Looking into a hellhound's eyes conjured a manufactured fear that rendered me as helpless as a fish caught in a net, unable to move. I'd assumed that my magic would make me immune. I'd been wrong. *Ah, fuck.*

Sweat slid down my brow as I fought to regain control over my own body, but my rational mind knew that my magic invariably surfaced in life-or-death situations, and this definitely qualified as such. The hellhounds might come from Faerie's darkest corner, but so did the power that lived within me. *Come on,* I thought. *Come on, magic.*

When the hellhounds got close enough that their warm, foul breath brushed my face, energy surged up my arms, wrapping me in blue tendrils. My grip on the blade tightened as the immobilising effect slid away and my reflexes sharpened beyond those of a regular person. In one movement, I leapt, impossibly high, and cut the hellhounds' throats in a single, devastating strike.

I landed on my feet the instant before their bodies slumped downward, my veins buzzing with energy. Threads of blue spiralled upward from my skin, circling me like smoke.

"If there's any more of you, come and fight me," I called into the now empty alleyway.

"I don't think that'll be necessary."

I froze—not literally this time. The voice was human and belonged to a tall broad-shouldered man wearing a long black coat that stopped at knee height, short enough not to get in the way but long enough to leave an impression. He stepped out of the smoke, hardly a hair ruffled by the magic potent in the air.

Oh my god. It was Lord Colton himself. Head of the mages. The man who'd spurned Swanson and sent me on this ill-advised quest in the first place. Not so much as a hint of recognition showed in his expression as he eyed the bodies of the fallen hellhounds.

"Who are you?" he enquired. "A human couldn't possibly have killed those monstrosities."

"Pleasure to meet you, too." I'd never reckoned on drawing enough attention for a face-to-face chat with the Mage Lord, but given the choice, I'd have preferred our first encounter to be on my own terms. Not covered in blood in an alleyway and glowing with the neon aftermath of faerie magic. "I'm here to help the Swanson family with magical difficulties."

A job he'd turned down, I might have added, but picking a fight with this dude was as inadvisable as summoning a pack of hellhounds into a human-only corner of town. *Why me?*

"The Swanson family," he repeated. "I was under the impression they'd requested assistance from the Mage Lords."

"I was under the impression you didn't give a shit about them." My mouth spoke without permission from my brain, my body humming with the aftermath of the fight even as the buzzing high faded with every passing second.

Confusion flitted across his face for an instant. Then he regarded me with eyes cold as pools of icy water. My heart sank a little. I didn't scare easy, especially where humans were concerned, but this guy gave me pause. Possibly because of the giant blade he presumably kept hidden somewhere nearby.

Or maybe because he might have seen my magic.

I drew myself up to my full five-foot-four height—not that it made a difference considering he was at least six-two —and said, "I'm a private investigator the Swansons hired to investigate their son's disappearance. They came to me after you turned them down."

"Is that so?" The Mage Lord gave me a once-over. "Show me your licence."

"Ask me nicely first." This time I couldn't blame my tone on the adrenaline surge from fighting the hellhounds, but I truly hated being ordered around. Especially by people who didn't have any authority over me.

"If you weren't already aware," said the Mage Lord, "I am Vance Colton, head of the mages in this region, and it's required by law for all magical practitioners to come to me for a licence."

"I have a licence," I said, digging in my pocket. "But I'm a consultant and freelancer, not a magical practitioner. I don't work with mages."

"That's unfortunate, because this situation has drawn my

attention. It seems there's more to the situation than a simple missing person's case."

"The hellhounds didn't give you a clue?"

I fought back a laugh at the incredulity that crept into the Mage Lord's—Vance Colton's—expression. But all he said was "Your licence."

Resisting the impulse to roll my eyes, I handed the paper over. His eyes roved over it, a crease appearing between his brows.

"Yes, I don't have blood in my hair in the photo, but it's me." I held my hand out pointedly. He handed the licence back, not taking his eyes off me.

"Two witnesses saw you use magic," he said.

"Witnesses can be mistaken in times of trauma. Can I go now?"

"No," he said. "You're to come to my office for an interview."

"Er, no." He had to be joking. "I have a job to do, and I told you that I don't work with mages."

"You're a witch, aren't you? More than a hedge witch, if that stunt proves anything. I just watched you jump ten feet into the air."

Damn. As I'd feared, he must have seen the tail end of the fight. "Yes. It's a temporary spell for speed and accuracy."

He had nothing on me. My cover story was airtight, and besides, he had no recourse to drag me into his office like a lawbreaking human who'd decided to dabble in necromancy.

The trouble was, someone nearby *had* been dabbling with necromancy, and he only had to stick his nose into the Swansons' house to assume the worst. Like it or not, the mages made and enforced the laws across the whole magical community, regardless of their relative scarcity. They'd held authority long before the invasion, presumably because their ancestors had used their skills to their advantage in the old world and made a fortune, while 'witch' was the label assigned to any non-mage with a rudimentary magical talent and no one particular skill. The result was an implied hierarchy. The mages practically owned the city, while witches like Isabel could barely scrape together rent payment. And while half-faeries and shifters lived in their own territories under their own rules, everyone in the region was subject to the mages' rules. To this man's rules.

One piece of information to file away for later… the Mage Lord, for all his talents, didn't have the Sight. He couldn't see my faerie magic. I mean, I practically glowed blue, even underneath all the blood. A faerie would have spotted me a mile away.

"All the same, I'd like to interview you," he told me. "Come to number Fifteen, Oak Drive. Clean yourself up first. It's tiresome getting bloodstains out of the carpet."

I laughed. "You're not serious."

He frowned, then his eyes widened as he looked over my shoulder. "Step aside."

Normally I'd have told him to quit ordering me around, but anything that could startle the Mage Lord, I didn't want behind me. I spun around as another huge, furred body leapt over the wall at the alley's other end. I tensed, lifting my sword. The hellhounds' bodies must have attracted more of the bastards from whatever hole they'd crawled out of. This one bared its teeth at me, and the Mage Lord stepped to my side so that we blocked the alleyway. The hellhound snarled, knowing it was outnumbered.

Or not, I thought, as a snarl behind me warned that another hellhound had stalked up to the bodies of its fallen kin. I didn't dare push my luck with faerie magic this time, but with those corpses ready to fuel the newcomers' power, I needed to finish this fast.

Climbing onto one of the fallen bodies to better reach

my target, I stabbed the hellhound's leg then went for the neck. Not quickly enough. The beast roared and flailed, and my sword remained stuck in its throat as it expanded to such a size that the fences on either side of the alley groaned.

"Watch out! They get bigger and stronger the more of them you kill," I yelled at the mage. He might be a dick, but I didn't want to watch him get his throat torn out.

I managed to free my sword and drove it into the roof of the beast's mouth. Drool sizzled onto the pavement as it collapsed, its paws knocking into the other corpse I was using for balance. I jumped down, landing at a crouch, and looked up into the other hellhound's eyes. *Oh, damn.*

The second hellhound had closed the distance between us, its fetid breath on my face—but the mage was suddenly in front of me. He moved *fast*. And—holy shit. For a moment, I gaped as what looked like black scales slid down his hands, encasing the knuckles and the fingers wrapped around the hilt of the blade in his hands. As if being an adept mage and swordsman wasn't enough. Judging by the scales, the guy must be part shifter, too.

His blade flashed out, blood spraying, and I finished the beast off with a swift stab to the throat. Blood poured from the crimson slash, and it sank to the ground, the blue tendrils of magic fading away like wisps of smoke blown away on the breeze.

The sound of steel meeting flesh drew my gaze to the alley's end. Though the mage hadn't moved an inch, two more hellhounds slumped, their throats cut by a blade that reappeared in its owner's hand in the time it took me to blink. *Did he just... kill them from all the way over here?*

"Jesus." I gaped at him. "What the hell kind of power is that?"

The Mage Lord ignored me, surveying the alley. "I'll call

someone to remove the bodies and clean up the blood. Are you hurt?"

"No." I refused to be deterred. "How'd you do that?"

"I take it you're reconsidering my offer?" He cleaned the blade on a handkerchief I swore he'd conjured up from thin air. Which, given the ease with which his blade had flayed a bunch of hellhounds without him stepping near them, might not be that far off the mark.

"No." I slammed a lid on my curiosity, knowing that no answer he might give would be worth getting myself entangled in the Mage Lord's business. "I said I don't work with mages, and I meant it. Thank you for your assistance."

Focus, Ivy. First and foremost, I needed to check on the Swansons and make sure every piece of magical equipment in their son's room was removed. The guy behind me might only be ninety percent arsehole and not a hundred percent, but I didn't trust him not to have them arrested for possession of necromantic props.

I'd hoped the Swansons would have hidden inside the house, but instead I found them cowering on the doorstep. At least they'd had the sense to get back behind the iron ward encircling the house, but the crimson stains shining from the hallway had probably deterred them from going back in.

"Ivy?" Swanson's face was greyish pale, and his eyes lingered on my bloodstained clothes and hair as I approached. "Are you... all right?"

Good question. The buzz of the fight was rapidly fading along with my brief rush of energy, and with that came a heightened awareness of the decaying stench the hellhounds had left on my skin. At least I hadn't got any of their drool on my clothes. That shit ate through fabric like it did through skin or paper, and I couldn't afford to lose another pair of jeans.

"I'm fine," I said. "Before I do anything else, I need to clear all traces of faerie blood from this place and get rid of everything in your son's room. The mages are sniffing around, and there's no way to prove you weren't involved with setting up those illegal spells."

The Swansons wordlessly moved aside to let me past. Both were trembling, but it was probably for the best that I'd given them the bad news first. Most people, when it came down to it, would rather know the truth. I know I would.

I started by using one of Isabel's highly effective cleansing spells on the hellhound blood in the hall and headed upstairs to retrieve the necromantic props from Dustin's room. My nerves remained on edge, expecting the head of the mages to come bursting into the house, but with a little luck, he was too busy dealing with those hellhound corpses. Or someone was. If the way he'd acted was any indication, he likely had an army of servants waiting to clean up any bodies he left behind. And, perhaps, to teach a lesson to any smart-mouthed mercenaries who had the nerve to give him attitude.

It's required all magical practitioners come to me for a licence. Bullshit. I'd obtained mine from the coven, which was perfectly legal. I'd have expected the Mage Lord to be too busy to hand out licences to hedge witches, surely, but I'd scarcely had time to stash the props in my rucksack before the doorbell rang.

I zipped the bag and backed out of Dustin's room. "Don't answer the door."

Mr Swanson halted in the doorway and gave me a questioning look as I came downstairs. "Why?"

"Do you have a back door?" When he offered a confused nod, I added, "The head of the mages is in front of your house, and I think we'd both rather he didn't see me carrying this."

I indicated my backpack, and Swanson paled. Since I'd

used the only cleansing spell I had on the hallway, I still had blood all over me, and catching the bus home was out of the question. I hoped the pair of them would keep the mage talking for a while.

His wife showed me through the dimly lit kitchen to the back door.

"Thanks," I said to her. "I'll be back tomorrow."

I ran through the back garden, scaling the fence at the far end and hoping that the Swansons would shake off their unwanted visitors. Including the hellhounds. Who'd summoned them? Someone who wanted to deter anyone from helping find their missing son, evidently, but no ordinary faerie would dabble in that kind of magic.

Emphasis on 'ordinary'.

The hellhounds' appearance banished all doubts that my worst fears were right on the mark. That this wasn't, had never been, a practical joke played by a harmless outcast. An outcast had certainly engineered this, but 'harmless' was not a word anyone would use to describe the literal grey zone between the realms, the lawless place ruled by Faerie's exiles. The natural home for monsters like those hellhounds.

Humans might be mere apes in comparison to the powerful immortals that lived over on the other side, but even the Sidhe of the Courts had been oblivious to the threat presented by those who were considered too depraved even to live among their own kind. Until the doors between worlds had torn open and the exiles had brought their ruin and cruelty here, to this realm.

And in the process, they'd taken everything away from me.

5

One restless night later, I woke to the sound of pounding on the flat door. My sleep-addled brain told me that Swanson must be back, but I would have expected him to call first rather than trying to break the door down. More thumping followed, and I winced, sliding out of bed.

"What the hell?" said Isabel sleepily from behind her bedroom door. If she was half asleep, it must be early. I checked the time. Six in the morning.

"What the hell indeed." Or rather, *who* the hell. Three possibilities stacked up in my mind, none of them appealing. One: the landlord. Two: Larsen. Three…

I opened the door to find Lord Colton stood outside. As usual, he wore a fitted suit and his ridiculously long coat.

"Do you wear that thing in the summer?" I asked, acutely aware I'd only had the chance to shove a dressing gown over the shorts and T-shirt I wore as pyjamas. He hardly seemed to notice, though, and his cool grey eyes met my gaze.

"Ivy Lane, I'm retracting my offer of an interview and turning it into an order."

I almost laughed in his face. "I don't take orders. Free-lancer here. I pick and choose my clients." And my working hours. Six a.m. was as uncivilised as you could get.

"Swanson told me that he came here and hired you to help him find his missing son. You then went over to his house yesterday and attempted to use a witch's tracking spell. You failed, and instead those faerie creatures appeared."

"Yes." Damn, he was thorough. And persistent. I'd have expected him to have given up by now, but it sounded like he'd subjected the Swansons to a thorough grilling after I'd slipped out of their house. "And?"

"I'd like to make you an offer. The mages can be of assistance in this case."

This time, I did laugh. He couldn't sound more pretentious if he tried. "Sorry to disappoint you, but I work alone."

Lord Colton blinked. "You won't consider a partnership? Look at the resources I have at my disposal. I can command every mage in the district."

"Yeah, no. Not interested. This isn't something you can help with."

Annoyance flashed in his eyes. "That wasn't a request. You will partner with the mages, and with me, or you'll lose this case." His tone took on a steely edge that would have made me step back if I wasn't royally pissed off. Who the hell did he think he was?

Only the most powerful human magic user in the city.

"You've got to be kidding me. Why would I work with you?" I put every ounce of derision possible into my tone. I didn't care if he was practically royalty. He couldn't order me around in my own house.

For a heartbeat, I expected him to conjure up a sword and skewer me the way he'd done to those hellhounds. Instead, his forehead creased, like he genuinely couldn't fathom why I wasn't kneeling at his feet in gratitude for his offer.

"Why wouldn't you? You'll have every—"

"Every mage in the city. I get it. Look, I'm sure you have a grand plan, but it won't work. I know what I'm doing."

"Was almost being mauled to death by faerie dogs part of the plan?" he queried.

Oh, he had a sarcastic streak, did he? "We hit a snag yesterday."

"Your changeling got away, I'm told."

"As I said, we hit a snag." What the hell did I have to do to get rid of this guy? I was kind of tempted to engage one of Isabel's trespasser spells, but getting on the shit list of the head of the mages wasn't a wise move.

Then again, neither was working with him. Until now, I'd got by without anonymity because nobody who knew me before the invasion was still alive. A hell of a depressing way to get a new start in life, but one I utilised to its full extent. I didn't need every mage in the district to know my name, much less start poking holes into my history.

The Mage Lord took one step towards me so that we stood face to face. Or rather, face to chest. He cut an impressive figure, mostly thanks to the coat, but also because of the breeze that had kicked up behind him, cutting at my bare skin, threatening to send me into retreat. I held my ground. I'd stared down too many of Faerie's nightmares to flinch away from an arrogant human.

"You're to come to my office before nightfall for a meeting, or you'll be formally charged with obstructing an investigation."

My jaw unhinged. "You what?"

He stepped down the doorstep onto the path. "Think on it, Ivy Lane."

And just like that, he was gone.

Holy shit. Never mind my resolution not to piss him off— I'd done so, and then some, and I hadn't even broken the law.

All I'd done was take a job he'd turned down in the first place. A job that… okay, maybe the mages *could* help, but they likely had no experience with faeries beyond the superficial everyday stuff. Trolls in the sewers and piskies in the attic were normal enough sights, and while the Mage Lord had undoubtedly been skilled enough to kill those hellhounds, even a mage was no match for Faerie's most depraved monsters.

"The fucking cheek," I muttered, closing the front door firmly.

"What is it?" Isabel peered out of the flat into the dingy hallway, her hair dishevelled from sleep. She wore a lacy top and a flowery skirt, but not her charms. Unlike me, she didn't sleep with weapons.

"The head mage showed up here and practically bullied me into working with him. He thinks he has the right to *my* case."

"What a dick," she commented. "Wait… you insulted the head mage?"

"He insulted me first."

Isabel grinned at me, though worry lingered in her expression. "Are you still going over to Swanson's today?"

"Hell, yes. I'm not about to let His Highness steal my job from under my nose."

"You told him you were a witch, right?"

"I had to. He saw me use magic against the hellhounds."

"Shit."

"I know, right?" I walked after her into the flat. The mages didn't usually pay much attention to anyone outside of their elite circle, and nobody would take me for a magic user if they didn't see me in action. But he'd seen me do more than fight. He'd seen me turn the faeries' magic against them. If he poked around and asked another witch if what I'd done was possible, he'd get a 'hell, no'. And then I'd be in trouble.

Sighing, I went into my room to dress properly and get my head together. I did need to talk to Swanson again. I hadn't dared go back after I'd dropped off all the dodgy spell equipment at clean-up yesterday, which had earned me raised eyebrows from Larsen. I'd told him I'd caught a bunch of teenagers staging an exorcism, but I'd had an inkling he hadn't bought my excuse. Swanson, thankfully, had disposed of the dead rats himself, though I did still have the bottle containing the changeling's silvery hair I'd taken from the scene yesterday. It sat on the coffee table next to a tracking spell Isabel had left me, but I wouldn't use the spell inside the flat if I could help it.

"Ivy!" Erwin the piskie flew past, blowing a raspberry at me. "You stink of hellhound."

Still? I'd scrubbed myself raw in the shower yesterday.

"Job hazards," I said. "You haven't seen a changeling around, have you?"

The piskie flew into the ceiling light, shrieking as the heat burned his skin. "No bad faeries, no!"

"Good." Sometimes I felt like I had 'faerie bait' tattooed on my forehead, but it figured that the one faerie I *wanted* to find was eluding me. I'd need to find an isolated area before I attempted to track down the changeling. Preferably without the Mage Lord getting involved.

"I have better news," said Isabel from the kitchen. "There are cookies left over from yesterday."

"Brilliant." My mood improved a hundred percent. Isabel's cookies were delicious, stress-relieving, and calorie free. Now *that* was witchcraft.

Naturally, the doorbell rang before I reached the kitchen. I went to answer, just in case the mage had come back, but this time it was Larsen who glared at me from the doorstep. As usual, he wore jeans and a dirty T-shirt that smelled like he hadn't washed them for a while.

"Ivy Lane. What's this?" He dropped a bag that I belatedly recognised as the one in which I'd stashed the props I'd brought in from the Swansons' house.

"A spell." I nudged the bag off the doorstep.

"It's death magic." He reached down, grabbed the bag again, and flung it into my arms. "We don't deal with necromancers. You know that."

I caught the bag on reflex, my body shuddering. "Neither do I. That's why I was getting rid of this."

"I'd say that mouth of yours will get you into trouble, but it looks like it already has." He moved close enough that his stale breath wafted in my face. "If you've been consorting with *them*, you won't be welcome at the guild any longer."

"I haven't spoken to any necromancers. I just didn't want to leave this crap in a house full of normal humans."

Larsen narrowed his eyes at me. He was allegedly part shifter and always claimed he could sniff out lies, but since he couldn't so much as shift a fingertip, I figured that was bullshit. He hated the mages as much as he did the necromancers, so telling him about the Mage Lord would go down as well as a confession to consorting with the dead.

"Get rid of that spell," said Larsen. "And if you bring anything like that near the guild again, I'll throw you into the canal."

Mouth agape, I watched him shuffle away from the flat, leaving me with my arms full of unwanted contraband. "Dramatic, much?"

"No kidding." Isabel appeared, wide-eyed, in the flat's doorway. "What was that about?"

"No clue." I stared at Larsen's disappearing back until he vanished through the front gate. "I need to get rid of this shit when I'm on the way to the mages. Know anywhere I can toss a bunch of dodgy props without any kids picking it up?"

"The coven will help… wait, you're actually going to see the Mage Lord?"

"What do you take me for?" I closed the front door once again. "This case is mine. The guy's a dick, and he's not taking my job from me."

"What's going on?" Henry Cavanaugh peered from the top of the stairs to the upper flat. He was a wolf shifter, so he'd probably smelled Larsen's stench of cheap beer from the door. He and his wife were friendly enough, if a little too willing to let their four-year-old son get too close to Isabel's spells, but they'd lasted the longest of any neighbours we'd had.

"Ivy!" Little George ran downstairs and threw his arms around me. Evidently, *he* didn't think I smelled like hellhound. "What's that?"

Oh, crap. "Nothing."

I awkwardly shunted the paper bag behind my back. Isabel, noticing my dilemma, reached out and took the necromancers' contraband out of reach of George's grasping fingers.

"I'll ask the coven to get rid of it," she said. "What was Larsen's problem?"

"Hell if I know. Thanks, by the way." I tilted my head to watch Henry come downstairs after his son. "You haven't seen any faeries around here, have you?"

After my spate of unwanted visitors, it wouldn't surprise me if the fae decided to get in on the fun.

"No." He took George's hand. "Didn't you bash a troll's head in the other day?" Shifters were generally more accustomed to violence than most other people, which was why they hadn't fled in horror the first time I'd left a decapitated redcap's head on the porch.

"Nah, I just knocked it out. Trolls' heads are as hard as concrete."

"Come in," said Isabel. "I made cookies. Henry, do you want some?"

I led the way into the flat and helped myself to Isabel's glorious cookies. They tasted like cinnamon and divine goodness and restored my faith that today wasn't a complete wreck after all.

Henry didn't take the cookie she offered him. "Has another shifter been here?"

"No." Not strictly a lie, and I didn't want the whole world to know the Mage Lord had taken an interest in me. Henry's wolf senses were highly attuned to any shifter presence, though, and from the flare of his nostrils and the tension in his shoulders, he'd picked up on my visitor's scent. "I mean, unless Larsen actually *does* have shifter blood."

He didn't, but the Mage Lord did, if those reptilian scales I'd glimpsed on his hands during the fight had been any indication. The last thing I wanted was to set foot on his turf, but if I refused, I'd lose my sole independent case at a time when Larsen was already threatening to kick me out of the guild. Trapped on all sides. I took another cookie as casually as I dared, smiling at George as he launched into an excited babble about his new friends at school. Considering shifters turned into hairy or scaly monsters on a monthly basis, the Cavanaugh family had their lives together a damn sight better than I did.

Isabel pushed a cookie into Henry's hand and tilted her head. "Can you always smell when another shifter's been nearby?"

"Here I can," said Henry, taking a delicate bite of his cookie. "If it's a lone shifter, it's more noticeable. On our own territory, there are too many of us, and the Ley Line jumbles our senses, too."

Isabel nodded. "Yeah, I figured."

The Ley Line amplified the abilities of all supernaturals,

with mages being the sole exception that I knew of, and their powers generally waned the further they ventured from its orbit. Faeries were no exception; in fact, it had been the Ley Line the Sidhe had used as a conduit to open a gate into our world. Might the person who'd summoned the changeling have done the same? If anywhere contained enough energy to summon a changeling, the Ley Line did, though the Swansons' house was nowhere nearby.

George tugged at my hand. "You look sad, Ivy. Have another cookie."

I loved that kid. "Sure," I said, taking one. "Just thinking about the job I'm working on. Looking for someone," I added vaguely to Henry. "It's to do with the faeries."

"Bad faeries!" Erwin flew through the room and nearly knocked himself out on the kitchen cupboard. Shaking my head, I picked him up by the wing and deposited him on the counter, where he helped himself to a handful of cookie crumbs.

"I thought I smelled one of them," said Henry. "It's not as distinctive as a shifter's scent… are you *certain* a shifter didn't come here? Whoever that scent belongs to is powerful."

Power had a smell? That was news to me, but evidently, shifters' finely tuned senses were capable of making that distinction. I gave a casual shrug, trying to ignore the curious look Isabel shot at me. "Not that I know of. You and Disha are the only shifters I know. Can you really identify the type of shifter by scent?"

"Yes…" Henry paused, nostrils flaring as he inhaled. "That scent belongs to someone at the top of the shifter hierarchy. They're rare enough not to form their own packs. Tend to be loners. Predators."

I thought of the Mage Lord. *I can see that.*

Not all shifters banded together. Most still lived in similar packs to the ones that had existed when they'd hidden from the world before the invasion, but like witch blood, shifter blood had been diluted enough that a significant portion of the population had carried the gene without even knowing it before magic had gone haywire twenty years ago and exposed their latent talents for the world to see. Being able to partially shift into a beast didn't disqualify one from full pack status, but the majority of part-shifters opted to play human instead.

The image of those black scales and claws flashed through my head. The Mage Lord clearly didn't care who saw what he was. That made him the stark opposite of every shifter I knew.

"I'm heading out anyway." I could tell Henry wasn't fooled by the evasion—nor Isabel either, come to that—but I needed to put the tracking spell to good use and find that changeling and I wasn't about to do so with a small child nearby.

First, though, I had a mage—or shifter—to get off my back.

ere we go. I looked up at the mages' headquarters, an impressive manor house whose whitewashed walls gleamed in the weak sunlight. Its balconies, tall windows and manicured lawns belonged to a time before the faeries, but the elaborate wards set up around its perimeter told me the mages took their security seriously. That, and they wanted to keep riffraff like me out.

The memory of my last visit remained seared into my brain. The day I'd crawled out of Faerie with the dried blood of the Sidhe I'd killed on my hands. I'd wandered around the streets in numb horror and confusion until I'd stumbled upon this street. To this day, I still remembered the harshness of the sun burning the back of my neck and arms. I'd been under shade for so long that the world held an unreal haze, and the manor might have been a mirage. The same went for the sharply dressed men who stood talking outside. Until one said the word *faerie.*

It had been the first time I'd heard someone audibly acknowledge the beings that filled the strange new world I'd stumbled into. Piskies fluttered around in packs, imps and gnomes peered from bushes, and nymphs lurked beneath the rivers' surfaces, eyes glittering. Try as I might, I couldn't connect this surreal new world with the one I remembered from before. The few cars on the road were broken down and battered, and when my gaze landed on the sleek black vehicle with tinted windows, I'd zeroed in on the people climbing out of the back seat. A pair of women in fine clothes, who joined the three men standing outside the manor.

I ran towards them, forgetting that I wore nothing but a ragged dress I'd stolen when a bunch of fire imps had burned my clothes off. The mages ignored me outright, save for one, who halted outside the gate and regarded me with one eyebrow raised. Like the others, he wore a tailored black suit and a long cloak, his hair crisply parted to the side. "Who are you?"

My throat dry, I croaked out, "Ivy. Please, you have to help me. I don't know where I am."

"You're at the headquarters of the Mage Lords," said the man. "Whose blood is that? Not yours?"

The words had stuck in my throat. *A faerie lord. I killed a faerie lord.* "I just want to go home. Do you—do you have a telephone I can use?"

"We're not a charity." His face showed nothing but contempt. "You can't come into the manor. You're filthy."

My heart sank. "It's not my fault. There's… my home has gone."

I'd expected it, deep down, but the level of change the faeries had wrought went beyond a mere few days of destruction. Words echoed in my mind, spoken by the man to whom I owed my escape from Faerie. *To the Sidhe, a mortal's lifespan is nothing more than a blink. Decades pass in our world, but this place remains endless.*

The mage watched me, his expression a mixture of distaste and wariness. "Go back to your coven."

"I don't have a coven," I said. "When... when did the faeries come?"

"Ten years ago."

His words burst the dam in my mind. I dropped to my knees and screamed. And kept screaming, sure that someone would come running and help.

Nobody did. The mages had retreated into the manor and closed the door on my screams, leaving me alone, burning on the outside, icy cold on the inside, with faerie blood on my hands.

Another decade on, the manor looked exactly the same. Trimmed hedges lined the path, and a wrought-iron fence kept out any intruders who weren't already deterred by the glowing wards. I hovered on the balls of my feet, angling myself so that anyone inside the grounds would be able to see me.

A man appeared on the other side, quiet as a ghost. He hardly looked older than twenty, and his perfectly even teeth shone pure white, disconcertingly inhuman. His smooth dark hair flowed to shoulder length, his eyes like ice-blue chips. No human had eyes that unnatural bright shade, either, unless he wore contacts. My body tensed.

"Back off, faerie." Did the mages employ faerie guards? I'd thought they had nothing to do with the Sidhe, but this guy sure as hell wasn't pure human.

The man's dazzling smile disappeared. "I'm no faerie. What are you doing lurking outside?"

"I have an invitation from your leader, the *esteemed* Lord Colton," I said. "And believe me, I don't want to be here."

"Don't talk about my boss that way." His eyes narrowed. "I think you should leave."

"I've been ordered to come here." I shifted on my feet so that he could see the sword at my waist.

A knife appeared in his hand, drawn from its sheath with faerie-swift speed. "Don't threaten me, witch."

I stepped towards him. "Then put the weapon away, faerie."

"I'm not—"

"What is going on here?" Vance Colton appeared behind him, and the gate creaked open as though he'd given it a verbal command. He didn't wear the long coat this time, but a tailored shirt and trousers. "Ralph, step aside."

The faerie boy shot me one final glare and shuffled to the right, leaving the path through the gate clear.

"Ivy," said Lord Colton. "I hoped you'd see sense."

I ignored his smug tone and walked over the threshold into the manor's grounds, shooting his unfriendly guard a glare. He'd already melted into the surrounding hedges as swiftly as he'd arrived. *Not a faerie indeed.*

"Your delightful faerie guard pulled a knife on me," I said to Lord Colton as we walked past a row of hedges sculpted into the shapes of mythical beasts. Curling magical glyphs decorated the manor's walls, shimmering like starlight on water. The mages could easily afford unobtrusive wards, but they evidently wanted to send a clear message to any potential trespassers. "You might want to teach him some manners."

"Faerie?" Lord Colton frowned at me over his shoulder. "If you mean Ralph, I assume you tried to frighten him off?"

"If your guards are running scared from me, there's something wrong with your system."

"There's no reason to be so hostile." He reached the doorstep. "I'm offering you a favour."

"By threatening to take away my livelihood." I refused to

let him play word games with me. "I took on the case first. You turned it down."

"Before I knew magic was involved." He pushed the door open and beckoned me into the hallway.

"Faeries," I corrected. "I'll bet you don't know the difference between a boggart and a brownie."

I took a careful step over the threshold, recalling his previous comment about not leaving blood on the carpets. The stains on my boots were old, but the hallway was pristine enough to make me wonder if the mages had cleansing spells etched on the walls like those protective glyphs outside.

"If you're an expert, tell me the name of the species that attacked us yesterday." Lord Colton began to walk down the hallway.

After a moment's hesitation, I followed. "Hellhounds. Faerie dogs."

He gave a brief nod that might have meant approval coming from anyone else. "I wasn't aware witches were experts on faeries."

If he was trying to probe me for information, I didn't take the bait. We reached an office panelled in cherrywood. Sunlight filtered through the drapes onto the bookcases and filing cabinets surrounding the neat desk and chair. Given the stories, I'd expected something less... mundane.

"So the rumours weren't true," I remarked. At least, there didn't seem to be any troll heads anywhere so far.

"Rumours?"

"The shifters say you keep the heads of the trolls you've killed hanging on the walls. Unless they're in a hidden room somewhere. Like the Bluebeard story."

Could I picture him butchering people and storing their corpses in cupboards? Maybe. After Henry's claim that the aura of a supremely powerful shifter was almost overpowering, I'd kind of expected to pick up on the same vibe. But while the Mage Lord's personality might be grating, dragging me into his office seemed more in line with someone who wanted to show off his authority and wealth, not mount my severed head on the wall as a warning to anyone else who crossed him. If he wanted me dead, he didn't need to go to this level of trouble.

"That's a new one." The corner of his mouth twitched.

"It wouldn't surprise me if you did," I went on. "If you're about to pull out that weapon of yours and decapitate me, I'd like to be forewarned."

He cocked a brow. "You think I'm going to kill you?"

I considered this. "No, but I'd be ready if you tried."

He laughed this time. "I hate to disappoint you. I had no idea my reputation was so dire."

Had to be a lie, right? He, unlike the faeries, could tell all the lies he wanted. "The first time I saw you, you were threatening someone with a sword because they wanted you to find their missing kid."

His smile faded. "You were there? In the Singing Banshee?"

"Yes." No point in pretending otherwise.

"Every hour, about thirty people show up here trying to convince me to use magic to solve their problems," said Lord Colton. "If I accepted all those cases, I'd have no time to take any meaningful action to keep the city safe. The number of parents who've come to the manor begging for help finding their runaway teenager is not insignificant either, and none of those cases have had any magical involvement."

"So you scared him into running straight to me."

"Clearly," he said. "Does that answer your questions? As for the rumours, you carry a reputation of your own. You single-handedly knocked out a bridge troll two days ago, didn't you?"

Don't tell me he called my boss. "Yes. Now, can you tell me why you felt the need to threaten my livelihood?"

"You aren't registered as a magical practitioner, for a start. This case may require spellwork to solve."

"I live with the second most powerful witch in the local coven," I said. "She's doing the spellwork. I do the investigating."

"How long have you been working as a consultant?"

"Five years," I said. "Longer than you've been in this position, I'm told. I've solved over a dozen missing child cases."

"Changelings?"

I glared at him to cover up the creeping sensation that crawled down my spine at the very mention of the word. The one changeling case I'd been involved in, I'd been the victim, and nobody had solved the crime.

"No," I said. "But I've dealt with faeries before."

"Your full name's Ivy Lane, right?"

"Why do you want to know?"

"Before I form an agreement with somebody, I need to know certain information."

"Who said anything about an agreement?"

"Larsen. He's your employer, so I had to obtain permission from him to work with you."

"The treacherous bastard." He *had* called Larsen, and that would explain why he'd been so pissed off earlier, too. Larsen hated the mages, though he'd never dare to close the door on their leader. I had to admit I wouldn't mind seeing the Mage Lord pull a sword out of thin air in front of *him.*

"He's your boss, isn't he?" asked Lord Colton. "He told me you've worked for him for ten years, since you were sixteen. That's awfully young to be a killer."

"It's the legal working age, isn't it?" I'd become a killer because I'd had no choice, but he hadn't earned the details from me. "You might have noticed we live in a dangerous world."

"Fair point." He looked me up and down, though I couldn't for the life of me figure out what he was assessing me for this time. "You're certainly qualified for this job, but it's required by law for the Mage Lords to intervene if magic is involved in any capacity."

"Fine," I said. "If I get the compensation from Swanson. He offered the job to me first."

"That seems adequate," he said. "I should warn you, however, that if I think you're endangering anyone, I have licence to take any magical props you own away from you."

Props? He assumed I was using regular hedge witch spells. A laughable assumption, but one he was welcome to believe. "That seems adequate."

His eyes glittered with amusement. "This is going to be interesting."

The arrogant arse. "You got your wish. Now you'd better follow through on your end of the bargain. I need the money. I'll bet *you* don't." I looked pointedly at the chair's fancy furnishings, the embossed bookcases—hell, everything in the room stank of money and privilege, and made my tattered jeans and top with one too many holes in the sleeves look even shabbier.

"I keep my promises," he replied. "If you keep yours. What's your experience in this area?"

"You don't get my life story." I straightened my spine and looked into his eyes, refusing to let him gain any more ground than he already had. "You just get my expertise. Believe it or not, I'm good at my job, but I'm not your employee. You can't order me around or make me play by your rules."

"That remains to be seen," he said. "Your skills. Tell me about them."

"I can use any spell. As you've seen."

"Anyone can buy a spell from the market."

"And half of them are duds. My flatmate and I make them from scratch. And I'm good at killing things."

His gaze dropped to the blade sheathed at my waist. "Evidently."

"Faeries," I elaborated. "I'm good at killing faeries. And I'd say whoever sent those hellhounds is in need of a friendly chat with my blade."

Lord Colton's mouth twisted into a smirk. "Well, if you're so certain," he said, "let's begin."

Were mages incapable of uttering a sentence that didn't employ excessive levels of drama? I almost returned his smirk, but I'd pushed my luck by mocking him already. I kept a neutral expression on my face when I spoke. "As you've probably gathered, my last attempt to find the changeling ended in us being ambushed by hellhounds. The Swansons' house is warded with iron now, so I'd prefer to use a tracking spell in an uninhabited area, just in case."

"To find the changeling," he said. "What does it look like?"

"I don't know." When he raised an eyebrow, I added, "Changelings are shapeshifter faeries. They're also not very bright, which tends to be how they get coerced or persuaded into impersonating humans. It's their masters you want to watch out for."

That was the issue. Those illegal spells set up in the Swansons' son's room didn't look like the work of a simple-minded changeling, but as to who had given the orders, I couldn't say.

"Masters," he repeated. "The fae. Sidhe?"

"Might be," I hedged. "So, I'll lure out the changeling, and you can do something useful like hold onto the trapping spell while I lay the bait."

"*Hold* the spell?"

I gave him my most charming smile. "It's nice to have an assistant sometimes."

"*Assistant?*"

"You don't have to repeat every word I say, sir."

He grunted. "I'm starting to doubt your expertise."

"You're the one who reeled me into working with you," I told him. "I work better alone. This is the best you're going to get."

"Fine," he said. "I'm putting a call through to the other Mage Lords to let them know there might be rogue faeries loose in the city."

I opened my mouth to object, but he'd already reached for the landline on the desk and tapped a string of numbers that I could only assume was some kind of mage code for 'shit's about to go down'. Placing the phone back in its cradle, he gave a satisfied nod. "We have backup on standby."

"Oh, good," I said. "Nice to know you have faith in me."

"Do you frequently walk out with no backup?"

"You're the backup." I hitched my smile back into place. "I did say I could do my job."

His brows rose. Probably, it had been a while since anyone stood up to him, but the head of the Mage Lords was likely surrounded by fawning admirers. Okay, I hadn't seen much in the way of that so far, but it was early days.

"We're partners," he said. "That makes it *our* job, not just yours. The other mages can step in and intervene if need be."

"They won't need to." I *hoped* not, as I didn't need all the mages figuring out my ties to the faeries. As long as Lord Colton proved more of a help than a hindrance, I'd tolerate his presence, but I drew the line at letting him bring a legion of underlings along for the ride.

"You seem certain," he commented. "The reserve team consists of two fire mages, one frost mage, two earth mages and an air mage. Would your skills be sufficient to make up for that?"

What was he doing now, trying to goad me into confiding the extent of my abilities? I glared at him instead. "Depends if *your* skills are up to scratch."

The mage bared his teeth in a grin. "*My* skills are more than sufficient, I think you'll find." His tone slid over me, unexpectedly seductive, and sent my thoughts right into the gutter. I fought to keep from blushing.

The gleam in his eye told me he knew exactly the effect he'd had. What in the hell was the matter with me? After the faeries, I knew better than to fall for a pretty face, but this guy... well, 'pretty' wasn't the word I'd use to describe him. Unless I employed the phrase 'pretty scarily attractive.'

Nope. *Not* going there. I shut the thoughts down and gave him a look. "We'll see about that."

I strode down the corridor without looking back, but I swore I heard him laughing at me as he locked his office.

What have I got myself into?

7

I called Swanson as we left the Mage Lords' house to let him know we were tracking the changeling but didn't give any more details. I'd rather avoid him getting involved in this any further. He'd had a damn close call, and the idea that the hellhounds had attacked him at home made me certain the faeries weren't done with his family yet. It'd be downright irresponsible to perform the tracking spell anywhere near his house.

Unfortunately, I couldn't go to one of my usual haunts, because of the obvious presence of the Mage Lord who walked down the drab streets like he expected red carpets to unfurl themselves before him. His black coat made him stick out like a troll amongst humans, only with considerably more visual appeal. The only upside was that the faeries might think twice about attacking me when they saw him; although he didn't appear to have any weapons on him, his whole manner radiated power, and he projected an aura of absolute confidence with every step. It was difficult not to feel like I walked in his shadow, but I kept my head high. Partnership or not, the job was mine.

"Whereabouts did you plan to perform the spell?" he asked.

"Preferably as far from anywhere inhabited as possible."

Lord Colton indicated a nondescript black car parked near the manor. "I can drive us."

I snorted. "Yeah, right. If the changeling sees the pair of us zooming around in one of your cars, we won't have a hope in hell of finding its hiding place."

"Very well," he said, surprising me. "What, pray tell, is your exact plan?"

"I'll track the changeling, then if it's still in the area, I'll set up a trap to lure it in." That had sounded better in my head, I'd freely admit.

"A trap." Scepticism tinged his voice. "How much do you know of changelings, exactly?"

I looked away, annoyed at the way my skin grew cold and my chest tightened at the word.

"Enough. Like I said, they're shapeshifters, tricksters, and not overly bright. That means a basic trap ought to do the trick."

"I take it the changeling was the one who called those hellhounds to the Swansons' house yesterday?"

Damn. He must have some inkling that I'd covered up a few of the details. Had Larsen told him about me showing up at the office with necromantic equipment? *Bastard.*

"I assume so," I evaded, waiting for the blow to fall. If he did know, why not say so outright? He'd know what necromancy looked like, but he didn't speak as we walked out of the suburban area and into a more unsavoury neighbourhood with dilapidated buildings on either side. Unable to ignore his stares a moment longer, I gave in. "What?"

"Where'd you learn so much about the faeries?" he asked. "I asked all my contacts for information, and most of them don't even know what a changeling is."

"Clearly nobody reads faerie stories anymore." Considering most people nowadays had *lived* one, at least if they'd been born before the invasion, I could forgive that, but while obvious resistance to deception would be an asset while dealing with the fae, it was also a major nuisance. "I have a loud-mouthed talking piskie living in my flat. You tend to pick up a few things."

"Really." He framed the word more like an incredulous statement than a question.

"Yes." That was as much as I'd give. "Any ideas where I should cast the spell? I don't want to draw the changeling's attention towards any more innocent humans."

"I have a field set aside for spellwork."

"You *own* a field?"

"The mage council does." He led the way down a side street to an old car park, beyond which lay what appeared to have once been a football pitch. Abandoned after the invasion, I assumed. The houses bore shattered windows and overgrown gardens, but were otherwise in decent enough condition to make me wonder if everyone who'd lived in the area had been evacuated as a precaution and never returned. Or never had the chance to. We were close enough to mage territory to make me wonder if they hadn't suffered losses in the invasion, too. I'd never asked.

I shoved my own memories away and concentrated on not slipping in the mud stirred up from the recent rain. Lord Colton entered the field and trod through the mud without getting so much as a speck on his fancy shoes. Given that they remained black and shiny, I could only assume they'd been doctored with some kind of mud-repelling spell. Talk about over-preparing, though I definitely wasn't jealous by the time I'd pulled my boot from the mud for the tenth time, dirt splattering the legs of my jeans. They were barely washed-out blue by this point, and I'd applied so many repair spells that they were probably held together by sheer willpower. I yanked my boot free from the mud and glared at the Mage Lord when he turned around, presumably to see what was taking me so long.

Throughout the field, the scorched remains of spell circles marked the dead grass. A faint burning smell lingered in the air, tickling my nostrils. A scent I was familiar with, living with a witch.

I found a free patch of grass and set up my own spell while Lord Colton watched. It came as no surprise when he raised an eyebrow at the small container in my hand. "What's that for?"

"The changeling's hairs." I didn't miss his sceptical expression. "Blood's the most accurate method of using a tracking spell, but this is the best I could get. Anything containing the target's DNA will do."

He grunted, looking displeased. The mages didn't much care for blood magic, perhaps because it strayed too close to the sort of unpleasantness I'd seen in the Swansons' house. Namely, necromancy. While the necromancers did hold some level of status as far as supernaturals went, I figured the reason the mages didn't associate with their creepy neighbours was that half of them were too unnerved by the idea of animating corpses to want to share an office. Like mages, necromancers had one skill only, except theirs edged towards the dark and creepy end of the supernatural spectrum.

When the spell had expanded into a wider circle, I scattered the hairs onto the cracked soil. Light flared up along the circle's edge, as vibrant green as before, but this time a tingling sensation ran through my fingertips and green light bathed my hands. Images rushed through my head, muted of colour but recognisable as streets I'd seen the previous day, lined with well-maintained houses and neat lawns.

I blinked the images away and let the circle collapse into fine powder. "It's hiding less than a mile from here. I'll set up the trap, but there's no reason for you to stay and watch. It might take a while for the creature to show up."

He raised an eyebrow. "Are you that desperate to get away from me?"

"Yes." No point in hiding that I wanted the whole case over with as soon as possible.

"How flattering," he said. "You don't sugar-coat your words, do you?"

"I'm a mercenary," I said. "We're not known for eloquence and sophistication. We're also not that interesting when you get to know us."

I reached into my bag and retrieved the second spell I'd brought—a red elastic band, the colour Isabel used for traps—and placed it on the grass. At a tap from my finger, it expanded into a larger circle as the tracking spell had done.

"I'm interested in getting to know you," said Lord Colton, with the faintest emphasis on the word *you.*

The feeling isn't mutual, I told myself, but that was a lie. Hell if I wasn't curious about him—both his mage powers and the shifter side that remained all but invisible—and despite Henry's comments earlier, there wasn't so much as a trace of the predator that supposedly lurked beneath the surface.

"My life is pretty boring." I feigned checking the circle was perfectly symmetrical and tried not to imagine Isabel shaking her head at me. She'd have berated me for passing up the opportunity to get to know a handsome guy—with astonishing powers, no less—but I usually dated non-magical, unobtrusive guys who wouldn't cause me any more stress. Not that the faeries hadn't done a thorough job of destroying every attempt I'd ever made at pursuing a relationship regardless, but the mages were thoroughly off-limits.

Moreover, I didn't get on with predators. I'd spent too long being prey.

"I beg to differ," he said. "You work for Larsen Crawley, but you aren't a glory hunter. You hate faeries, but you have a piskie living in your house. You live with a witch, but you aren't one."

I stiffened at the last part. "Yes, I am."

"You don't belong to a coven."

"Witches can be independent. If I wasn't a witch, I wouldn't be able to use these spells." I indicated the circle, but his gaze never left me.

"No," he said. "An unconventional witch, then. I confess myself *very* interested."

A chill crawled up my spine. Last time I'd heard those words, they'd come from the mouth of a Sidhe lord. I looked away from him, suddenly wishing I was anywhere but here.

"I told you," I said, my voice brittle, "you don't get my life story."

His arms dropped to his sides. "What's the problem?"

I blinked, determined not to look at him, and aware that my behaviour would look downright bizarre to an outsider. He hadn't meant to speak like one of *them*. He'd plainly never seen me in his life before we'd met in the alleyway, and he hadn't been present the day his fellow mages turned me away ten years ago. I'd put him at between thirty and thirty-five, so he'd probably been a fully-fledged mage, but not yet a Mage Lord.

I rummaged through my bag to avoid catching his eye. "You've been nothing but disrespectful, and now suddenly you want to have a friendly chat."

"I'm letting you do your job, aren't I?"

Maybe I needed to give him the benefit of the doubt. "If

you get to ask me questions, then I get to do the same to you." I lifted my head. "What's your ability?"

"I'll tell you, if you tell me what yours is."

I fell back on my usual explanation. "You've seen me fight. As for magic, I have the bare minimum. I can use most witch spells, but I don't know the coven rulebook by heart. My friend Isabel does, though."

I could tell he didn't quite believe me, but my explanation made perfect sense, and even he, for all his resources, would never guess the truth. Not in a million years.

"I'm a displacer," he said. "It means I can manipulate space and matter to some degree."

I raised an eyebrow. "You can mess with the rules of physics?"

"Not on a large scale. Some people think I'm a conjurer, but it's a matter of displacing an object from one place to another."

Wow. I'd never heard of an ability like it, but what he'd done—sliced hellhounds' throats from a distance, conjured objects up from nowhere—was way more impressive than standard mage tricks. Not that I'd admit so to him. He had a high enough opinion of himself already.

"So you can fetch that stone over there?"

His eyes followed my hand as I pointed across the field. "Yes. Technically. It'd be a waste of power."

"There's a limit, is there?"

"All magic has a limit," said Lord Colton. "Most usefully, my ability allows me to move around the city without drawing attention."

"Because your giant sword's... where? Back at the mansion?"

"In the weapons room, yes."

"Weapons room. How fancy."

"You have quite the collection yourself," he commented,

glancing at the daggers at my waist and the ones strapped to the sides of my boots.

"Can't be too prepared," I said.

"They're all made of iron, or an alloy?"

"Does it matter?"

"You mentioned you mostly kill faeries," said Lord Colton. "Either everything you fight with is made of iron or you have a suit of armour somewhere."

"Funny." I returned my attention to my bag and fished out a container of miscellaneous spell ingredients. From inside, I selected a couple of sylvan leaves, which I placed inside the circle. Those things were practically catnip to most small faeries and their scent was potent enough to reach every fae within a mile, so I'd have to apply iron to fend off any piskies or other beasts who might venture near the trap. "There's our bait. All we need now is a cloaking spell to hide the circle."

I set the second circle up around the first, conscious of him watching my every move. Flattering in a way; I rarely got an audience. Sure, it was Isabel's spell, but I still grinned at the mage as the concealment spell flashed a smoky grey once and then vanished, along with the faint red lines giving the trap away. To anyone who didn't know better, the sylvan leaves lay scattered in the middle of a bed of grass and nothing more.

I then sprinkled more sylvan leaves at intervals throughout the field, leading up to the fence closest to where I'd seen the changeling roaming in the vision shown by the tracking spell, and left a similar trail across the road until I was certain I'd covered all routes by which the changeling might approach. Lord Colton followed my lead, eyeing the trail of leaves with scepticism. It couldn't be plainer from his manner that he disliked not being the one in control.

"Are you sure that will work?" he asked as we returned to the field to wait for our target.

"I'm sure." *Eventually.* I was banking on the changeling continuing to move in the same direction and not take any detours, but I already glimpsed a few piskies flitting around the nearby bushes who'd taken an interest in the sylvan leaves. I reached into my bag for a jar of iron filings—another essential tool for anyone who ventured near the fae —and flicked them at the winged fae until they fled with shrill screams.

Lord Colton watched the piskies take flight. "This method seems... inefficient."

"I did tell you it might take a while." And evidently, he intended to stay for the duration. Oh, joy. "It's that or jump on the changeling from behind, but it's likely to cloak itself in glamour as soon as it realises there are humans around."

His expression remained unimpressed. Maybe he was right and we'd better off using a more direct method of catching our prey, but I'd learned from living with a piskie that they could slide out of almost any trap, no matter how airtight. Simple worked best.

Unless, perhaps, you had a mage on your team. After a long pause, I tilted my head at my companion. "Out of curiosity, if you can displace things, can you reach through thin air and grab the changeling?"

"No." His tone was surprisingly curt. "That's not how it works."

Ooh. "Can you grab *people?*"

"No."

Ha. See how he liked being bombarded with questions. "Well, you can hardly lecture me on using inefficient trapping methods."

"We've got company." He spoke matter-of-factly, but he

shifted on his feet in a way that indicated he was ready to fight at any second.

A small figure appeared at the field's end. Not a piskie this time, but a wingless creature the size of a child. That, though, was where the similarities ended. Its ears were long and pointed, as was its face, while its legs were spindly and delicate enough for me to wonder how they supported its lanky body. It wore ragged clothes, the sort you might pick up at a jumble sale, and its eyes—black, twice as big as a human's—locked onto the sylvan leaves.

Satisfaction rushed through me when the creature ran towards the trap with a gleeful cry.

That was easier than I expected. It hadn't gone far from the Swansons' at all, and there weren't many other wild fae in this area. As the trap snapped closed in a sudden flash of red light, I walked towards the circle and grinned at our captive. A pair of bulging dark eyes stared back from within the red.

"Humans," the changeling whimpered.

"That's right," I said. "Mind answering a few questions?"

The faerie writhed and screamed. I'd have felt sorry for it, except the bloody menace was faking its reaction. The circle wasn't designed to hurt, only to keep it contained.

"Humans, cruel humans, let me go."

"Does the trap hurt?" asked Lord Colton.

I hadn't pegged him for the pacifist type. "No. It's an act. Stop being so bloody melodramatic." I took out my sword, letting the creature see the iron, and it fell silent. "You answer my questions, you get to leave. Simple."

The changeling gave another shrill wail.

"None of that," I said. "You were told to take the place of a human teenager. Who sent you?"

The changeling's wail reached such a pitch that my ears throbbed. I drew a knife and hurled it at the circle. The point missed the changeling by a hair's breadth—intentionally—

and buried itself in the soil. The changeling's answering shriek died when the mage pulled his sword from thin air again and pointed it at the beast's neck. "Who are you working for?"

"Nobody."

"I can put you under a compulsion spell." A lie—those spells were hellishly tricky to make and definitely not among my supplies—but it gulped, its bulbous eyes larger than ever. "Just tell the truth. Who sent you?"

"I didn't see his face," said the changeling. "He had silver hair, and he carried a blade forged of ash."

Lord Colton's expression said *that's interesting.* I hoped mine said the same, not what I was really thinking: *oh, crap.* As far as I knew, only the Sidhe lords themselves used weapons forged from the hearts of their trees.

"And he asked you to impersonate a teenage human?" asked Lord Colton.

"I hadn't a choice, mortal," the changeling croaked.

Really. Faeries were unable to lie, but that didn't stop them manipulating the truth if it served them. "You said you didn't see his face. You didn't say you never heard his name."

"Clever, mortal." The changeling's gaze shifted to me. "Are you fae-blooded?"

Oh, shit. Lord Colton glanced at me out of the corner of his eye.

"If I was, I wouldn't be carrying iron." I held up Irene, and he whimpered. "Who summoned you? Tell me the truth, or I'll cut you."

The changeling tried to speak, but only gasping noises escaped its throat. I froze, my heart sinking. I knew what a tongue-tying spell looked like. Someone had cursed the creature so it physically couldn't speak the name of its summoner.

"I get it, you can't answer," I said quickly, aware of Lord

Colton watching my reaction. "Can you say *where* you were summoned? And when?"

"Some days ago, mortal," the changeling answered. "Near the home of the fae-blooded."

Ah, shit. That could only mean half-blood territory, the closest place to Faerie in this realm. In other words, exactly the kind of place where somebody with a lot of magic and a lot of guts could summon up a changeling.

"Did you see the human child you replaced?" My heart began to pound, cold sweat gathering on my back as I instinctively prepared for the worst.

"Yes."

"Where'd they take him?" My heart beat faster with each word.

"I don't know." The changeling burst into tears. "Let me go, cruel human."

"Only when you tell me where the child is," I said in my coldest voice. "Who has him? Got any names?"

It took everything I had to speak clearly and confidently despite the sweat running down my spine and the memories threatening to claw their way free. *No. He's not dead. You can still find him.*

The changeling started to speak and choked again, beating its tiny feet on the charred soil.

Lord Colton studied the creature. "What's wrong with it?"

"Tongue-tying spell," I said. "Whoever's behind this figured their changeling might get caught." Not that I'd expected this to be easy, but if I couldn't track the Swansons' son and the changeling couldn't speak the name of his captor, we were at a dead end.

"I see," said Lord Colton, lowering his sword. "If the changeling can't speak the names of anyone involved, can it describe them? It claimed the faerie had silver hair?"

"Yeah, like half the faerie-blooded population in this realm."

"Aside from the ash blade," Lord Colton reminded me. "Trinkets like that aren't easy to come by."

"True." I had to hand it to him for picking up on the details. He'd likely never encountered this kind of spell before, but one didn't get to be the leader of the mages by being a fool. "It'll be faerie-made, but where would a half-Sidhe even get that?" I snapped my mouth shut before I gave too much away.

"Was anyone else there?" Lord Colton asked the changeling. "You don't have to give names."

"My brothers." The little beast cast a shifty look around. "They're here, too."

Sure enough, I spied two more small figures creeping across the field. Three feet tall with long, spindly legs, they waved pointed knives at me. Not regular knives—faeries couldn't touch most metals—but sharpened twigs. *How threatening.* I nearly laughed, some of the tension in my spine easing.

"Get in the circle." I paced towards them, holding out my sword. "This contains enough iron to make your skin fall off your bones."

Two shrill screams followed; a glance confirmed Lord Colton was watching me with amusement in his eyes.

"Come on, get in the circle."

Fire exploded from nowhere, and the faeries screamed, bolting across the field and straight into the path of the circle. I opened my mouth to shout a warning, but the cloud of fire disappeared as suddenly as it had arrived. A hooded figure approached in the manner of a movie star walking away from an explosion.

Lord Colton regarded the man with a frown. "Must you be so dramatic?"

I snorted. He was plenty dramatic himself. I watched the new mystery guy, who lowered his hood to reveal a crop of dark-red hair. His coat was similar in style to Lord Colton's. He must be another of the Mage Lords.

"You're Ivy?" He held out a hand. "I'm Drake, Vance's second-in-command."

"And a fire conjurer?" I shook his hand warily. His skin was warm but didn't burn to touch. Interesting. His casual stance was a sharp contrast to Lord Colton's uptight attitude, but he must pack some serious firepower to have the title of second most powerful mage. Pun intended.

"That's me. What's with them?" He indicated the changelings lying in a shrieking heap within the circle.

"We're questioning suspects," said Lord Colton.

Drake grinned at the changelings, and they howled and dived away from him, pitching against the circle's edges. "Isn't that a witch's trap?"

"It's not worth expending my own power on an interrogation," said Lord Colton.

"Ha. More like you overextended it in the fight with those hellhounds."

I glanced at him, surprised. So the Mage Lord did have a limit, and his fellow mages didn't mind pointing it out. I stowed that information away for later.

"Anything else you want to ask them?" Lord Colton directed this at me. *Changing the subject, huh.*

"I think we've covered everything." By that, of course, I meant we hadn't learned a damn thing. "Care to help carry the changelings back? I can turn the trapping spell into a cage so they won't escape."

He raised an eyebrow. "You want to keep them in your house?"

"I thought you arrested faeries who broke the rules."

"We don't," he replied. "Technically, minor infractions are for the mercenary guild to handle."

That figured. Larsen wouldn't be pleased with me, but letting those changelings run free would be out of the question. "Fine. I'll drop them off at the guild."

"Drake, you're supposed to be at the manor," Lord Colton said to his companion. "What happened?"

"It's bad news," said Drake, his smile fading. "A second child has gone missing, this time from necromancer territory."

8

"Who?" I asked immediately. *Oh. Shit.*

"The daughter of two necromancers, apparently," said Drake, pocketing his phone. "Two of our people are at her house. I'd be with them, but I heard you'd decided to go wandering off with a witch in search of a changeling."

Necromancer territory? That was way over on the other side of town from the Swansons' place. "How d'you know it's linked to this case?"

"Because I followed those little buggers here after I unmasked them," he said. "One of them was trying to impersonate a teenage girl. Not very successfully, I might add."

"A teenage girl?" My voice rose on the last word, much as I tried to hide it.

"Yeah. Her name's Melanie Climes. I've just spoken to her family."

"You followed this creature all the way here?" asked Lord Colton.

"In a car," he said. "Little bastards move fast."

The changelings tripped over one another in an effort to

escape the circle. I rolled my eyes at them, trying to suppress the tightening feeling in my chest. Another child taken, and I'd come no closer to finding the culprit.

"Have you taken on the case officially?" I asked. "If so, I'd like to talk to the victim's family."

Drake tilted his head at Lord Colton. "What do you say, Vance?"

Lord Colton spoke to me instead. "What are you going to tell Mr Swanson?"

"That I caught the changeling. At least it won't be bothering him anymore." I faced the three small creatures in the circle. "Did any of you use magic *after* you were told to impersonate humans?"

It was the most roundabout way I could think of to figure out who was responsible for summoning the hellhounds. These creatures were at Faerie's lowest rank. They'd been set up as much as we had, I was certain. Somebody else had laid the trap.

"No magic, none," said the first changeling as its brothers howled and beat their fists upon the grass. "Can't use magic."

"You can't?" I'd known most lesser faeries couldn't so much as conjure up a spark, but it was good to confirm that the changelings were no exception. On the other hand... "What about those illegal necromantic traps in the Swansons' house? Did you have anything to do with them?"

Lord Colton's gaze shifted to me, but I kept my attention on the changeling. It gave a frantic head-shake. "No. Wasn't us."

"Did you see the person who did?"

The changeling shuddered. "Don't like bad magic!"

"I was under the impression that all faeries could access a certain amount of power even while in this realm," Lord Colton said to me.

"Not all of them can." At a sharp look from him, I added,

"The piskie in my flat can't use magic. Generally, small fae don't have the skill or the brains."

Three shrill voices protested, but Lord Colton cut through them. "I see. Perhaps an interrogation from the mercenary guild will loosen that tongue-tying spell."

"Unlikely." Larsen would never have seen one in his life, but I could hardly leave them in the middle of a field either. "We need to remove them either way. Did you say you brought a car?"

Drake grinned at me. "Someone's angling for a lift?"

I shrugged. "Figured it'd be easier to get to the Climes' house that way. Saves time."

"The Climes case isn't yours," Lord Colton said pointedly.

"It's connected, isn't it?"

"I'd say it is," said Drake. "Come on, then."

Lord Colton glared at me. "If you're volunteering to carry those changelings, you're welcome to."

"No problem," I lied. If it got me in on the Climes case, I'd deal with the irritation of handing the changelings over to Larsen. When I crouched down, they leapt upward and beat their fists against the invisible barrier of the trapping spell. What with their flailing and shrieking, I had to close my eyes to concentrate on picking up the spell circle without accidentally deactivating it. I rested my hands on either side of the edges, and the lines wrapping around the circle folded inward, forming a cage. Three screaming voices hit my eardrums as I lifted the makeshift cage in my arms.

"Quiet," I snapped. "If you don't shut up, I'll pitch you into the canal."

Drake burst out laughing. "Where'd you find her, Vance?"

The changelings' ongoing shrieks drowned out the Mage Lord's reply. Once we left the field, we came to a black car parked in the deserted street. Drake climbed into the front.

To my surprise, Lord Colton didn't call shotgun, but joined me in the back.

"What?" I asked him over the cage of squirming changelings. "This isn't a good time for conversation."

A sharp knife appeared in his hand, resting above the cage. "Be quiet."

All three voices fell silent.

"Nice." I adjusted my grip on the changelings' cage, settling back in my seat. "Now are you going to explain why you keep glaring at me?"

"Did I hear you say you found necromantic equipment at the Swansons' house?" I didn't miss the accusation in his tone. Ah, shit. Now this new disappearance had happened right on necromancer territory, the omission would look even more suspicious.

"Yes," I said, as the car rumbled to life. "At the time, I thought you'd arrest them on suspicion of practising dark magic, so I took the burden off their hands."

"You thought I'd do that?" His mouth turned down at the corners. "We never arrest anyone without an investigation. We'd make inquiries within the Necromancer Guild to start off with."

Really? I'd been so wrapped up in disposing of the evidence, I hadn't stopped to consider the unlikelihood that the Mage Lords would arrest a family of clearly non-magical people like the Swansons. While my first encounter with the Mage Lord had not inspired confidence that they weren't susceptible to abusing their power and authority, it seemed obvious in hindsight that they'd have some level of restraint.

I drew in a breath. "Do you have contacts in the Necromancer Guild, then?"

"We have regular meetings with the other leaders within the supernatural community, yes," he said. "Now that I know the necromancers might have been involved, I'll certainly be in touch with them." His accusing stare remained intact, but I refused to be cowed.

"You threatened to charge me for obstructing an investigation just for doing my job," I said. "When I found all the dark magic crap in the kid's room, I figured you'd burst in and arrest everyone on the scene, including the Swansons."

Displeasure underlaid his voice. "What *did* you find in that room?"

"A couple of defunct summoning circles and a lot of dead rats. I already cleaned them up and disposed of the props in a secure manner." He didn't need to know the coven had taken care of it. The witches wouldn't thank me for sending the Mage Lord to poke into their business next.

"I'll certainly be making enquiries." A phone appeared in his hand. I supposed he didn't have to bother keeping anything in his pockets if he could bend the laws of physics whenever he felt like it. "Lord Evander. I shall be stopping by the guild later. I trust you'll be present. No, I won't accept excuses. I'll see you then."

I arched a brow at him as he ended the call. "Not on friendly terms, then?"

"They're necromancers," he said, as if that explained anything at all.

"And?"

"If dark magic's involved, it's on them. Ninety-nine percent of the time."

Fair. "One of their kids was a victim. You sure nobody wanted to set them up?"

Faeries and necromancers had nothing to do with one another. No surprise when the faeries were immortal and the necromancers dealt in death magic, which effectively meant they stood at opposite ends of the magical spectrum. A changeling using a necromancers' equipment stank of foul play. For all I knew, the person responsible was banking on the mages' distrust of necromancers to obfuscate the true culprit.

"You seem to have given this a lot of thought," the Mage Lord said.

"Are you accusing *me* of being involved?"

"No," he said. "But you did cover up what you found at the Swansons'."

"I told you why. If you made a better first impression, I might not have jumped to conclusions."

Drake turned around from the front seat of the car. "What did you do, Vance?"

"Refused to help rescue a missing kid," I said. "And pulled out his sword on the kid's father in the middle of the *Singing Banshee*."

"Really, Vance?" Drake smirked at him, nearly crashing the car in the process. I gripped the seat with both hands to keep from being sent flying as he veered away from the tree he'd almost hit. "You're usually better at giving a nice first impression to pretty ladies."

Oh, please.

"The first time I saw Ivy, she jumped ten feet into the air to cut a hellhound's throat," said Lord Colton, leaning back in his seat. "Make of that what you will."

"Damn." Drake jerked the steering wheel before we collided with another tree. "You're a witch, right? You don't act like one."

"You're one to talk." I almost added, *You don't act as stuck-up as I thought all mages did, like your boss,* but I managed to hold my tongue.

"Just curious," said Drake. "We haven't hired a witch as our assistant... ever, I don't think."

"Drake, for god's sake, pay attention to the road," said Lord Colton, as we veered into a main street and the car's side scraped against a broken-down lamp post.

"Hey, not all of us can take shortcuts through space-time." Drake didn't appear ruffled by his boss shouting at him. Maybe the mages weren't as uptight as I'd thought.

"Space-time," I said. "I gather he can grab people or animals and haul them across the city? He wouldn't answer."

Lord Colton shot me an irritated look.

"Ha," said Drake. "Technically, he can, but it expends all his power. Living things take a lot more out of him."

"How far can he reach? The other side of the world?"

Drake shot him a grin. "Nah. The city, maybe, but he won't let me get a tape measure and check."

Lord Colton scowled. "What did I say about watching the road?"

"Okay, okay."

I glanced down at the cage. Three angry faces glared up at me. "If you're handing these changelings over to Larsen, I want to talk to him first. They might be nuisances, but some of the mercs are downright brutal to any non-humans we drag in there."

"I thought you hated faeries," said Lord Colton.

"Strongly dislike," I corrected. "These little bastards were in the wrong place at the wrong time, sounds like." I didn't trust them at all, but neither did I want to subject a living creature to the mercenaries' petty cruelty.

Lord Colton didn't look angry anymore. "You're not like his other mercs."

"In what way?"

"Half of them have been arrested for public aggression, haven't they?"

"I don't know. They're not my colleagues." I treated my fellow mercenaries with politeness if they extended the same courtesy to me, but most of them were more into killing monsters for profit than helping people out. Not my style.

"I suppose not." He glanced up as we drove through

shifter territory, recognisable by its tall fences and gates fitted with elaborate lock systems. "I did say you don't strike me as a glory hunter."

Probing for information again, was he? "I'm not hunting for anything except enough cash to keep a roof over my head. So are most mercs, come to that."

"And the time you killed the hydra in the canal?"

Just how much had Larsen told him? It seemed as though he'd heard my entire resume. From the tilt of his head, Drake was listening in, too. Just bloody perfect.

"It was eating people. Nobody else wanted to get too close. The other mercs made all kinds of excuses." Nobody else had wanted to step in—including the mages, actually. "Guess your firepower wouldn't do much good against a giant water beast."

Drake grinned. "Now I know why Vance is so keen to spend time with you. You don't tell him he's wonderful at everything."

"And other people do?" I smirked. "If you ever want brutal honesty from me, you need only ask."

To my consternation, Lord Colton laughed. As did Drake.

"Can we keep her?" said Drake.

"In your dreams."

We turned into a road bordered on one side by a high fence warded with iron. This area had been hit hard by the war, but on the orders of the Mage Lords, the necromancers had gathered as many of the victims as possible and interred their bodies behind walls designed to prevent the undead from flooding the streets the way they had during the invasion. Didn't always work, as evidenced by the zombie infestation a few years ago, but the wrought-iron gates and high fences were sturdy enough to repel most would-be graverobbers.

At the end of the fence stood a squat building of dark

brick. The necromancers' main headquarters. Thick leafless trees framed its entrance, and its unassuming exterior formed a stark contrast to the mages' elaborately decorated manor. A chill wrapped around me. I doubted a single person inside would remember my face, but the memory of my last visit left a bitter taste in the back of my throat.

Upon my return from Faerie, my hopes of ever seeing my family again had plunged to zero until I'd learned the necromancers were capable of calling back the dead. I'd saved an entire month's pay for their services, but the sleazy fucker I'd hired had taken my money and then revealed that too many people had been killed when the human and faerie worlds had collided for him to contact a specific ghost. I hadn't been back since.

"I have to say, I think we have better taste in decor," Drake commented as we approached the gloomy-looking building. Up close, its bricks were the colour of soot, as though someone had liberally applied dye, though my sharp eyes picked out the glimmer of a spell circling its base. Evidently the city's necromancers were egotistical in their own way, except instead of employing glittering wards to put off outsiders as the mages did, they'd opted for a permanent spell that made the place look like a goth nightclub.

"Nice." I glanced at the skull-shaped door knocker. "That's how you play up to stereotypes."

Lord Colton rapped on the door, which swung inward, revealing a short, balding man dressed in a smart suit that was more rumpled than the ever-immaculate Mage Lord's. He looked, ironically, like a funeral director.

"What?" he snapped.

"As you gathered from my call earlier, we're here on urgent business. Someone illegally obtained necromantic equipment from your guild."

"Nonsense," said the man. "I've logged every piece of

equipment that's left the place, and only my own necromancers have made use of them."

"I gather you missed some," said Lord Colton, with a surprising bite to his voice. "They were found in a human home. At a guess, somebody was attempting a summoning."

The necromancer shrugged. "Kids try to do that all the time. I can't police everyone."

"That's your job, Lord Evander," said the Mage Lord.

"And it's not your place to dictate what my job entails, Lord Colton."

Oh boy. At this rate, I'd get to witness a mage-versus-necromancer standoff with my own eyes. Lord Evander's short and unimpressive stature appeared pathetically outmatched compared to the tall, imposing mage, but necromancers allegedly held power over life and death. Regardless, my money was still on the Mage Lord.

"Excuse me," I interjected. "I'm the one who found the equipment. While I was dismantling it, a group of hellhounds attacked me."

The necromancer narrowed his eyes at me. "Hellhounds are faeries."

You don't say. "You aren't concerned someone might have been trying to frame your necromancers?"

"No."

That was it? He wasn't even going to pretend to care?

"Fine," I said. "But don't blame me if a hellhound decides to show up here and take a bite out of you."

Drake snickered behind me, covering it up with a fake cough, while Lord Evander's scowl deepened even further.

Lord Colton stepped forward. "We suspect the perpetrator attempted to use blood necromancy. Several dead animals were found at the scene. Usually that's a sign that someone has attempted to summon a violent spirit."

"I know my own branch of magic," snapped the necromancer. "Most summoning circles drawn by amateurs are flat out wrong. All my necromancers are accounted for. They know the horrors hiding over the veil, and I can assure you none of them would be foolish enough to attempt anything of the sort."

I blinked. "Horrors?"

He gave me a withering look. "The invasion took place not a mile from here. I can assure you that my people are well aware that nothing but trouble lies over the other side of the veil."

"The veil." That was where most people went when they died, but occasionally, a spirit was left behind and decided to stir up trouble. That was allegedly the necromancers' purpose, but since spirits were a rarity, they were more likely to be found charging a small fortune to anyone who wanted to say last goodbyes to dead loved ones and spent the rest of the time walking around in their dark cloaks, being creepy. The only requirement to join their ranks was the ability to see spirits, their own equivalent to the Sight that allowed me to see the fae. Personally, I'd have preferred to see ghosts instead of faeries, but if having the spirit sight required spending all my time at this place, the necromancers could keep it.

"Your people pass through the veil all the time, do they not?" said Lord Colton.

"Only the first layer," said the necromancer. "None are foolish enough to venture beyond the gates. If your client wishes to hire me to extract a poltergeist, I'm more than happy to oblige, but I don't think this is what's happening. I think you're trying to accuse me of breaking the law."

"I'm not accusing you," said Lord Colton, his voice both steely and calm all at once. "I'm simply trying to get to the bottom of this case, and your guild is certainly involved in some manner."

"I beg to differ," he said. "I have a summit to conduct tomorrow, and I have more important business to concern myself with than the whims of paranoid mages."

Without another word, he shut the door in our faces.

"Who pissed on his grave?" I asked in an undertone, earning an amused look from Drake.

Lord Colton swivelled to me. "Have you encountered the guild before?"

"Not in a professional capacity." True enough. "I thought all necromancers could walk into death at any time. I didn't realise the veil was… subdivided. Is that what he implied? Something about a gate?"

"Yes," said Lord Colton. "Most spirits exist on the first layer of the veil. It's my understanding that the necromancers opened the gate to the world beyond when the invasion claimed a significant number of lives in a short time, to keep them from overwhelming the living, but that they never venture to the other side of the gate themselves."

So that's how it went. I held my hands at my sides, clenching my fists to stop them shaking.

"Is that it?" said Drake. "I can't say I'd like to spend any more time in this hellhole, but maybe we ought to interrupt that summit of theirs tomorrow to get their attention."

"First we need to talk to the Climes family," I said. "I can use another tracking spell to see if I can find their daughter." I'd left the changelings in the car, which probably hadn't been the best idea, but I could hardly bring them up to the necromancy guild's doorstep.

"Didn't know you were an expert in tracking as well as decapitation," said Drake.

"Technically, my flatmate is," I said. "She's second in line to the Laurel Coven."

Lord Colton gave me a sideways look. "You live with Francine Blackwood's Second?"

"Yes." It might have surprised me that he knew the coven leader's name, but if he regularly met with the local supernatural community's leaders, he'd likely met Isabel's coven leader if not Isabel herself. "Should I try a tracking spell?"

"I doubt it'll work, given the last time."

He had a point, but I had no intention of abandoning the effort. "Giving up, Lord Colton?"

"No, but we need a new strategy," he said. "Whereabouts are Rod and Bailey?" he asked Drake.

"Combing the city, like they've been doing all day," Drake responded. "Er, I should probably let them know we caught the changelings."

"You mean you've had your people walking around looking for them all day when a simple witch's spell trapped them in half a minute?" I asked, finding this absurdly funny. Not for the first time, it struck me that mages were surprisingly oblivious to magic outside of their immediate circle.

Drake grinned. "They won't mind. Vance was kind enough to put them on patrol together even though they've been flirting hardcore for weeks. He's not as stringent as he pretends to be."

"Witch spells are usually the most direct," said Lord Colton, ignoring Drake's comment, "but that doesn't mean they're the first idea we'd think of."

Hmm. I'd thought he didn't possess an ounce of humility. Maybe I'd been wrong.

A shout made me spin around. Drake marched away from the car, sparks of fire flying from his hands. "The little bastards have gone."

Damn. Behind him, the car door lay open, and the changelings were nowhere to be seen.

9

I stood outside the hedge bordering on half-blood territory and took in a steadying breath. I'd never been to this part of town—at least, not beyond the hedge's boundaries—but short of wandering around hoping I ran into a friendly half-blood on the street, my only option was to walk right into their home and hope they didn't shoot at trespassers.

Most half-bloods lived in here, but the only ones I'd encountered were the few who mingled with humans. Their ethereal beauty didn't look like it belonged in this battered world, and each of them stood out starkly against the mundanity of the ordinary streets lined with worn terraced houses.

In contrast, their own territory had been adapted to mimic Faerie so effectively that all my instincts warned me to run as fast as possible in the opposite direction. On the other side of the hedge, golden sunlight shone despite the pale-grey clouds smothering the sky above the road outside, and beyond, I glimpsed lush, bright flowers blooming at every corner.

The most eerie part was the faint tinkling of faerie music, the plucking of a harp or some similar instrument. I did my best to tune it out, wishing I'd brought earplugs and also, absurdly, that I hadn't come alone.

Don't be ridiculous, Ivy. Like hell would I bring Lord Colton here. He'd come too close to guessing my secret already, and I'd already survived a dressing-down from Larsen when I'd been forced to tell him that I'd captured a group of changelings and then let them escape. I could get through this, too.

The front gate, nestled between thick hedges, wasn't made of metal but from intertwining branches as though it had grown out of the hedges themselves. A tall figure sidled into view on the other side. Well over six feet tall, pale and silver-haired, he fit the changeling's description so exactly that I stared for a moment, forgetting my mission.

The gate creaked open, and the faerie glided out, frosty eyes raking over me. Up close, I could see the human in him; his ears were rounded, not pointed, and his face wasn't perfectly symmetrical, but enough of him resembled a pure faerie to make my fingers curl towards my weapon.

"Your name?" His voice rang in my ears like a melody. Ugh.

"Ivy Lane," I said. "I'm here to speak to…" I fumbled for the client's name. "Alain Delian."

The faerie whose beautification spell I'd recovered hadn't exactly been personable, but talking to someone whom I'd done a favour would win me more brownie points than walking in here and waving my sword around.

"Aren't you one of Larsen's lackeys?" said the faerie.

Lovely. "I'm here to talk to one of my former clients about a confidential matter."

The guard's eyes lingered on the blade at my waist. "No iron in here. Leave your weapons there." He pointed, and a hole formed in the side of the hedge, branches creeping backwards to expose a nest-like shape.

Abandoning my weapons went against all instinct, but I had my magic as backup and no faerie would be foolish enough to steal anything made of iron.

I gathered my daggers together with my sword—the faerie guard raised an eyebrow when I pulled the spare one out of my bra—and put them into the hole in the hedge. I felt naked without them, especially my sword. Poor Irene would have to cope without me for a bit. "I take it your people won't harm me?"

"I can't make any promises," he said.

I'd bet not. The fae took their promises seriously, and a human delivering herself into their hands would be taken as either a threat or an opportunity to play a prank. I was under no illusions there, and while the territory might hide a hundred changelings for all I knew, I'd talk to Alain and then get the hell out. Anything more would risk ending up with my head impaled on that gate.

I followed the guard into a wide-open space far bigger than should by rights have fit between the hedges, and a full-on assault on all my senses almost sent me running back for my weapons. The scent of a thousand flowers created an eye-watering perfume that stung my eyes and nose, while the sound of birdsong turned up to full volume played in the background. Had to be a spell, because I didn't see any birds behind the thick fields of flowers and grassy lawns.

"This is Seelie territory?" I surmised. "Do the Unseelie live somewhere else?"

"No," said the faerie guard. "We have this one area as our territory." There was an unspoken accusation in his voice. Why? Because his kind had been restricted to one territory? They hadn't even lived here before the war.

"So you alternate between Summer and Winter?" I

guessed, looking around at the ever-blooming bright flowers. Sure, it might look beautiful, but Summer hid its fangs behind sweet smiles. Winter showed their fangs for the world to see. I knew which I'd rather face upfront.

The half-faeries' homes ranged from ordinary blocks of flats to literal holes in the ground that might be troll nests. There weren't numbered or named streets either, so I'd have to ask for directions to Alain's house. The sense that I'd made a huge error in coming here drove its claws into my skin the further I walked. The sound of a lyre or some similar instrument punctuated the twittering of birdsong, my skin itched from the heat, and I had the overall impression that someone had plucked my definition of the ninth circle of hell from my head and thrown me into it.

When I came across an enormous fountain, I stopped to ask for directions from a group of nymphs who appeared to be engaged in some kind of naked dance class that I belatedly discovered had half-turned into an orgy. Faeries had almost no taboos around modesty, and I'd learned from my time on the other side that they regarded human social customs with mild confusion at best. Public fornication was an improvement on starting a fight, so I disentangled myself from their attempts to get me to join in and continued until I reached the apartment block in which Alain lived.

The buildings were unlocked, and I walked right in through the front door and found the correct flat.

"Hello?" I knocked on the door. "I'm Ivy Lane, here to see Alain."

A male voice replied from the other side. "You're who?"

"I'm the person who helped find Alain's missing beautification charm," I clarified.

The door opened, revealing a masculine face that would have been inhumanly stunning if not for the scowl twisting his mouth. "And why does a human want to talk to her?"

Who was he, her boyfriend? Like most half-faeries, he wore his hair long, while his cheekbones were sharp enough to cause papercuts and his eyes resembled chips of green glass. With his face, he ought to be wearing medieval armour, not a T-shirt and jeans, though given what I'd seen in the fountain, I should be grateful he wore any clothing at all. It'd take a while to scrub that mental image from my eyes.

"I want to ask a couple of questions." Faeries took everything literally, so I had to tread carefully to avoid giving offence or sounding like I was making an accusation. "Have you seen any… any shapeshifter faeries imitating humans?"

"Why would anyone want to imitate one of you?" he said in disgusted tones.

How friendly. "They were changelings. You know, the sort that sneak into human families' homes and replace their kids as a joke."

The crap I'd found in Swanson's house was far more than a prank, but I had the distinct impression that this guy would not take kindly to me insinuating that one of his fellow faeries might have been dabbling in necromancy.

"I need to know if you've seen any shapeshifter faeries around here," I added. "Someone summoned a changeling. As Alain is the only half-faerie I've spoken to recently, I hoped she could help."

"She hasn't seen anything," was his only response. "Will you go away now?"

I pulled out my last card. "Have either of you seen someone wielding a blade made of ash?"

"Is that a joke?" His mouth twisted into a snarl, and green light crackled to life in the palms of his hands. "You have some nerve, human."

"That's not necessary." I resisted the urge to step back, wondering what the hell had offended him so badly. "I'm here investigating a human child's disappearance and heard that someone carrying an ash blade was involved, so I wondered if you'd seen..." I trailed off at the dangerous glint in his eyes.

"You're accusing me of stealing mortals?" He lifted his hands, the green glow splitting into twin balls of light in his palms.

"I'm not accusing you," I said as calmly as possible. "I'm stating the facts. Believe me, I wouldn't be here if I had a choice."

Wrong thing to say. He turned his palms outward, and twin green bolts of magic shot at me. I dropped to a crouch, my knees scraping against paving stone, and his attack soared over my head. A wall of brambles sprang up behind me, conjured from the sizzling green light.

"What the hell was that for?" I pushed to my feet, fighting a wince as my knees protested. My jeans had torn again. *Just great.*

"A warning." A growl entered his voice, and the green glow in his eyes mirrored the energy building in his palms.

"I did your girlfriend a favour," I said, cursing myself for stripping all my weapons off before entering. "I'm asking for one in return, not making an accusation. If you can think of anyone else who might help, I'll talk to them."

"We paid for your services already," he said. "We're done."

"Can't I at least talk to Alain? You haven't even asked her opinion." Wasn't this her flat?

He muttered under his breath. "Fine. Alain, there's a human here. Should I throw it out?"

"She has a name." My fingers itched to conjure up some magic of my own, but he knew I was human, and using faerie magic would drag up questions I didn't want to answer.

After a short pause, Alain sloped into view, wearing a sullen stare. "What?"

So much for gratitude. "I wanted to know if you'd seen

anything suspicious recently. There was an incident involving a changeling replacing a human child."

"No." A shifting movement behind her revealed something long and thick dragging on the floor at her back. Was that a tail? She hadn't had one of those before.

Angry tears flared in her eyes when she caught me looking, and the guy stepped in front of her again. "Is that all? Will you go away now?"

Probably I should have, but I was pretty sure I'd have noticed she'd had a giant rat's tail during our last meeting, and a sudden suspicion seized me. "Was that spell I retrieved for you a dud? Who sold it to you?"

"Come to laugh at us, have you?" he growled. "Get out. We don't want you here."

"All right, I won't help you find the—" I broke off, spluttering, as a sudden wave of icy water drenched me from behind like someone had switched on a shower above my head. Pulling sodden strands of hair out my eyes, I turned to see the water in the fountain behind me spilling over the edges.

I whirled back to Alain's boyfriend. "Did you do that?"

In answer, he shut the door in my face, at the same time as a growl sounded behind me. *Shit, don't tell me they have a guard dog.*

Worse. As I watched, a giant horse arose from the fountain. Make that a guard *kelpie.* I shielded my eyes from the spray, taking in its sleek form, its hooves skimming the now-drenched grass, and the madness in its dark eyes.

Now I was in trouble. Without my iron weapons, I had nothing but a few spells in my inside pockets that had no doubt been drenched beyond use, a bunch of useless ingredients, and a canister of salt. The latter was very effective against the dead, but this beastie was very much alive.

The horse studied me. Its flanks were blue-black, its

mane thick and soft. There was wild beauty in its movements, but its teeth, when it opened its mouth, resembled sharp white razors.

As it began to charge, I threw myself to the ground and rolled into the building's shadow, shouting for help. Unsurprisingly, nobody came to my aid. I rolled over, and the beast's hooves skimmed my back as it veered sideways to avoid crashing into the wall.

I jumped to my feet, and a whip-like tendril of water latched itself around my ankle, yanking me into the air. The contents of my pockets—spells, jars and all—fell to the ground and smashed. Blood rushed to my head and my wet hair clung to my face as I fought to free myself. Sharp teeth closed around my other ankle. I screamed and cursed, but before the teeth could chomp down and take off my foot, the beast's hooves slipped out from underneath it.

I fell, landing in a forward roll on the grass. Confused, I watched the kelpie flail and howl, its hooves skidding out from underneath it. Then my gaze snagged on the array of spells that had fallen out of my pockets. Ah. My jar of iron filings had smashed, too, the shards embedding into the kelpie's hooves.

As I climbed to my feet, wincing, the kelpie gave one smooth leap into the fountain. Another wave of water crashed over my head. I spluttered and gasped, held my breath, but the faerie horse didn't reappear.

Spitting out water, I brushed sodden hair from my face and checked the damage. Its teeth had pierced the skin of my ankle and left puncture marks above my boot, but I was lucky it hadn't been worse.

I spun back to the block of flats, anger rising. "Thanks a fucking lot, both of you. I hope that tail is permanent."

Alain's face appeared in the window and she mouthed

something at me. I moved closer, my ankle throbbing with each step, and tried to read her lips.

"What?" I snapped. "Speak louder. You owe me."

"I saw something," she whispered.

"What—the missing kids?" I asked, disarmed. "Or the changelings?"

"No… the Lady of the Tree." I had to press my ear to the window to hear her speak. "She's one of the most powerful ancient Summer faeries in this part of the country. She lives in the old Botanical Gardens, but she rarely leaves. I think some magical disturbance caught her attention, but I don't know what it was."

A shadow appeared behind her—her charming boyfriend —and she vanished from the window. Getting the message, I turned away. I didn't need to stick around long enough to find out if they had a guard chimera as well as a kelpie.

All right. She'd given me a clue in the end, but anger still burned inside my veins as I hobbled across the lawn to the exit. Whoever this Lady of the Tree might be, like hell was I ever walking into a faerie's lair without my sword again.

By the time I got home, my ankle was bleeding worse than ever. Luckily, Isabel had a few insta-dry spells left, and when I applied one, all the water immediately vanished from my clothes. Living with a witch had some major perks.

Isabel raised an eyebrow as I limped across the living room in search of a healing spell. "What happened this time?"

"Faeries." I spat out the word like a curse. "I've had bloody enough of them."

"You're bloody enough," she commented, looking at my ankle. "I'll get a healing salve."

"You're incredible, you know that?" I staggered to the sofa and collapsed onto it. "Word of advice? Don't do a faerie a favour."

"I could have told you the same for free." Isabel was rarely fazed by my tendency to get injured at least once a week and kept her first-aid kit on the shelf behind the sofa for precisely that reason.

One healing salve and a microwaveable meal later and I felt slightly less like death. I applied yet another repair spell to my jeans while I watched Isabel kneel on the floor and draw out some fresh spell circles. Our version of home entertainment, since our old TV had broken months ago, and its habit of flickering and randomly turning on and off had made me jumpy as hell on bad days anyway. That, and Erwin's habit of thinking the people on the screen were real and starting arguments with them had been grating to say the least. I looked for the little bugger and saw him hiding behind a biscuit tin.

"You stink of kelpie," Erwin yowled in my general direction.

"That's because one tried to take a bite out of me," I said. "Have you ever heard of the Lady of the Tree?"

"The Lady of the Tree?" He darted out from behind the tin and spoke in a reverent tone. "She's the wisest of Summer's faeries."

"Summer, huh." I'd never had reason to really think about the distinctions between Seelie and Unseelie, but it might be good to know which of the fae had called upon the changelings. Both Alain and her delightful boyfriend had been from Summer, too, given the vibrant green magic he'd employed against me.

My mood dimmed again when Swanson called and I had to admit that I still didn't have any new leads, save for a nebulous clue and a name. Considering the way my luck had gone so far, I couldn't count on this Lady of the Tree, however wise, being able to help.

My phone buzzed again as soon as I set it down on the coffee table. I suppressed a sigh. As I'd already called Swanson, it must be either Larsen or some new client, neither of whom I particularly wanted to talk to.

Isabel picked up the phone. "Since when did you have the Mage Lord's number?"

What? "I don't," I said, taking the phone from her. "He doesn't have mine either… *Larsen.* I'm going to kill him."

"Who's on your hit list next?" asked Vance Colton. I'd hit the 'accept call' button while still speaking.

"Larsen." I pressed the phone to my ear. "He should know better than to give out my number to strange men."

"Strange men? I'm insulted. I think you know me quite well by now," he said. "What are you doing?"

"I'm at home." No reason to mention my little excursion.

"Come to the manor."

"Was there a 'please' in there somewhere?"

"Please do me the honour of coming to the manor. I've left you alone for a few hours, which means you've likely got yourself into trouble."

"He's got a point," said Isabel, who was listening in.

I sighed. "Right, fine. I'll be there in half an hour."

10

Lord Colton didn't answer the door this time and neither did his unfriendly faerie guard. A young woman dressed in smart casual clothes greeted me with a friendly smile. "You're Ivy, right? I'm Wanda. It's been a while since we've had any new blood here."

Speaking of blood, my ankle had finally stopped bleeding, though the crimson stains on my ankle and my left boot was more obvious when contrasted with the polished hallway. Wanda didn't offer any commentary on my appearance, though her own demure appearance was more akin to a regular office secretary than a mage.

"Ah—is Lord Colton waiting for me?" I asked her.

"He's in there." She pointed down the hallway.

I wondered why he hadn't invited me into his office this time, but the answer became obvious when I passed by the door and saw a group of people waiting inside. Their eyes followed me curiously as I walked to the corridor's end, where I found an open conservatory that looked out across bright-green lawns and flowerbeds Isabel would be proud of.

Inside, a grand piano sat next to a display of potted

plants. Lord Colton paced behind with his phone in his hand, giving some incomprehensible order to the person on the other end. Nothing new there. How many mages did he command? He was responsible for the whole region, and I assumed this house must be their main headquarters, but it didn't look as though many other mages were present. If they were, I would have thought someone would have been helping the people waiting in his office.

Lord Colton saw me and nodded. "Yes, I'll speak to him later. I've got a client bleeding all over my floor."

Bleeding? Ah. Now I looked down, I'd left a trail of bloody footprints on the conservatory floor.

"What did you do?" he asked. "I spoke to you five minutes ago. You can't have been attacked already."

"You called me when I was in the middle of healing up," I said. "No chance to wash my shoes."

Technically I had, but I must have missed a few spots, and Larsen usually didn't care if I wiped my shoes on the doormat when I walked into the mercenary guild.

Lord Colton called out, addressing someone out of sight. "Quentin, please clean the blood from the floor."

A short figure popped out from behind a plant pot. He was as tall as my knees, and his bark-like, knobbly skin made me recoil.

"Faerie," I hissed.

"I'd kindly ask you not to insult my assistant," said Lord Colton. His phone had vanished from his hand, though I hadn't seen him put it away. More mage trickery.

"What? Me or him?"

The faerie bristled, glaring at me with beady bird-like eyes, but didn't speak.

"Quentin here is my assistant."

"You have a faerie slave?"

"Slave?" Quentin repeated, his growling voice sounding affronted.

Lord Colton eyed me in surprise. "I thought you knew all about the faeries. Brownies have a compulsion to clean the building in which they live. Once they've moved into a home, they see themselves as guests of whoever lives there and take care of household chores in exchange for shelter and other favours."

"And that's not exploitative?" Sure, I knew brownies, but I'd never have pictured one in a place like this, much less expected the mages to understand how they operated.

"Not if I give him the choice in the matter. Quentin, you can leave."

The faerie looked up briefly, shrugged, and carried on cleaning. Lord Colton gave a satisfied nod. "He does as he wishes. Not unlike yourself. Did I hear you were poking around the half-bloods' territory?"

Had he sent someone to tail me or simply guessed? "They're the closest to the faeries, so I figured they'd know if anyone decided to pop over here for a visit from the other side."

"And did they?"

"No clue. They refused to answer my questions, and one of them sent a kelpie to take a bite out of me."

"You're good at making enemies, aren't you?"

I glared at him. "You try reasoning with the fae. It's like expecting common sense from a troll."

The corner of his mouth twitched. "Perhaps. I've spoken with half-bloods before and found them amenable, but perhaps they're more respectful of authority figures."

He did *not* just say that. "Wish I'd called you first. See how you like getting chewed on by a kelpie."

He cocked an eyebrow. "You're giving me that look again."

"What? Like I'm about to skewer you?"

"You look more like you're pouting."

"I'm certainly not." What game was he playing this time? "You know there are people outside your office waiting to talk to you, right?"

"Unfortunately," he said.

"What, isn't that your job?" I'd thought he was dedicated to his work. Obsessively so, even.

"We've dealt with all the priority cases today," he said. "These are people asking for favours. It's our policy to help any mage who needs assistance, but there are always those who take advantage."

"Because they can afford it?" I sure as hell couldn't. Even if someone blew my house up in a magical explosion, I'd have to go to Larsen and beg for help.

Lord Colton frowned at me. "Our rates aren't extortionate. Your boss underpays you."

"You're welcome to tell *him* that and see how it goes, but keep my name out of it." Larsen was pissed off at me enough already. "If you constantly get people coming here to ask for favours, do you ever leave?"

"I live here," he said, indicating the open conservatory. "The house is mine."

"It is?" From outside, I'd guessed the place had at least twenty rooms. Maybe more. Surely too many for one person. "You live alone?"

"I inherited the house from my parents."

"Really? So they're dead?"

"They were killed fighting the Sidhe in the invasion."

Well, crap. I didn't know what to say. *I'm sorry* wouldn't cut it, seeing as it'd come out insincerely. "But you only became leader of the mages this year, right?"

"The house has been the mages' main headquarters in this city since my father's time," he said. "Mages often aren't able to easily hide their abilities the way witches can, and they have the potential to be a danger both to themselves and to each other. As a result, we obtained properties across the country to train new mages and to ensure that everyone is taken care of."

Oh. I'd assumed the mages' exclusionary manner came about because they thought of themselves as belonging to a higher tier than anyone else in the supernatural community, not out of a desire to protect themselves that reached back long before the invasion. Admittedly, the mages themselves had done little to mitigate that assumption, but I filed that information away in my mind. "So there are others here?"

"Not at the moment. Aside from yourself, Wanda and Quentin. I think you scared Ralph off."

"I wasn't that bad. He does look like a faerie. No teenage boy has skin that clear."

Lord Colton looked at me with amusement in his eyes. "You're a menace," he said. "He's quarter-blooded—three quarters human, one quarter faerie. He never met his faerie ancestors. His mage side came out on top, as it usually does."

"I did wonder. You're partly shifter… right? I saw during the fight with the hellhounds."

His expression was unreadable. "Quarter-blooded, yes."

I recalled Henry's claim that Mage Lord carried the scent of the most powerful branch of shapeshifter. I couldn't sense a thing myself, but most shifters were indistinguishable from ordinary humans until they transformed. *Ordinary* wouldn't be the first word that came to mind when I thought about Vance Colton, but still.

"I know a family of shifters," I explained. "They live in the upstairs flat. That's why I wondered." I didn't quite have the courage to mention Henry had sniffed him out. God only knew how he'd react to *that*.

The Mage Lord tilted his head. "Yes, you live near shifter territory, don't you?"

"Yes. Do you have family over there?"

He paused before saying, "Not that I talk to on a regular basis. Are you faerie-blooded?"

The question was so unexpected, I gaped at him for a good thirty seconds. *What did I say?* I hadn't given anything away—at least, I thought not—but why else would he ask *are you faerie-blooded* like it was as ordinary as asking *is it raining outside?*

Clenching my sweaty hands at my sides, I said, "No. Why?"

"The changeling asked the same question."

Oh, right. *Come on, he can't have believed that.* Sure, I cleaned up okay when I wasn't covered in monster innards, but even quarter-blooded faeries looked more faerie than human, if his security guard proved anything. "You can see for yourself that I'm not a faerie. No pointed ears or horns here."

He couldn't see my magic, I knew, but his stare burned through me all the same. To change the subject, I asked, "What about the missing kids, then? Got any other leads?"

"Have you?"

I hesitated. I didn't *want* to tell him, and this crap was way too dangerous to involve anyone else in. Even Isabel, who was the only person I'd trust to walk with me into the faeries' territory.

If I was forced to leave my weapons behind again, though, it wouldn't hurt to have someone with me who could grab a sword out of nowhere.

"After the kelpie incident, one of them took pity on me and said they saw this 'Lady of the Tree' walking around," I said. "According to them, she rarely leaves her own territory, so her appearance is a sign of some kind. That's all I've got."

"Whereabouts does she live?"

"The Botanical Gardens, apparently." I vaguely recalled visiting a couple of times as a kid, with my parents, but the place had doubtless changed beyond recognition in the interim, like everywhere else in the city.

He nodded. "Very well. I'll see to my clients, and then we'll leave."

And that was that. I left the conservatory and spied Wanda beckoning me through a side door. Taking her cue, I followed her into a room that contained several chairs of polished wood and some low tables, like a lounge. "You'd think Lord Colton would have offered his guests a seat."

Wanda grimaced. "Is he finally dealing with those people? He told me not to, so I've been hiding in here to stop them glaring at me."

"Yes, he is. Are they really asking for favours, or is he just trying to get out of work?"

"I think he wants to prioritise the missing person's case," she said. "He hates that we've made no progress at all. It makes us look bad."

"I'm the one who originally signed up to investigate," I said. "And I haven't got too far either."

Aside from some useless clues and a sore ankle, I had nothing, and frankly, it bugged the hell out of me. In addition to the children's plight, my own future looked like a line of dominoes ready to collapse. If I failed the case, more kids would be taken, and whoever was behind the kidnappings would walk free. To top it off, Larsen was on the brink of turfing me out of the guild, and if he did, Isabel and I would lose our flat and become homeless. All in all, the situation was as bleak as the underside of a troll's foot.

"What's he like to work with?" I asked Wanda, to take my mind off my own failings.

"Lord Colton? He's good at his job."

"I mean, personally," I said. "I was under the impression you didn't work with witches, yet he hired me for this case." I also wanted to ask if he regularly spoke to business partners the way he'd spoken to me.

"For him to take a personal interest means he thinks the entire magical and supernatural community may be affected," she said.

"Really?" I shouldn't have been surprised, considering the way he and the necromancers' leader had almost blown up at one another, but it still didn't explain his personal interest in the case—and in me. "I thought he only dealt with cases people paid him for."

"Technically, the money goes to the mages as a collective and not one individual person. This case, though... it's odd. I've never seen him go to this much trouble before."

Hmm. "Doesn't he often deal with cases himself?"

"As many as he can, but one person can't be in seven places at once. I get the impression he *would* be, if he could. He has a protective streak a mile wide, and he dislikes sending his people into danger."

That, I hadn't expected. "Seriously?"

She nodded. "Why is that a surprise?"

I shrugged. "I don't know. You guys always struck me as..." Self-centred. Exclusionary. Probably not a good idea to use either of those terms. "I mean, he's not exactly the friendliest of people. He and the leader of the necromancers got into an argument. Does that happen often?"

"Every other Tuesday," she said. "I joke, but the necromancers are awful people. All they care about is watching the veil, not this realm. The faeries could invade again and they'd lock themselves in their basement and look the other way."

"They did that last time?"

She nodded. "The Mage Lords persuaded them to come

out and help. I was young at the time, so I don't remember much."

"You're a mage… obviously you are." I suppressed the sudden surge of anger that lanced through me. The necromancers had looked the other way while my parents died, had they?

"Yes, I'm a frost mage apprentice." She smiled. "I'm told you're a talented witch."

"Who told you that? Drake?" I doubted it—he'd never seen me use magic—but the mages' leader had shown me nothing but disrespect.

"Lord Colton, of course. He said your tracking spell's the best he's seen."

Oh. Figures. "My friend made it," I said. "Didn't think the guy handed out compliments. He seems to strongly dislike me." Judging by the way he'd instantly accused me of foul play when he'd found out I'd covered up those spells I'd taken from the Swansons' house, anyway.

Unless he showed different sides of himself to different people. Which made him dangerous. Untrustworthy.

Intriguing, some part of me said. I paid it no notice.

"Are you ready?" Lord Colton entered the room. "I've seen to my clients."

That was fast. "Sure. You mean we're going to follow my lead?"

I glanced at Wanda, but she didn't look cowed by the Mage Lord's presence as I might have expected. I could only assume he didn't intimidate his staff if they could speak openly to me about him, too.

"I haven't heard back from Rod or Bailey, or any of the others I sent to patrol," he said. "Since your lead is the best we've got, we might as well pursue it."

"Way to give me a backhanded compliment," I said, rolling my eyes.

He shrugged. "You yourself said it's an unlikely source. I've sent a mage ahead to scout, so he'll let us know if the coast is clear."

I eyed him. "Probably won't be, if you show up wearing that fancy coat. Every faerie in town will know something big's happening."

He frowned. "I'll leave the coat behind."

I grinned.

11

Even unarmed and without his coat, Lord Colton's immaculate suit drew attention wherever we walked, especially when put next to my torn-up jeans and faded leather jacket. If that was his idea of casual dress, he'd missed the mark.

"You're staring," he said. "Do I meet your approval?"

"If you're asking for fashion advice, I'm not your girl." I indicated my own worn clothes. "Does everything you wear come with a dirt-repelling charm?"

"Quentin usually puts one on to stop me from leaving mud on the carpet."

"Ah." I looked away, because I couldn't trust my eyes to stop lingering on the way his tailored shirt showed off his muscled arms and broad shoulders. "Right. Come on. Let's get this over with."

"I'm flattered that you're so delighted to spend time with me."

"Please. You give yourself too much credit. As I said, I'm using you as a backup system should things get ugly out there."

"Are you always this polite to your colleagues?" he asked.

"Nah, you made it onto my special list." *And you're one to talk.* I clamped my mouth shut and crossed the front garden to the gate.

One of the mages' black cars waited outside. I didn't recognise the driver this time around, though he wore the same smart-casual attire as Wanda did. A pair of glasses perched on his thin nose—a surprise, as I'd assumed the mages had ways to compensate for mundane issues like eyesight problems—and he gave me a curious look when I opened the door. "Hi. I'm Bailey. You must be Ivy."

"Did you tell *every* mage about me?" I asked Lord Colton as he climbed into the front, leaving me alone in the back. I might have put my feet up to prove a point, though a container of what appeared to be high-grade witch spells stuck out from under the seat in front of me, next to a worn paperback that presumably belonged to the driver.

"Only the ones whose cars you're likely to get bloodstains in."

I snorted. The interior of the car smelled strongly of air freshener, which suggested someone had had to clean up already. "Don't you use dirt-repellent on your vehicles as well as your fancy clothes?"

Bailey watched me through the mirror with one eyebrow slightly raised as though surprised that I'd address the Mage Lord in such a casual manner. "I did just get back from the necromancer district. That place requires a dirt-repellent charm without even opening the door."

"Oh, fun." Once again, I revised my assumption about all mages being joyless stiffs. Unlike the necromancers. "No trouble over there?"

"No." He nodded to Lord Colton. "Rod's still patrolling, but I came back as soon as I got your call."

"Where's Drake?" I asked as the car rumbled to life.

"Also patrolling," Lord Colton said. "We've got everyone on the lookout for those changelings."

The changelings… had they been taken, or had they seen a chance for freedom and taken it? They'd left no other traces behind, but that someone had gone to the trouble of putting a spell on them to ensure they didn't give away their master's identity suggested that they'd expected the creatures to get caught.

"You look like you're thinking hard," Lord Colton said from the front. He must have seen my reflection in the wing mirror.

"Trying to work out what possible traps we might run into." I didn't know how much he'd told the driver, though Bailey at least appeared committed to the car arriving the right way up, unlike Drake.

"The Botanical Gardens aren't listed as belonging to a particular group," he said. "They're more or less abandoned."

"Makes sense that the faeries stepped in, then." Faeries flocked to places where nature had reclaimed the land from humans, and gardens and parks certainly fit that description. While you'd think the city itself would have been a deterrent, faeries adapted surprisingly well, and even a warren of concrete and steel could become a forest, given enough time.

When we reached the Gardens, Bailey pulled up at the side of the road. "Let me know if you need backup," he said to Lord Colton. "I'll make a call."

"I doubt that'll be necessary," the Mage Lord returned.

"Sure about that?" I muttered as we climbed out of the car.

I might have asked Bailey if he minded sitting around to wait for us, but by the time Lord Colton closed the door, he'd already retrieved the paperback from the seat behind and seemed content to sit and read. I hoped he'd be ready to jump in at a moment's notice if the Mage Lord and I came running back to the car with hostile fae on our tail.

As we approached the Gardens, I ran through my inventory. I was running low after losing all the spells I'd carried into half-blood territory and my jar of iron filings was gone, too, but Irene rested at my side, ready to bite into anything that might attack us.

Unlike half-blood territory, the Botanical Gardens looked deceptively ordinary, if abandoned, a spread of dead grass and trees under dull grey sky. An old play area complete with seesaws and swings covered in rust and overgrown with weeds lay beside a crumbling path with grass peeking through the cracks.

"Looks like a cheerful place for a Summer faerie to hang out," I commented as we stepped out of the car. "They tend to prefer brighter areas. With sunshine."

Lord Colton joined me. "What about the Winter faeries?"

"Creepy dark forests are more their style."

"Hmm."

He eyed the wooded area a few metres away, inside which the Lady of the Tree presumably lived. Given her name, she was likely a dryad or something similar. They were usually mild-mannered as far as faeries went, but I wouldn't take any chances after the kelpie incident. Irene rested in my hands as I walked towards the forest as though I didn't want to run as fast as possible in the opposite direction.

It just had to be a bloody forest. My instincts snapped on when the branches closed over my head and cut out the sunlight, and every sound set my teeth on edge. When I sank into a marsh that sent a wave of sharp pain through my sore ankle, I bit down on my lower lip hard enough to draw blood. Spitting curses, I advanced onward, gripping my sword with both hands.

A rustling sound made me jump, but it was only my

companion. He'd grabbed a weapon of his own, the same hand-and-a-half blade I'd seen him pull out beforehand. Evidently, I wasn't the only one on edge. Somewhat gratified, I continued.

"Wish someone had given us a map," I muttered. My sense of direction wasn't terrible when the laws of physics made sense, but with the faeries, that was no guarantee. Most public parks or similar spaces within the city before the invasion had never been this size, but I had the suspicion that the place had been warped with the same trickery that had given half-blood territory its expansive reach.

Lord Colton and I navigated our way through the maze of trees in silence, skirting around piles of fallen leaves and over rotting tree trunks crawling with insects. Despite its extent, the forest appeared to reflect the season outside—early autumn—so it couldn't entirely be a conjuration of faerie magic. I watched the trees as we walked, but they didn't appear any different from ordinary English oaks. I'd heard stories of Unseelie's creeping dark forests of ice or the achingly bright colours of Seelie territory, but another forest entirely lurked in the crevasses of my mind, nudging unwelcome memories to the surface. Aside from our rustling footsteps, not a sound disturbed the silence, and a chill crept up my back. When had the birds stopped singing?

A few steps later, the whispering started. Lord Colton didn't appear to notice, but the faint sound tickled my ears and lifted the hairs on the back of my neck.

"You hear that?" I asked.

"Hear what?"

I shook my head. The whispering was quiet enough that I couldn't make out any individual words, but either my ears were more sensitive than I'd thought, or only people with faerie magic could hear the sound. Considering my track record with faeries, I'd bet money on the latter. "Might be hearing things, but I feel like someone's watching us."

Lord Colton glanced at me and lifted his blade. Either he trusted my judgment, or maybe he was being extra cautious. I didn't blame him a bit.

The tension in my shoulders eased a fraction when the whispering quietened, and the trees thinned out around the edges of a clearing. In the centre lay a huge oak that extended into the canopy and beyond.

This is our tree. The roots were thicker than my body, fanning out and all but swallowing up the trees around it. I didn't want to climb over them in case it came to life and tried to eat me—as happened on a disturbingly regular basis in Faerie—so I gingerly approached from the side.

A smiling face appeared in the bark, so sudden and grotesque that I jumped violently. I'd assumed all Summer faeries were beautiful, but her face was as gnarled as the tree trunk, her mouth a sneer, and her eyes were black pupil-less pits.

"Such strange visitors," she crooned, her voice harsh as nails scraping against wood. "A mage and… why, what lovely creature are you?"

Instinct screamed at me to flee, but I took a step forward. "We're here to ask if you've seen any mortal children stolen away by the fae." No point in wasting words.

"Mortal children. Pretty mortal children." She grinned. "He needed them, he said, but I know not why."

What? I stared a moment, heart freefalling. *He needed them.* Who needed them? I hadn't even mentioned the Swansons, nor the other missing girl, but she couldn't possibly be referring to anyone else, could she? I hadn't heard of any other mortal child being taken.

"Wait," said Lord Colton. "We need more details before we jump to conclusions."

I might have agreed, but as a pure faerie, she couldn't lie. That didn't mean I'd take anything she said at face value, however, and I held back my desire to sink my blade into her grinning face. "Who—who needed them?"

"The Lord of the Grey Vale."

Ice shot down my spine. My throat closed up, my skin going clammy. *No. Not there. Anywhere but there.*

Deep down, though, I'd already known. The odds of a rogue sneaking in from Summer or Winter had always been low, and it had been grimly obvious that the outsider had come from between the realms.

From the place I'd escaped.

"His name?" I croaked.

The lady's mouth fell open, but nothing more than a choking noise came out.

My lungs tightened, lightheadedness sweeping through my body. I tried to step away, but my feet didn't seem inclined to move. *Dammit, pull yourself together, Ivy.*

"Where did he take them?" Lord Colton's sideways look made me certain he'd seen me freeze up, but for once, I didn't care what he thought. Nothing else mattered but the horrible truth the faerie had spoken.

My hands tightened on the solid iron of my sword's hilt. Wisps of blue magic flared around me as a tremor surged through my fingers. "Are they still... are they still in this realm?"

"Not anymore." She gave me a mournful look. "Not anymore."

I jerked back, her words hitting me like bullets. We were too late. The faeries had already taken the children out of this realm.

We'd failed.

Tears stung the corners of my eyes, but I forced the words

through numb lips. "Did you see… did you see them being taken away yourself?"

"I did," croaked the Lady.

"And you did nothing?" Blistering rage rose white-hot and melted every last drop of fear away. More blue wisps of smoke arose from my skin, thickening by the second as my anger climbed. Of course human lives meant absolutely nothing to her, like every fucking faerie I'd met.

Her face crumpled. "My power is limited in this mortal plane. Like the rest of my kin, I cannot go back to my own realm, and we are doomed to wither and die as you mortals do. I did what I needed to do to preserve my own life."

"You let kids get captured to preserve your own life?" I stepped closer. My legs trembled with fury, but the weapon in my hand was steady. I'd cut down her entire tree, branch by branch, if it meant getting those kids back.

A hand rested on my arm. "Wait." Lord Colton, though evidently surprised by my outburst, faced the tree and spoke in calm tones. "Why would aiding the capture of the children preserve your life?"

A valid question. I'd thought faeries were immortal, but this realm wasn't their natural home. Could they really die if they stayed here too long? Even if that was true, I couldn't begin to figure out how mortal children would ever be a factor.

"He made a promise," she said. "I know not why he needed the children, but I aided the one with the ash blade, in return for my life back."

"How?" My voice was brittle. "Your life back? What does that mean, a way back to Faerie?"

"Blood," she whispered. "Blood from the heart of our own realm."

Blood. An image burst to life in my head, of crimson-blue

faerie blood exploding all over my hands and my blade as I delivered the killing blow to the lord who'd taken me.

"The blood of an immortal can restore my life." She gave a sad smile. "It is my only hope."

"You're saying if another faerie gives you their blood—a pure faerie from your own realm—it'll make you immortal again?" asked Lord Colton. "Do I understand that right?"

She bowed her head. "Yes."

That can't be possible. Can it?

"Why did this faerie want children in the first place?" Lord Colton, at least, had managed to keep his head together.

Once again, the words choked her before she could speak, but I didn't pity her in the least. I found my voice. "Whatever spell's on you, you're going to tell me where to find those kids, or I'll kill you."

I moved towards her, and the ground collapsed underneath my feet. A scream jammed in my throat as I dropped a good five feet before rolling over onto a sliding earthen shelf.

Hands grabbed me—clawed hands—and drew a startled scream from my mouth. I kicked out, waving my sword around without caring what I hit, but no body followed the clawed hands.

Wait. Those weren't hands. The tree's roots were attacking me.

I kicked again, the movement dislodging more soil and causing me to drop further into the ground. Shit. The only way back to the surface was to climb *over* the roots, but their ends were as sharp as spears. As one jabbed at my head, I dodged, and two more grabbed my ankles, yanking me onto my back. I hung onto Irene and attempted to stab them, but the blade missed. Digging my fingers into the hilt, I sliced downward, trying to cut my way free.

The roots dragged me into the air and threw me against the earthen wall. My back hit packed earth, knocking the wind from me, and the roots seized my legs again before I could catch my breath.

I dodged another stabbing root and aimed the side of the blade at the root wrapped around my right ankle. This time the iron cut into the bark and a spray of bluish red brightened the roots. As I'd suspected, the roots were part of the Lady herself, not mere weapons.

A sword materialised next to my face and stabbed the root sneaking up over my shoulder, slicing it in two. *About time, Lord Colton.* He must be standing above me somewhere, and I took advantage of the pause to dig my blade into the root on my right ankle again. This time, Irene sliced through as easily as a knife through butter, and a horrible keening sound rose up around me. The root blackened, permanently damaged by the iron, but there were plenty more where that came from. When one tried to take my eye out, I raised my arm, and the root glanced off the thick sleeve of my jacket.

Lord Colton's sword appeared again and struck out, almost slicing through me as well as the root.

"Dammit!" I yelled up at him. "Be more careful before you make a sword materialise next to my face."

The root around my left ankle tugged me into the air, and I hung upside-down, swearing. I waved my sword, but I couldn't get at the right angle to free myself with the blood rushing to my head.

Lord Colton's blade swung and severed the root that held me, dropping me into the gaping hole in the ground. I yelped, hand scrambling for purchase on the edge. The touch of the soil on my hands triggered unwelcome memories of thorns rising from the ground to pierce me all over. Rotting bodies of past victims splayed out on the thorny mat, their sightless eyes watching me. The scent and taste of my own blood as I scrambled, trying to hold on, but falling—

"Ivy."

Lord Colton. I couldn't see him, but his voice came from nearby, and I steadied my grip on the ledge and caught my balance.

I wasn't in Faerie. I was in the mortal world, and I wouldn't be bested by a fucking tree.

Hands grabbed mine and pulled me upward out of the pit. I caught my balance and swung Irene at the thick root, drawing a fresh wave of red-blue blood. Then I aimed for another, slicing downward, working my way towards the tree's heart. That was the way to kill a dryad, as far as I knew.

"Ivy," said Lord Colton from behind me. "Wait. She might be the only person who can tell us where the children are."

"She can't," I spat. "Thanks to the tongue-tying spell. She's no use to us."

Lord Colton stepped past me, his cool grey gaze locking onto the Lady's face. "Is there no way to remove the spell?"

"No," she croaked. "This spell can only be removed by the caster. However"—her mouth split into a grin—"perhaps there's a way around it, if you are willing to offer something equally valuable in exchange."

In exchange? Did she mean a vow? If you made a promise to a faerie—or vice versa—then the vow itself took on a kind of magic that went far beyond a simple tongue-tying spell.

The pulsing anger in my veins told me to ignore her attempts to ensnare me, but Lord Colton was right. She *was* the sole person around with information on the missing children, and a binding vow spoken in clear terms would be my only chance at getting around that silencing spell. If she promised to tell me the truth, the promise should loosen the magic binding her tongue. It wouldn't stop her from enacting any more trickery, of course, but I saw no other way ahead that would lead me to those children.

"All right," I said. "You tell me where the person who took

the mortal children is hiding, and I'll owe you something in exchange. Anything in particular you need?"

Not the wisest question to ask a faerie, but until we spoke the vow, no word I spoke would be binding.

"A favour," she said. "You will owe me one favour, to be claimed at a later date. Do you accept?"

My heart thumped. I of all people knew the risks of making a deal with one of *them*, yet years might pass before she claimed that favour, and she'd already told me she was dying. I'd have to take the risk. "Yes."

At once, her roots began to withdraw into the soil. "Ask your question, mortal." Her words were punctuated by creaking and cracking noises as her roots were swallowed up in the thick, churned-up mud.

"Tell me exactly where the person who stole the children took them."

"To a place the mortals long abandoned," she crooned. "A place that once spawned roaring beasts of iron and steel that poisoned the world."

"Come again?" Beasts of iron and steel? "I don't follow."

Vance's brow furrowed. "She's talking about machinery of some sort, I'm guessing."

"Right." Faeries weren't fans of technology as a general rule. "Roaring beasts? What, cars?"

I'd only half-guessed, but she bared her teeth in a grimace. "Giant monstrosities that roared on poisonous tracks."

"Train tracks?" I surmised.

"I imagine she means the nearest train station." Lord Colton said. "We can drive there from here."

"How'd you figure that one out?" No faerie would make a nest in a train station, surely.

The Lady grinned in response. "The mage is correct."

"And the favour?" I asked warily.

Her grin widened. "I will call upon you when I need it."

Roots shot from the ground and sent me tumbling head over heels once again. I pitched against a tree at the clearing's edge and lifted my blade, but no further attacks hit me, and I looked up to see the Lady's face vanish into the bark.

Lord Colton reached to pull me to my feet. I let him, my mind fixed on the improbable mental image of a Sidhe walking around a train station.

"Are you okay?" He let go of my hand, making me abruptly conscious that I was covered in mud from head to toe. Somehow, not a single speck had landed on him. Kind of impressive.

"I'll live." I shook dirt out of my hair and brushed it from my clothes, mostly to avoid making too much of a mess when we got back into the car. Not because I felt like a reanimated undead when put next to the Mage Lord's impeccable appearance.

"You made a deal," he said.

I shrugged, more dirt sliding off my shoulder. "Yeah, promises are serious business. I figured that might loosen her tongue a little."

"Did you?" He didn't sound accusing, more curious, and despite his posturing, he'd accepted my expertise and let me take the lead. He'd also helped me in the fight, even if his sword had almost taken my head off in the process. Maybe having him along wasn't such a bad deal.

Maybe I didn't mind not being alone for the walk back through the creepy forest.

"Yeah, and we actually got a lead. What d'you say? Should we go to this train station?"

He stared at the tree, a crease between his brows.

"Lord Colton?"

"Call me Vance," he said.

Huh. I hadn't expected that. "All right. Do you think we

should follow her lead? She's a full-blooded faerie, so she can't lie."

"She might have concealed the truth, though. Right?'

I smiled despite myself. "Now you're getting the hang of it."

"What do *you* think?" he asked. "Should we go?"

I thought then nodded. "I'd say we go. But get backup."

He flashed me a smile, too. "Now *you're* getting the hang of it."

Touché.

12

One terse phone call later, we returned to the car. I climbed in the back, still shedding dirt, but Lord Colton—Vance—didn't comment on the mess I left behind. Neither did the driver, though I noticed he stashed his paperback book on the front seat this time after Vance joined me in the back.

"Where to now?" Bailey asked.

"Nearest train station, apparently." I met his eyes in the mirror. "Does he always have you play chauffeur, or did you just get lucky?"

"I'm also your backup." He glanced over at the Mage Lord. "Which station?"

Vance leaned forward to give him directions, to which he responded with a frown. "Don't faeries hate any kind of metal? Why hide in a station?"

I tensed, though Bailey didn't so much as look in my direction. Evidently Vance hadn't told him much about what we were investigating.

"Yes," was Vance's reply. "I'm assuming they want to evade attention."

"Seems to be working for them," I commented. "Didn't you say you had people searching the whole city?"

"Yes, but nobody lives in that district anymore, so I never thought to send anyone there," he said. "Maybe that was a mistake. If the person responsible is operating from the abandoned part of the city, it opens a lot of other possibilities."

"Yeah." I kept my eyes facing the front, my hands clenching on my lap. Too many possibilities existed when it came to the exiled fae, and even my extensive experience hadn't prepared me for them all. To suppress my own bad memories, I addressed the Mage Lord's companion. "What's your ability?"

"I'm an earth mage," Bailey replied. "And you...?" He trailed off when Vance gave an imperceptible head-shake. Weird. Did he want to ensure he was the only one who got to ask me probing questions?

"Witch," I answered anyway. "Earth mage? Can't you tunnel underground instead of driving to save on time?"

"Sure, if I wanted to risk taking an accidental detour through a sewer."

I snorted. Between him, Wanda and Drake, I had to admit the mages were much more fun to be around than I'd expected, and even Lord Colton—Vance—wasn't all that bad. Not that he needed to hear so from me, when the other mages already seemed ready to respond to his every command. Bailey drove us into the city centre without a single complaint even when we had to navigate roads half-destroyed in the invasion.

By the time we hit the thirtieth pothole, I was starting to think detouring through a sewer might not have been the worst idea after all. When we reached a street blocked with debris, the car dropped us off on the corner that Vance claimed we could walk from. Given the torn-up roads, walking would be much easier than driving, though I pitied Bailey for having to sit in the car alone in this creepy place. Granted, he was already up to his nose in the same paperback he'd been reading earlier.

"He's the backup?" I murmured to Vance as we left the car. "What if *he* needs backup?"

"I asked Rod to wait on standby. He's our best air mage."

"He can fly?" I hid a smile at the mental image of a cloaked mage soaring over the city like a witch on a broomstick from an old tale. Of course, those stories had been proven false within five minutes of meeting a genuine witch for the first time.

"More hover."

"I guess it'd be unfair if you could *all* grab weapons out of thin air." I clamped my mouth shut before his ego grew too inflated to fit down the street. "Have you been here before?"

"Not recently."

He continued to walk past broken-down houses, his polished shoes a stark contrast to our grim surroundings. The stripped remnants of an advert for some decades-old TV show hung in tatters from a board above a road lined with debris. Further along, signs of the war became more obvious. Doors askew on their hinges, ground torn into claw-shaped furrows, holes in the road the size of giant footprints. Overall, the place was a ghost town. Hopefully not in the literal sense. *Glad I'm not a necromancer.*

To distract myself, I said, "None of my cases have ever given me this much hassle."

"Not even the hydra?"

"No. Have you been reading my records?" *Thanks for that one, Larsen.* Bastard had probably handed them over without a thought.

Vance's eyes lingered on me. "As I said, I looked into your

history. I'm curious. From the rate of your jobs' completion, you ought to be earning twice what you do. Working for Larsen is limiting you."

Yeah. Well, I might be out of a job by the week's end if I don't dig myself out of this mess. "I thought I said not to tell me how I should be doing my job."

"That wasn't my intention," said Vance. "I was merely making a suggestion. Clearly, working for Larsen doesn't make you happy."

I gave a short laugh. "It pays the bills." *Not that you'd know what it's like to live hanging over the edge of poverty.* He'd been born into a family of privilege and power, never in danger of being trampled underfoot when the faeries invaded. I didn't lay the blame for the invasion upon anyone but the perpetrators, but damn if he wasn't getting on my every last nerve. Even if he had a point. I *hated* being dependent on Larsen for a living.

"There are other options," he said.

"For a witch with basic skills?" I tapped the sword at my waist. "It's not that bad. Irene would rust if I left her behind to go and work at a bar or shop."

"You named your weapon?" he said, a bemused expression on his face.

"You didn't?" His own weapons had disappeared after we'd left the forest where the Lady of the Tree lived, presumably back to the manor. "Guess you own a hundred swords. I have one. Irene's been with me since I started working for Larsen."

"Hmm." His eyes shifted from the sword, and I flushed when I realised the side of my top had ripped open at some point during the fight. What with the mud, I'd forgotten my clothes were also shredded from being thrown around by the tree roots.

Hoping he couldn't see my blush, I said, "Now you've got my life story, I get to know yours. How'd you get elected to the top of the Mage Lords?"

A moment passed. "I killed the last guy."

I blinked, startled. "You what?"

"He lost control." Vance's manner was casual, but something in his tone suggested he didn't welcome further questions. *Okay...*

"Is that possible? I thought..." I didn't know what I thought. Hell, I didn't know much about mage abilities at all. Not that it was possible to lose control over their own powers.

"Everyone has a limit," he said. "Some more than others." He peered down the road ahead. "We're almost there."

A chill crept up my arms. The old station lay at the road's end, its cracked windows reflecting the sliver of sunlight peeking through the grey clouds in the sky. It looked like the least obvious place for a faerie hangout, though nature had done its best to claim the husks of long-abandoned cars parked outside and vines crept up the walls. The shivers intensified, as if that kelpie had hurled another wave of icy water over my head.

I gave myself a mental shake. We hadn't even set foot inside yet. No obvious threats presented themselves, and yet I wanted nothing more than to get away from here. Far away.

"Ivy?" Vance gave me a curious look. What had I been doing, staring vacantly at the building?

"Just got a bad vibe." Obviously. Since there was supposed to be a child-stealing evil faerie hiding here. *Focus, Ivy.*

The door had been kicked in already, but Vance pressed his foot to the dangling remains and shoved it aside.

"Stealth isn't your thing, is it?"

"It is when I need it to be." He shrugged. "We want them to know we're here."

The creeping vines over the door gave the uncomfortable sense of entering a forest rather than a building and made the place feel enclosed, not at all like the station it had once been. Inside, I didn't see any platforms, or ticket desks, just a dark corridor littered with debris. The smell of mildew mingled with something else, like rotten flowers. Decaying roses.

The hairs on my arms stood up. Was I imagining the smell? Possibly. Faeries had a way of reaching into your thoughts, extracting your deepest fears and making them manifest, but I'd never felt it so acutely. Not in this realm, anyway.

Damn. After ten years, all it took was the smell of roses to send me sliding back into the shoes of that scared, helpless little girl the faeries had tormented. I clenched my teeth together and gripped Irene, stealing comfort from the way my hand fit snugly to the hilt. *I'm not her. I'm not that girl anymore.*

Vance Colton's presence was reminder enough, but my bravado would only stretch so far before it snapped like cheap elastic.

"Was the station always this big?" The pitch darkness made it impossible to tell where we were, but if faerie magic had warped the building despite the presence of so much metal, we were in trouble.

A rattling sound echoed through the corridor and made me jump. I told myself to get a grip. Even if it was a spirit and not just the wind, ghosts were harmless compared to anything *living* that might lurk in the darkness.

"Don't like haunted houses?" The dim light made it hard to see the Mage Lord's face, but I heard the smirk in his voice.

"This isn't a haunted house, it's a den for dark faeries.

Imagine the most twisted poltergeist possible and you aren't even halfway there."

Wisely, he shut up.

The dim light revealed a fork in the corridor, both routes indistinguishable from one another. Other than cobwebs, there were no signs of life, but the smell pervaded, the scent of rotting roses tinged with something more sinister. Something that shouldn't exist in this realm.

"Left or right?" My voice held steady, to my relief.

"Right."

He sounded confident, but then, he always did. We had a fifty-fifty chance, so I turned eastward and continued. Faint blue light spilled across our path, lighting the area immediately in front of us but leaving everything else in darkness. I didn't see the source of the light, but the decaying smell grew worse with every step, along with my certainty that this place had absorbed Faerie's taint so thoroughly that I could all but taste it in the air. This wasn't the pale imitation of the half-blood district, but one hundred percent faerie. Not Summer nor Winter, but the place between.

The place that no matter how hard I tried, I could never outrun.

The dizzying smell of rotting flowers surrounded me like an invisible cloud, and I expected the moment when the music started. A familiar piano tune that crawled down my spine like a thousand ice-cold spiders and slid into my very bones.

I shook myself fiercely. Vance gave me an odd look, which I ignored. Being oblivious to glamour would be a blessing. The worst part was that I still couldn't see where we were going. The corridor appeared to have no end, and I turned around and saw that the path behind us had been replaced by a solid wall.

"Vance… do you see that?"

"What?" He followed my gaze and stiffened, which told me he'd noticed, too. "Where did that come from?"

"With the faeries, it's usually best not to ask." I shivered harder. "I guess this is the way we have to go."

The sense of being herded into a trap intensified as I surveyed the corridor ahead. The eerie blue light conjured a dreamlike atmosphere, the same haze of unreality that surrounded all my memories of Faerie. Sometimes I wondered if the only reason I hadn't lost my mind was because it was easy to pretend it *was* a dream, that those events had happened to someone else.

Here, though, drenched in the smell of rotting roses and with the sound of a piano caressing my ears, it was the real world that felt like a dream instead. As though Faerie was all that had ever been real.

"Ivy?" Vance watched me, and in the dark, I couldn't tell how much he read from my face. "What do you see?"

"Nothing." I shook my head again. "That's the fucking problem. The faeries are screwing with us."

I made myself step forward, one foot in front of the other. Whatever fear held me back, those kids needed me. I kept that knowledge in mind, held onto it as we walked deeper into the building. The blue light showed the way, but only up to a metre in front of us, leaving everywhere else cloaked in shadow.

Vance kept his weapon out, too, his shoulders tensed. "Do you hear that?"

"The music?" The faint melody persisted, as much as I tried to ignore it.

"No, it's more like… whispers."

A chill raced up my back. "No, but Faerie can be pretty fucking specific with its hallucinations."

Vance glanced sharply at me. He didn't look scared, he looked pissed off. "Right."

A thin black object appeared in his hand, catching the blue light as it sliced the air in front of us.

"I don't know what that is, but I think it's broken."

"It's a dispeller," he said. "Reveals and negates hostile spells."

"Really?" If it was witch-made, it must be a custom job, and not one I'd seen before. "Faerie magic doesn't usually react to witch spells."

Though now I listened out, the music had stopped. I had my doubts that the dispeller had cut through their illusions. No, it was more likely that the faeries had decided to change their game.

Sure enough, the corridor dead-ended at a wall. An opening on our right-hand side showed an identical corridor heading southward. Vance peered ahead. "We've been walking in a circle. Or a square."

So we had. "Yes, and I think we left reality behind a long time ago. This isn't a train station by any stretch of the imagination."

The words had scarcely left my mouth when the blue light shifted sideways to reveal another door branching off the southern corridor, this one appearing to point towards the building's centre.

Vance overtook me and walked straight past the door as if it didn't exist. *Glamour.* The fae had intended for me to see the door, and not him. All right.

I faked stumbling and pretended to grab the wall for balance, intentionally angling myself so that the door pushed inward. "Hey—Vance. Look."

He backtracked, eyes widening as we took in the improbable sight on the other side of the door. It had plainly once been a platform, judging by the low-hanging roof and the crooked remnants of a bench, but the area below was covered in a white haze, not train tracks.

I looked closer and recoiled. *Cobwebs.* Thick webbing formed a mat across the area that had once encompassed several train tracks, extending as far as my eye could see and swamping anything that might lie beneath.

"Now that," I murmured, "is a trap."

A gust of wind stirred. Vance lifted what appeared to be a fountain pen and pointed it into the gloom. "This detects life forms. It'll tell us if anyone's hiding in there, and as far as I know, it works on faeries, too."

Good to know. "Why not use it before?"

"It only works up to ten feet ahead." He gave the pen a shake, but no obvious effects showed. "Nothing living in here."

"You've got to be kidding me." Despite his claim, I had my doubts that any spell would detect a faerie who didn't want to be found. "Wait. Have you only used it on half-faeries before?"

"Yes… why would that matter?"

"I mean, the spell might not count true faeries as living because they're technically immortal." Not that witch spells could usually get to that level of specificity, but something told me I'd made an obvious oversight.

"Are you serious?" he asked.

"Dead serious." Wait. *Dead.* The spell only detected the living.

A heartbeat after the thought crossed my mind, a hand reached from within the cobwebs, clawing at my ankle. On instinct, I stabbed downward, severing the wrist. A human-sized figure followed, rising upward jerkily, its half-severed hand dangling by a thread of sinew. A second rose behind the first, faces sunken, bodies emaciated. Undead. *Oh, lovely.*

As a third joined them, I struck out at the first undead I'd attacked. Its head tilted sideways as my blade sliced into its neck, but it kept moving despite the decaying muscle spilling from its slit throat. The foul smell dove down my throat and made me want to gag.

Vance lashed out, his sword disappearing and decapitating two undead in one swipe. His sword reappeared in his hand long enough to send one of their bodies flying, head over heels, into the mass of cobwebs below.

"There'd better not be more under there." I kicked another down to join it. They were flimsy creatures, despite being persistent little buggers, but they had no autonomy of their own. Somebody must be controlling them, but surely not—

Another, bigger figure rose upward from the mass of cobwebs, tall and spindly with long legs that put me in mind of a spider cursed into a human shape.

"Have you come to join the dead, mortals?" whispered the creature.

I stilled, dread curling around my heart. "Who are you?"

"Show yourself," said Vance.

Huh? I cursed myself inwardly for forgetting, again, that Vance didn't have the Sight. To him, the room was still empty of all life, and our enemy unseen.

"What the hell are you?" I repeated. "What are you doing here?"

"I am bound to walk amid these mortal ruins until I expire," the spindly faerie said. It was unclothed, its ribs as protruding as one of the undead, and its legs crept closer to us with each word it spoke.

"You're banished here?" I guessed.

"Mortals ask too many questions," said the creature. "It would be my pleasure to watch you die."

Cobwebs came to life, rising upward and grabbing my

legs. I struggled, but the webs climbed up my thighs, wrapping around me like thick ropes as they pulled me off the platform's edge. I twisted left and right, slashing with my blade, to no avail. Unlike the Lady of the Tree's roots, the webs weren't part of the faerie, because no blood spilled from each cut I made, and the sticky aftermath slowed my swings. Fear flooded me when I realised that my sword, my beloved Irene, was swamped in webs and I couldn't pull the weapon free.

Vance's sword appeared and slashed, but he had no more luck than I did. The cobwebs rose upward between us, forming a wall. I heard a muffled sound as the blade struck the solid webbing, but even Vance's sword couldn't cut through it.

The faerie's spindly form loomed over me, its bulbous eyes gleaming. "What would you give me in exchange for your life essence, human?"

My life essence? That implied the beast had once been a Summer faerie—Summer fed on life, after all—but stealing my life would hardly be a replacement for the immortality of Faerie. This fae wouldn't be the first exile I'd encountered desperate enough to suck the skin from a mortal's bones for an extra day of life.

Not that I'd give it the chance. After all, the faerie had made the mistake of thinking I was a normal human.

I let the web pull me in, holding my breath as the faerie bared sharp teeth in a grin. Then I called the faerie magic.

Bluish light rose like smoke and snaked around my sword. The webs loosened, a hundred strands severed at once, and a stream of blue light flared from my other hand, pushing the fae backwards. The stickiness vanished from my legs, and I caught my balance upon the webbed surface, a flood of new energy flowing through my veins.

The faerie's grin barely faded. "Did you truly think

wielding Lord Avalin's magic in your traitorous hands would spare your life, mortal?"

"Actually, yes." My heart caved inward, my mind fighting the instinctive horror that struck at the sound of his name. *Avalin.* How could this faerie know of *him*, much less recognise his magic?

"You're the human who survived," whispered the faerie. "An offer I will make you. A drop of our blood will more than suffice to make you immortal, should you desire."

Make *me* immortal? "No thanks. Know anything about missing human children?"

The faerie laughed. "What use would I have for mortals?"

"You tell me. Did you take them?"

"I took no mortals captive, save for you."

"You must have seen the person who took them," I pressed. "A faerie with a blade of ash? Are they here?" If not, why had the Lady of the Tree sent us? To die, obviously, but I'd thought pure faeries were incapable of speaking untruths. We'd both made a promise, hadn't we?

"No," he said gleefully. "I have not."

Screw this. I brought Irene down, slicing the rest of the cobwebs binding me, and leaped forward.

The faerie directed another cobweb skein to block my path, and I veered to the side to avoid being grabbed. Vance must still be trapped behind the wall of cobwebs, so I whipped around, bringing the sword down in a diagonal slash fuelled by the magic surging in my veins.

The wall of webs collapsed in a white mass, and Vance leaped at the faerie with a ferocity that startled me. The beast must have revealed itself fully, because even Vance couldn't have aimed so accurately without being able to see his adversary. He crashed headlong into the faerie, and the beast gave a shrill scream.

More cobwebs rose upward, pushing Vance backwards and reforming into a wall once again. How could a creature that was supposedly dying draw on this much power? Magic couldn't exist in a vacuum, and the faerie had to be fuelling the cobwebs somehow. It had been a Summer faerie at one time, judging by its twisted offer. *Wait.* The undead who'd attacked us, the bodies under the floor… how long had they been there? Had their life force been sucked out to fuel this cobwebbed hell? Bile rose in my throat. Summer faeries used life as an energy source, but draining that energy from a *person* was the sort of depravity only an outcast would be capable of.

I moved towards the faerie, which vanished in a flash as Vance's blade sliced down through the cobwebbed barrier, his arms now covered with black scales.

"It's glamoured." I squinted, but the fae had hidden itself even from my sharp eyes. "This dickhead has way too much power for an outcast."

Vance shook his blade, sending strewn cobwebs everywhere. "Where are all these webs coming from?"

"I'm pretty sure our fae is drawing power from the dead," I said. "It told me that it intended to take my life force, which would mean it used to live in Summer once."

"How'd you work that one out?"

I'd said too much, but I refused to let the faerie get the upper hand on us. "Instinct. That, and it's obviously too scared to face us head-on instead of resorting to trickery."

I spoke with pointed derision, goading the fae to come out of hiding again. It did so, striking at Vance from behind. He flew backwards, fetching up against a fresh wall of cobwebs.

"Hey!" I ran forward, my speed enhanced by the faerie magic still flowing around me and propelling me to the spindly creature's side.

My blade brushed the faerie's neck, but cobwebs rose to seize my weapon hand before I could deal the killing blow.

"You humans always cheat," the faerie spat. "As you did when you took the life of one of our own."

Blue light sprang from my non-weapon hand. "What, are you mad that I killed Avalin?"

"The Lord of the Grey Vale should have been more than a match for a mortal," hissed the faerie.

"Clearly not."

More tendrils of cobweb wrapped around my waist. I kicked, grappling to get a hold on my own magic, but I'd never figured out how to use it as a weapon the way the faeries did.

The cobwebs released me abruptly, uncoiling from my waist and carrying with them one of the knives I carried at my belt.

"Give that back!" I lunged and missed, the blade's hilt sliding through my fingers.

Straight at Vance.

I didn't stop to think. I twisted my arm free of the cobwebbed skein and ran, shoving Vance out of the way. The knife grazed past, and pain blossomed up my right side. In blood-dampened fingers, I caught its handle, took aim, and threw it at the faerie.

This time, I didn't miss. My blade skewered it through the throat. The spindly fae crumpled, uttering a coughing laugh. "Lord Avalin… I wish I could live to see the moment your power is ripped from this hateful mortal's corpse."

With another cough, its chest rattled to silence, its last words ringing in my head.

The fae knew. They knew I'd killed Avalin, knew what I'd stolen in the process. Such was my horror that I took my blurring vision as shock until I looked down and saw crimson soaked my side. *Ah. It did cut me.*

Vance's face swam before mine. "We're going back. Now."

His hand gripped my arm, and my weak protest died on my tongue as the world vanished in a gust of wind. An instant later, we stood in the manor's hallway. He'd transported both of us across the city. He'd used magic...

Oh, shit. He'd seen *me* use faerie magic.

Vance loomed over me with eyes as dark as a storm cloud and a voice to match: "What the hell was that?"

13

"What?" I said, intelligently. The bleeding coupled with the draining effect of the faerie magic wearing off forced me to lean against the desk to keep from falling to my knees.

"What did you do?" Vance looked tired but not injured, which would have been a relief if not for his furious expression. The black scales on his hands hadn't receded yet either, which accounted for the throbbing pain in my arm where his nails had dug in when he'd transported us out of there. "That magic you used on the faerie. I saw it."

Yeah. Of course you did. "I killed the faerie," I croaked, my throat raw. "Don't I get a 'thank you'?"

There was no way to cover up what I'd done. None. All I could do was spin what I had left into a coherent story, which would have been a tall order even if I hadn't been covered in my own blood and reeling from the knowledge that the fae knew my worst secret. I'd never be safe again.

"So," he said. "Faerie magic. You didn't mention that on your licence."

"I guess I have faerie ancestors somewhere." I was at my

lowest ebb, but for all he knew, I *might* have faerie ancestors. My family tree didn't exist anymore, after all.

"You told me you were human."

"What do you want, a DNA test?" The room swayed, but he didn't appear to notice the blood dripping from my side onto the plush carpet. His eyes were narrowed to slits in an animal-like manner, and the part of me that wasn't about to faint from blood loss turned to watery terror. My hand rested on the desk, leaving a bloody handprint. "You're not human yourself, so it'd be hypocritical of you to judge me for the same."

He glanced down at the black scales on his hand like he'd only just noticed them. "I never denied what I was," he said. "But you're plainly doing exactly that. Is that why you only accept menial pay from Larsen?"

"What the hell does my job have to do with anything?" I shot at him. "I kill faeries. Magic helps me do that sometimes."

"You're not a witch at all," he said. "Are you?"

"You're the one who came up with the definition," I returned. "You define 'witch' as any magic user who doesn't belong to your little cult. I'm not a necromancer, so 'witch' is the only label left. Not my problem if you don't like it."

"I didn't come up with the definition," he said. "But what you did isn't covered by your licence."

"I saved your neck, Vance. Even you can't deny that." I managed to shut my mouth before the accusation escaped— *your people abandoned me when I was desperate.* He'd pried enough secrets from me already, and while he might think I possessed a dangerous power, I was a walking survival story, not a war hero. Even if he didn't hold my abilities against me —and I couldn't yet be sure those claws wouldn't make a reappearance—the very last thing I needed was pity.

I wasn't that scared girl anymore, but I'd reverted into her back in the faerie's lair, and it irritated the crap out of me. Almost as much as the fact that I'd thrown myself into the path of a knife on Vance Colton's behalf and not had so much as a word of thanks for my trouble.

"No," he said, "I can't deny it. Nor can I deny you deceived me and put us both in danger. Did you know what we'd find inside that station? Had you met that faerie before?"

"Don't be ridiculous," I said. "I figured *something* evil was waiting for us in there, since you don't go into a creepy abandoned train station expecting a surprise birthday party."

His eyes narrowed a little at the sarcasm. "You're an infuriating woman."

"You're not exactly a stellar personality yourself." The room swayed. "Also, your carpets are tacky."

"Cheap insults will get you nowhere."

"This is the best you're getting from me today." I attempted to walk. My wound disagreed. I bit down on the pain, refusing to let him see how dependent on his mercy I was.

"Where are you going?"

"Home." I ground my teeth when he moved to bar the way.

"If you think I'll honour your whims after that, you're mistaken." His tone rang with anger.

"Whims? This is my safety I'm talking about. You think the faeries will leave me alone if you tell the whole city I can use a tiny bit of their magic?" If all else failed, all I had left was the guilt trip. "Every faerie in the region will come down on me in a swarm. With me dead, those kids will be trapped in Faerie forever, and your reputation will take such a hit, I doubt you'll ever recover."

His mouth parted a little. "You think I care about my reputation? I was under the impression we were going to find two missing children in the train station. Instead, I found out you were deceiving me."

"My heart bleeds for you." Bad choice of words. Crimson soaked into my waistband, and if I stayed on my feet much longer, I'd humiliate myself by passing out.

He frowned. "You're bleeding on the carpet."

I drew in a shaky breath. "Oh, I'm terribly sorry. I'll try to bleed to death in the hall next time."

"There won't be a next time." His tone went deadly quiet. "Sit down."

"What?"

"Sit down." He pulled a chair out of thin air, startling me so much I fell into it without meaning to. Blood soaked into the upholstery, but he didn't even seem to notice. "Stay where you are."

I slumped to the side, closing my eyes against another wave of dizziness. "Have you ever spoken a single sentence that didn't involve ordering someone around?"

He didn't answer, because he'd disappeared. Not going to kill me, then. Okay.

Next thing I knew, cool hands pressed against my side. My limbs were too numb to move, though I feebly pushed the hands away.

"Don't move. You'll make it worse."

"Huh." I must have lost more blood than I thought. If I didn't know better, the Mage Lord knelt beside me with his cold hands over the wound. A fragrant aroma filled my nostrils. A witch's spell. Since when did the mages keep hedge witch healing remedies?

Probably because they work. Within seconds, the blood flow halted, the world stopped spinning long enough for me to open my eyes, and I jumped. Vance leaned over me, my blood dripping from his hands, and it hit me that my clothes were shredded worse than ever. Indecent, even. I was practically topless, the ruins of my T-shirt hanging from my side and exposing my bra. At least it was plain black, strapless and, god forbid, without any holes. I shakily grabbed my jacket and pulled it tighter around myself.

"A thank you would be nice." Vance hadn't even looked at my exposed skin. Not in more than a cursory manner, anyway. One point in Vance Colton's favour, plus another for healing me. My insides warmed, but I cautioned myself against letting my guard down. I wasn't entirely sure he was done accusing me of being buddies with Faerie.

"Thanks."

He grunted and turned away, conjuring a handkerchief to wipe the blood from his hands.

"I have to call Bailey and ask him to drive back to the manor, and then I'll go and shout at the necromancers." He remained close enough to make me self-conscious about the amount of skin I had on show. "Are you intending to tell me how you knew how to beat the faerie's spell? Even my sword couldn't cut through those cobwebs easily, and I thought all faeries were allergic to iron."

"They are," I said. "I reckon that creature had been there feeding on people's lives for years. The cobwebs were a defence mechanism. It only had a few good attacks left in it, I think, otherwise it'd have been more aggressive from the outset."

"And *your* magic? What can you do?" His tone didn't sound accusing this time, but I knew I needed to clear up the matter before I found myself sitting before a committee of angry Mage Lords.

"It's mostly defensive," I said. "In certain situations, my magic acts like a temporary shield, and my speed and accuracy increases. Just lasts a few minutes, usually. Iron is more lethal, so I mostly use my sword instead. You can put me under all the tests you like. I'm telling the truth."

He studied me, and it struck me that the aura of barely restrained power that had surrounded him had disappeared like it had never existed. Instead, there was only Vance and the faint scent of the witch spell he'd used to heal me.

"Did you know what was waiting in the station?" His gaze remained steady, but warmer than before.

"No, of course not. The Lady of the Tree either lied or told us a half truth."

"I believe *that,*" said Vance. "I'm less convinced you aren't hiding important information."

"What good would that do?" I asked. "Don't you think if I'd known how to get those kids back, I'd have done it by now? I've been as upfront as possible, but you've given me no reason to trust you."

His brow furrowed, as if I'd bewildered him. Maybe 'don't accuse your employees of plotting against you and threaten their livelihood if you want them to trust you' wasn't taught in mage training school. I tried to put myself in his position, but I couldn't imagine having such a level of influence over other people. Besides, I was bone-tired and hadn't the energy for another argument. "I'd like to go home. We can pick up where we left off tomorrow."

From a whole heap of nothing. If anything, we'd *lost* momentum, and apparently the *faeries can't lie* rule was a lie itself. The Lady of the Tree had directly claimed the person who'd taken the children had gone to the train station.

Helpless anger simmered inside me, but tiredness won out. When I made for the door, Vance barred the way again, close enough I could smell *him* beneath the witch's spell, a scent unidentifiably masculine. Appealing. Unwanted.

I let out an impatient hiss. "Didn't I say I was done? I'm all out of fucks to give, Vance."

"Please," he said. "If you know anything about the faeries —anything that might help us solve this case—tell me. You can trust I won't spread the information. Part of my position is as a confidant to all mages, and I'll extend the same courtesy to you."

My head throbbed too much to figure out if he was employing mage social niceties or just being a decent human, so I shrugged. The movement didn't hurt my side, but my vision swam. I needed a major blood sugar hit, asap. "What do you want to know?"

"If we went to Faerie," he said. "Those cobwebs… they didn't come from this realm. We weren't in the station."

"It was a trick," I said. "Trust me, if there was another way to Faerie open in this realm, we'd still be there."

"Where did that faerie's magic come from?" he asked. "If not its own realm?"

He thought now was time for a quiz? "I thought you knew faeries had a certain amount of power within them. Pure Sidhe, ones from the Courts, have a metric shitload of magic. Wild creatures like trolls have almost none."

"That one wasn't a Sidhe."

"No, just an exile," I said. "I guess they shoved the bastard into the mortal world during the invasion. Can't imagine why."

"And the children?" he said. "The Lady of the Tree claimed the person who took them went to the station, and if they passed through…"

"That'd count as a half-truth," I agreed.

"Might that fae we encountered have opened a way into Faerie?"

"No. If just any faerie could do it, there'd be a second invasion. It hasn't happened in twenty years." Not strictly true, but what I'd done didn't count. I'd broken through the realms by using the lord's power in sheer desperation, and I still didn't entirely understand how it had been possible.

He watched me, eyes unblinking, and I held my breath.

"You don't look like a faerie."

Huh? Where had that come from?

"I didn't think I'd be glad to hear you say that." Oops. There went my filter. "Never mind. I've lost a shit-ton of blood and don't know what I'm saying."

"You sound pretty coherent to me." His eyes lingered on the bare skin at my waist, possibly on the pretext of examining the now healed wound. But the spark igniting in his eyes was the opposite of concern. The word *predatory* came to mind, along with a rush of warmth I couldn't entirely put down to the aftereffects of blood loss and nearly dying.

His gaze stripped the rest of my clothes from me as surely as though I'd read his thoughts. *Oh.* Heat crept up my neck, and I forgot how to speak, even to tell him to look the hell away. The scent of him grew stronger, and I inhaled almost against my will. *You don't get on with predators.*

Tell that to my thumping heart.

All Vance said was, "Will you be able to get home? I can ask someone to give you a lift."

I licked my lips, suddenly overcome with a fresh wave of tiredness. At least, I assumed that was why my legs wanted to fold at the knees.

"Uh. That'd be great. Thanks. By the way, what did you mean by 'shout at the necromancers'?"

"Somebody," he said, his voice dropping on the word, "is going to pay."

I had no doubt about that.

"And Ivy?" His eyes caught mine, captured my gaze like a moth in a sunbeam.

"Yes?"

"Don't ever take a hit on my account again."

Was that why he hadn't arrested me? Because I'd saved his neck? I didn't know, but now that I was fully aware that I was up against the worst of Faerie, I couldn't carry on working with him.

Vance watched me leave with his arms crossed over his chest. He wasn't smiling, but his open expression showed curiosity more than hostility.

There won't be a next time. When Wanda said he had a protective streak, I hadn't believed her, but now I saw it. Oh, boy. This was heading down a dangerous road. I wasn't the type to salivate over someone as unattainable and unpredictable as a Mage Lord, to say nothing of the years I'd spent taking pains to avoid the mages in general.

We're from different worlds, I told myself. All the mages I'd met until now had been ruthless and self-centred with little regard for anyone below their own social status. And I'd always been more than happy to remain at the bottom of the heap. Invisible. Safe.

Vance Colton was already too involved with my professional life. I didn't need him to shove his way into my personal life as well.

I turned my back on the Mage Lord and closed the door behind me.

14

By the time I got home, I wasn't tired anymore. I was pissed off. I slammed the door open, making Isabel jump out of the armchair she sat in.

"What happened this time?" Her eyes widened at the sight of my tattered, bloodstained clothes.

"Fucking faeries." I stormed past into my bedroom, tossed my jacket onto a chair and stripped off the ruins of my T-shirt. Grabbing a fresh outfit, I made for the shower.

The warm water somewhat calmed me, but the amount of blood streaming from my side reminded me just how close I'd come to dying. Because of the faeries, and because my self-preservation had run for the hills and made me jump between the Mage Lord and a knife. I shuddered, switching off the shower and watching the pinkish water disappear. Next time a faerie gave me an address, I'd torch the place instead of walking in.

Was the kidnapper at that station? The Lady of the Tree had said he'd been there at one point, certainly, but maybe the other foul creature had chased him off. Or sucked out his life energy and left him a withered husk.

Unlikely. For all its trickery, that other fae had been weak, comparatively. I hadn't realised how dependent most faeries were upon the source of their power: the Faerie realm itself. Without it, they'd wither and die like the Lady of the Tree. Really, I should have put her out of her misery, not made a deal with her. Now I owed her a favour... or not, because I'd made her the promise on the assumption that she'd give us the enemy's location, and what she'd told me had been a total lie. That's what I got for trusting faeries to keep their word.

Isabel raised an eyebrow when I stomped back into the living room. "I haven't seen you this mad since Erwin ate the last cookie."

On cue, the piskie zoomed overhead, shrieking about bad faeries.

"This is an epic clusterfuck like you won't believe." I lay down on the sofa and gave her a rundown of the last twenty-four hours. It sounded even worse admitting aloud that I'd failed twice over and almost got killed, and I hadn't told Swanson the latest, either.

"So in summary, the whole universe is crashing around my ears."

The microwave dinged, reminding me I'd shoved a pasta meal in there. I pushed myself up off the sofa and went in search of sustenance.

"I can brew something to help with the blood loss," said Isabel.

"That'd be awesome." I rubbed my forehead. "Erwin *didn't* steal the last cookie, did he?"

"Luckily, no."

"First piece of good news I've had all day." Nothing, not even all the denizens of Faerie, would stand between me and Isabel's heavenly cookies.

Isabel reached towards the bookshelves behind the sofa

and took out her go-to handbook for herbs and potions. "Well, this is definitely worse than the hydra case," she said.

"Tell me about it." I returned to the sofa with my meal. "At least then I had a clear target. I know faeries supposedly can't lie, but they manage to be deceitful little bastards anyway."

I dug into the pasta, shoving cheese-coated macaroni into my mouth. I hadn't realised how starving I was, but I'd barely had the chance to pause all day.

"Maybe the Lady of the Tree didn't mean it literally when she said you could find the children at the train station." Isabel's brows pinched together the way they did when she was thinking hard. "She claimed the person who took them had been there, but they might have passed through on their way somewhere else."

"She as good as said they were in Faerie." I tossed the empty plate onto the coffee table, wanting to scream. I'd failed in the worst way possible, and I'd doomed two teenagers to the same hellishness I'd suffered myself. Small mercy that the Lady of the Tree didn't know my address, so I wouldn't be dragged from bed in the middle of the night and forced to march through a swamp in pursuit of whatever heinous favour she decided to ask for. Probably a quest of some kind. Some faeries didn't get the memo that this was real life, not a storybook.

"Need a healing charm?" asked Isabel. "Looks like you took a real hit back there."

I'd been through worse, but I'd never sustained a wound from defending a mage, of all people. I didn't even know how to explain why I'd done it. Instinct. Sheer foolishness. Whatever.

"I wouldn't mind getting rid of some of these bruises." Now the pain from the stab wound had gone, my body decided to remind me I'd also been used as a punching bag by a bunch of tree roots.

Rather than applying a healing salve to each individual bruise, I opted for one of Isabel's fancier healing spells, figuring I'd more than earned it. She laid down the circle—this one a purple band-shape—and I stepped inside. Purple light flared up around the edges, and a cool sensation washed over me like I'd jumped into wonderfully cold water at the end of a scorching day. When I stepped out, I felt fully re-energised as well as considerably less achy.

"Much better," I said. "About those cookies…"

"In the fridge. What now?"

"I'm supposed to recover, then tell Swanson I failed to find his kid." Should I share everything the Lady of the Tree had claimed? That it was too late, and Faerie already had him in its clutches, might have been a lie as well. I couldn't trust a word she spoke.

With the return of my energy came anger, a familiar helpless rage at the monsters who ruined human lives for kicks. There didn't need to be a point to all this suffering. The kidnappings might not be part of a bigger plan… but my instincts said otherwise.

And, despite it all, those same instincts told me there was still a chance of saving those kids.

Isabel's arms folded around me. "Hey—you'll be fine. You've got out of worse scrapes. Don't count this as a lost cause yet."

My throat closed, choked with unsaid words. *I'd* been a lost cause, yet I'd escaped. I knew luck alone had saved me, though, and rationality warred with the same dogged hope that had kept me alive all those years.

"I'll try." I took in a steadying breath. "If the kids are in *Faerie*, though…"

"Summer or Winter?"

"No clue." *Neither.* Guilt choked my throat. I didn't deserve Isabel's faith in me, and my excuses for concealing the truth had shrunk to almost nothing. It was selfish and cowardly of me to carry on lying to my best friend.

And just what the hell was I supposed to do about Vance Colton? He knew too much. More even than Isabel did. No good could come of letting him keep probing into my life. Quite apart from my peace of mind, anyone else who knew my secrets would be endangered by association. That fact alone had kept my silence despite the number of times I'd almost confessed to Isabel, but I hadn't reckoned on a stranger being the first to find out.

Maybe not a stranger anymore, I thought, thinking of the burn of a knife in my side and the heat in his eyes when I'd left the manor.

Isabel released me, and I walked into the kitchen to retrieve the cookies. "Remind me of the difference between Summer and Winter again?" she asked. "Seems like they're equally evil."

"Pretty much," I said, sitting back on the sofa and taking a bite of cinnamon-flavoured goodness. "Summer is fuelled by life and their magic specialises in making things grow, while Winter feeds on death and their magic tends to involve freezing things. But exiles like that one in the station might have either sort of magic. They aren't beholden to the Courts, either."

"And it's one of the exiles who took the kids, right?" She propped her feet up on the coffee table.

"Has to be, but if I'm to believe the Lady of the Tree, they're already lost." I sank back onto the sofa again. "I can't do this on my own."

"You're not alone," said Isabel. "You're working with the best witches in the district, remember? I've got the whole coven involved. They managed to get something from the house where the second kid went missing. Turns out Shana's wife is friends with the Climes family, and she convinced them to let the coven look around her kid's room. They found traces of the changeling there."

I sat bolt upright. "DNA for a tracking spell?"

"That's right." She grinned. "It's at the coven's headquarters, but I bet I can convince Francine to let me bring it home."

Yes. "You might have just saved the day, Isabel."

"I do my best. Actually, I can't take credit for this one, but I'm sure Francine'll be happy to let me use a tracking spell myself. She trusts me."

"I should hope so, given that you're her Second." I wasn't so sure the coven leader trusted *me,* but we weren't out of the game yet. "Does anyone in the coven have any theories as to why that family was targeted?"

"No clue," she said. "They picked a human living in mage territory and a necromancer's kid. Doesn't really form a pattern, unless they were trying to make all the local supernaturals blame one another."

I shook my head. "Maybe they're banking on the necromancers taking offence at everyone suspecting them."

I couldn't for the life of me figure out the link, either. Faeries were notoriously unpredictable at the best of times, but why piss off multiple groups of supernaturals at once?

My phone buzzed. "Oh crap."

A new message read, *"If you've recovered, I'm coming over to your house now."*

"He's coming over now. Shit." So much for giving me time to recuperate. I was *not* mentally prepared to have the Mage Lord in my house.

"Wait, who's coming over?"

"Vance Colton."

"Holy shit."

"I know, right?" I groaned.

"Wow." She didn't appear as concerned about the mess as I was. "I never got to talk to him last time."

"You don't want to." Kinda harsh, but he might have given me a break before he came back demanding another favour. Then again, maybe he had more information, or a new lead.

"Is he that bad?"

"Stuck-up. Snobbish. Standard mage." I paced around the sofa with my phone in hand. "He thinks only of himself and can't speak a word without ordering people around."

"You're fidgeting," said Isabel. "You always do that when you're nervous."

"Hell, yes, I'm nervous. The Mage Lord's used to swimming in luxury. This place is practically a troll's nest to him."

"Since when did you care?" She snorted. "Is he attractive? They say he is."

Yes. Very. I shrugged.

"Aha." Her eyes gleamed. "So that's why you've been spending so much time at his house."

"Are you forgetting he coerced me into working for him?" I shot her a warning look. "He's rude, overbearing and terrifying."

"And smoking hot, from what I've heard." She flashed me a grin. "I said you needed to get out more. You haven't dated in months."

"Because the last time worked out so well." I'd made the mistake of inviting the guy over here, and Erwin the piskie had decided to make a nest in his hair. My romantic life was even unluckier than my professional one, though right now, 'nonexistent' was a better word.

"I warned you," said Isabel. "Regular humans don't get what we do. You need someone who's in the know about this." She indicated the general spell-strewn mess of our living room.

"Do I look like I have time for a relationship? My life's a

complete shit show." My phone buzzed again. "He's on the way."

"Excellent."

I flicked a piece of discarded spell at her. "We almost died. Twice. That's probably what he wants to talk about."

That sobered her up. "Do you really think we should clean the flat?"

I looked around. "Never mind. It's not worth it. If this place is good enough for clients, it's good enough for His Pretentiousness."

She snorted, but I felt an inexplicable twinge of guilt. He'd helped me. More than once. He could be a dick sometimes, but then, so could I.

Before I could gather my thoughts together, the doorbell rang. It figured that he'd have used his space-bending power to come here in five seconds flat.

I walked to the door and opened it to find Vance standing there in full Mage Lord gear, cloak and all.

"You must be Isabel," he said to her over my shoulder.

I tensed, but she smiled and accepted his handshake. "Hi. You're... Lord Colton? Sir?"

"Either."

So much for leaving his pretentious attitude behind.

"Vance," I said pointedly, but he reacted like I hadn't spoken. "We were discussing how you volunteered to help me deal with this particularly difficult case."

"I see." For a moment, I thought I'd pushed too far. Then he smirked. "Did you include the part where I saved you from bleeding to death?"

Oh, he had to go there. "And the part where you got beaten up by a wall made out of spiderwebs?"

Isabel's shocked expression said, *I didn't know you were on such familiar terms,* but she had the sense not to voice her thoughts aloud.

"I asked the necromancers about the train station, since we encountered undead there," he said, snapping back into professional mode. "Lord Evander said nobody's raised any queries around that area recently, but undead can't survive in the state we found them in for long. Days at most."

"Then he's lying." In the distraction of nearly bleeding to death, I'd forgotten about the zombies.

"I agree, and that's why I've sent people to check up on the necromancer guild," said Vance, surprising me.

"But why would a necromancer be involved with the faeries?" That made zero sense. It was as unlikely as a troll joining a community project.

"I intend to find out," said Vance. "As for the necromancers, we will be meeting with them after their monthly summit tomorrow. That should give me the opportunity to find out if anyone has been dealing in forbidden magic.'

"The necromancers are supposed to stop that from happening," said Isabel over her shoulder as she made for her open bedroom door. "They protect the veil. If one of them goes rogue, they're supposed to be expelled from the Guild. It's in their sacred oath."

"Clearly not sacred, then."

"No, it's true," said Vance. "They rewrote the laws after the invasion, since the necromancers had to do more than the Mage Lords to clear up the aftermath. I believe it's the only time they've taken on any responsibility."

Sounded about right. "Every necromancer in the region is a member of their guild, right?"

"Generally," Vance said, "but necromancy doesn't tend to be dominant in family lines, unlike with mages. As with witches, ordinary people might carry the gift and not know it."

"Hmm." I watched Isabel's bedroom door close behind her, leaving me alone with the Mage Lord. *Great.* "I still don't see how the faeries fit in. Winter magic feeds on death, and the necromancers live next to a giant cemetery, but otherwise I can't figure out any link between them."

"Especially as faeries are immortal," Vance added. "But the Lady of the Tree said she wanted her immortality back."

"From Faerie," I corrected. "A necromancer wouldn't be of any use. I don't think even *they* can stop someone from dying permanently, let alone a faerie."

"Exactly," he said. "I have mages patrolling every inch of necromancer territory, looking out for trouble. Lord Evander isn't happy with me."

"Tough shit," I said. "The necromancers should've thought of that before they made everyone suspect them."

"They care nothing for their reputation," said Vance. "As for the half-blood faeries, *they* refused to allow me to send anyone into their territory at all."

"Be glad they did. I nearly got eaten by a kelpie when I went in there."

"Can half-bloods lie? I know pure faeries can't."

"Yeah, they can. They aren't bound by Faerie's rules here. Even the Lady of the Tree lied to us, unless we seriously misinterpreted what she claimed."

Or unless someone really had opened a way back into Faerie inside that old train station. I'd have thought an event of that magnitude would have sent all magic along the Ley Line haywire, but how else to explain why we hadn't found those kids, nor their kidnapper?

Vance studied me. "You really think someone opened a door into Faerie."

"I can't think of another way to interpret her words," I said. "But—it's impossible. Magic alone wouldn't do it. The half-bloods dream of escaping this realm, but they can't. The invasion was the only time anyone's opened the doors, and everyone saw how that turned out."

Vance's phone buzzed. "I'll answer this."

He stood, pressing the phone to his ear. "What happened?"

A voice buzzed on the other end, and from Vance's tight expression, I could tell it wasn't good news.

"I have to leave." He switched his phone off. "Bailey never made it back from the station. Rod went there to look for him and found the car empty, and now he's not answering the phone either. Nobody's been able to get hold of them."

My heart plummeted. "Damn."

"Don't leave the house."

Before I could blink, he'd vanished. Without even opening the door. As Isabel came out of her bedroom, I sank onto the sofa.

"*Don't leave the house.* Unbelievable." I shook my head. "I'm not going to ground myself because two of his people went missing near the station."

Isabel joined me. "That station... it's in the abandoned part of the city, right?"

I nodded. "Why?"

Isabel reached behind the sofa, pulling out a dusty map. "This shows where the Ley Line is. Handy for figuring out where our spells will work best... or where to avoid." She unfurled the map upon the coffee table and placed a couple of glass bottles on top to keep it from rolling up again. The map showed a warren of streets that formed our corner of the city, and a line drawn in black ink cut directly through the centre. "I did wonder if the station lies over one of the key points."

"Key points?"

"Places on the line where magic is particularly strong." She traced the Ley Line with her fingertip and indicated several spots circled in black marker. "The first thing I learned when I joined the coven was not to attempt a spell directly on top of a key point. There's something in the necromancers' code forbidding them from using their powers there, too, I think because the veil's particularly thin."

"It's easier to raise spirits there… and undead." I mentally retraced the route to the station and jabbed a finger at one of the circled spots on the map. "That's the place. I bet faerie magic's stronger at those points, too. That's got to be our connection. I'll tell Vance—"

A blaring alarm from outside made me jump. Erwin the piskie flew through the room, shrieking. "Bad faerie!"

"What the hell?"

Isabel leaped to her feet. "Someone's attacking our wards."

I reached over and grabbed my sword. I hadn't left a trail of blood outside, or so I'd thought, but the alarm rang like a siren, and the smell of burning reached my nostrils. As I passed the window, a sudden blast of fire scorched the flowerbeds beneath.

"Hey!" Isabel shouted. "Those are rare herbs, you bastard."

She grabbed a handful of spells from the coffee table, shoved the window open, and flung one outside. Purple light spilled out, accompanied by a tremendous bang like a fire-work. High-pitched screams reached my ears, and several tall, twig-like figures danced across the front lawn, howling.

I knew it was the faeries.

Fire imps were something of an anomaly. Summer disliked them because of their destructive tendencies towards plant life, while Winter wasn't terribly enamoured with them either. Frankly, I didn't know where they came from, except possibly the land of the exiles. Nobody ever handed me a definitive guide to Faerie. I had to figure out most of it on my own.

This was far from my first encounter with fire imps, but they'd never attacked me at home before. I took pains to make sure that no faerie, no matter how weak, set foot in here.

I ran to the door, Irene in one hand and one of Isabel's explosive spells in the other. Those particular spells were reserved for the two of us, on the reasonable grounds that most non-magic users did a good job running into magical accidents without having access to the witch equivalent of a firework.

A flaming ball shot past my face the instant I opened the door, sizzling out on contact with the ward. *Still too close.* A fire imp danced close to me, teeth bared in a manic grin, and I sliced its head off with my blade.

"Bad faerie!" Erwin flew past, narrowly missing being torched, and threw a handful of what appeared to be paperclips at our attackers.

"You could have grabbed a weapon," I told the piskie. "They aren't all iron."

Not that the piskie was a reliable fighter. Another ball of fire sent him spinning out of sight with a shriek, vanishing into the smoking ruin of a bush.

"Hey!" I yelled at the aggressors. "Get out."

The piskie might be an annoyance, but that didn't mean I wanted to watch the fire imps set him ablaze. How the hell had so many of them got past the iron wards? Fire sparked all over the lawn, burning holes in the grass, and Isabel ran forward as another flowerbed went up in flames. She threw an explosive spell amid the dancing imps, which went off with a bang that sent bits of twig flying in all directions.

"Whoa." I stared, somewhat surprised at the result. "That's strong."

Another imp leapt on my head from behind, its sharp fingers stabbing at my eyes.

"Get off," I snarled, grabbing at it with my free hand. The imp's sharp little teeth sank into my finger, and I swung, sending its body tumbling to the ground. A stab finished it off, and I kicked its body towards the gate.

A gate that was decidedly *not* warded, though it should be. The glyphs that had been drawn on the back of the garden wall on either side had been scribbled out, as if someone had taken a sharpie to them. I nudged Isabel and pointed, and her eyes went wide.

A sudden flaming ball came flying at us from Isabel's side. I leaped in front of her, blue light flaring around my non-sword hand. The light spread, forming a barrier, and the fire harmlessly glanced off the blue shield now surrounding both of us. *You don't get to hurt her.* I'd kill them all first.

"Thanks," Isabel breathed, tossing me an explosive spell and employing one of her own.

Our twin explosives soared at the oncoming imp horde. Two blasts went off, and bits of dismembered imp flew left and right, some still holding fireballs in their spindly hands. One was left, and I ran forward, giving the beast a sharp kick on my way to the gate. A cursory glance outside confirmed none had escaped, so I brought Irene down on the last imp to put it out of its misery.

When the imp's head tumbled to the ground, Isabel walked over to me. "You're fast. I didn't see you grab a speed enhancer."

I said nothing, a heavy measure of guilt settling over me at the reminder that Vance Colton knew more about my abilities than Isabel did. More pertinent right now was that the faeries had done what I'd sworn I'd never allow. They'd attacked our home. Just how had these dim-witted creatures managed to deactivate a warding spell?

"How the hell did they take out our defences?" I walked over to the gate, peering at the spot where a ring of iron-laced magic had once circled the garden and finding nothing more than crumbling remains near the scratched-out glyphs.

"No clue." Isabel bent over the now-defunct ward. "I can use a tracking spell and see if someone came in."

"Good idea."

I watched her return to the house, one eye on the fence in case more assailants showed up. The house was still warded, but that they'd got so close was unacceptable. Nothing was a perfect defence, of course—especially against the faeries—but fire imps were simple creatures. They couldn't have taken the wards down themselves.

Isabel returned with a tracking spell, which she placed next to the gate. A circle spread out, and lines appeared within, a series of glyphs etched in green light dancing up and down Isabel's arms.

The light dimmed, and she shook her arms, scattering bits of spell-dust onto the path. "I don't believe it."

"Who was it?" I asked.

"Larsen," she said. "One of his mercenaries scratched out those wards."

My boss. Unless one of the mercs had gone rogue, he'd tried to kill us.

15

I wanted to confront Larsen alone first thing the next morning, but as per usual, Vance Colton put a wrench in my plans. I woke to a rapping on the door and groaned as the impact of the past twenty-four hours hit me like a rampaging troll.

"All right, all right!" I snapped at no one in particular when my ears rang with another sharp knock. I dressed in ten seconds flat and grabbed my sword in case another faerie contingent waited outside the wards. "Chill the hell out, Vance."

"When did you end up on first name terms, anyway?" asked Isabel, who stood in the kitchen with a mug of steaming hot chocolate in her hands.

"When we both nearly died." I wasn't mentally present today. Small wonder when my boss had tried to kill me, and I had no idea why. All my phone calls went through to voice-mail, and the fucker hadn't even been at his office when I'd stormed up there with my jeans still stained with the remnants of exploded fire imps. I'd planned to go back today and try again, but not while hiding behind the Mage Lord.

"What is it?" I asked as I opened the front door.

"Not a morning person?" Vance was as unruffled as ever, while I both looked and felt like shit. I'd taken a fair beating yesterday, and even Isabel's healing spell hadn't got rid of all my bruises. I'd stayed up late trying to get through to Larsen and helping Isabel replace all the explosive spells we'd used up on the fire imps, so an early wakeup call was not what I'd needed.

"A bunch of faeries tried to torch my house," I said. "Knocked the wards out. You didn't see anything odd when you came here yesterday, did you?"

"No." His mouth tightened. "Who did that?"

I hesitated. I didn't need to admit the boss he'd told me to ditch seemed to want rid of me of his own accord, but I had no other explanation to hand. I glanced over my shoulder to find Isabel had retreated into her room again and left me alone with Vance. *Damn.*

"Fire imps got my address somehow." I evaded the question. "They torched Isabel's flowerbeds. Did you find those two mages?"

"No."

Funny how he could pack so much meaning into one word. Specifically, *No, but I'm going to find who's responsible and eviscerate them.*

"You could have come to me," I said. "We have a dozen new tracking spells ready."

"We already tried," he said. "I believe there's some faerie trickery that's blocking them from working effectively."

That figured. "Isabel and I have DNA from the second changeling, from the necromancer family's house. We were going to use a tracker to find it."

"Now?" He looked over my shoulder into the flat.

"You can come in, but I'm not using the tracking spell in here."

I regretted my decision when I realised the flat looked even worse than yesterday, if possible. Vance raised his eyebrows at the sight of a dozen spell circles set up on the floor, surrounded by piles of herbs and other ingredients. "What are you doing?"

"Making tripwires," I said. "I'd watch your footing in here. They're anti-faerie defences for the flat. I was thinking of something that makes their testicles fall off."

"Wouldn't just killing them be a deterrent to the others?"

I smirked. "That wouldn't leave anyone alive to tell tales, would it?"

"You're more vindictive than I gave you credit for. What's that?" He indicated the map I'd left out on the table.

"A possible connection. Isabel had a theory about why the faeries picked the factory as their hideout."

"Tell me."

"Still forgetting to say 'please'?"

"Two of my people are missing," he said, his jaw tight with anger, as he studied the map. "The Ley Line. The train station is near a key point?"

"You know about those?"

"Of course. Doesn't the Ley Line give you the ability to use magic? That's how it goes for witches."

I didn't miss the accusation in his tone. A reminder of the lies I'd told him.

"I guess. I've never been away from it, so I wouldn't know. It doesn't give you *your* power, right?" Mages were the only magic users who could access their abilities to the same degree whether they were near the Ley Line or not.

"No, but I find it useful to keep track." He pointed to the spot on the map where the station lay. "This spot contains enough raw power that even the necromancers wouldn't have been able to sense that someone was summoning the dead. Was that your friend's theory?"

"That, and… it might have also concealed someone opening a doorway into Faerie." I dropped my gaze. "It shouldn't be possible, but that would mean the Lady of the Tree technically did tell the truth. I can't think how else she evaded the *fae can't lie* rule."

My phone went off. Larsen. Of all the timing. "My boss is calling me."

"Make it quick." Vance clearly wasn't going anywhere, so I moved away from him, phone in hand.

"Larsen." Try as I might, I didn't quite succeed at packing the word with menace the way Vance could. "Is your phone working again?"

"Don't be smart with me," Larsen growled. "I've had a job and a half dealing with the mess you stirred up, Lane."

"What mess?" I gripped my phone tightly. "Somebody sent fire imps after me and turned off the protective wards outside my house. I don't suppose you know anything about that?"

An ominous silence followed. Out of the corner of my eye, I glimpsed Vance talking to Isabel. He held out a hand to take something—a spell?—but Larsen's next words made me forget everything else.

"With the number of enemies you've made," he said, "it's a wonder that didn't happen sooner."

"What?" I stared at the blank screen in disbelief. "Fuck me sideways."

Vance raised an eyebrow. "What happened?"

"I have absolutely no idea." I swivelled to Isabel, who'd emerged from her room and gave me a questioning look.

"Larsen didn't admit anything?" she guessed.

"No, but he also didn't deny it. He can't be *that* pissed off about those necromancy props, can he? Or the changelings?"

"Might be." Vance paused. "You planned to track the changeling today?"

"I don't know if finding the changeling will improve his mood, to be honest." Though the changelings were also one of our few remaining sources of information on the kidnapper. "You can go after your people, and we'll do that."

Finally, an ironclad excuse to get rid of him. So why did the idea of heading after the changelings without Vance being there fill me with trepidation?

Vance studied me, his expression unreadable. "I can send someone to assist you, if you like."

I shook my head. "I'll be fine with Isabel." *I hope.*

When Vance had gone, Isabel and I opted to use the tracking spell outside the house this time, though it didn't make much of a difference to our chances of turning the place into Faerie Central again. There were laws around doing spellwork in public places and we didn't need any curious onlookers, but I hadn't thought to ask Vance to loan us the use of his field again.

"Guess we can't do much more damage than those imps already did." Isabel surveyed the scorched grass. "It'll take months to replace those herbs."

"Bastards." I set down a new iron ward outside the front door of the house, just in case. "Have you seen Erwin since yesterday?"

"No." A worried frown creased her forehead. "Did those imps chase him off?"

"Better than turning him into a fireball." Piskies were flammable enough that I worried they *had* torched him and we hadn't noticed. Yet another strike against Larsen and the mercs.

"Did the Mage Lord have any new theories?" Isabel asked as she set up the tracking spell.

"He said the energies around the key point on the Ley Line might have hidden that someone was summoning the dead," I said. "Like we already guessed. The Ley Line boosts the abilities of almost every magic-user, and faeries and half-bloods can't *survive* away from it."

It had to be the place someone had opened the way into Faerie, but surely not a permanent one. How? The Lady of the Tree had claimed she was dying, that she wanted to go home, but the person who'd taken the children had walked back and forth between realms with apparent ease and hadn't taken anyone else with them.

Unless their goal wasn't to return to Faerie, but to bring Faerie here.

Shivers broke out on my arms. *Enough paranoia, Ivy.*

The lines of the spell circle flared up. Isabel knelt on the lawn, green light dancing up and down her arms as she stared into the circle. She then blinked, lowering her arms. "That can't be right. The spell says the changeling's just around the corner from here."

I stared a moment. "Are you sure?"

"Pretty certain."

"Better get ready for another fight."

"I'll double-check the wards," she said. "There are some nasty tripwires if Larsen comes back."

"Good." I was doubly glad we'd spent half the night making a new batch of explosive spells. If this was another trap, I'd be prepared this time. I already had my blade, but I sheathed two more daggers at my waist. "I hope Larsen walks straight into that tripwire."

"Same here." Isabel slid on two more armbands, both for protection, and joined me at the door. My normally chilled-out best friend was dressed for battle, carrying knives of her own to go with her impressive collection of explosive spells.

Once outside the flat, I immediately spotted the blue light flaring like a beacon from the road's corner and ran ahead, readying Irene. The blood of last night's imps had barely dried, and the blade gleamed wickedly as I prepared to fight whatever Faerie threw at us this time.

Fucking Larsen. If not for him, the faeries wouldn't have found out my address. That light surely couldn't come from the changelings alone. They didn't have magic powerful enough to cause that big a spark.

Isabel followed my lead, and when we drew closer, a familiar smell slapped me in the face. Decaying roses. Faerie blood, drenched in magic. Dread wrapped itself around my body like a net choking the life from me. My legs locked into place, my skin going clammy. *Not again.*

"Ivy?" Isabel overtook me, and my instincts snapped back on. *She can't see the faeries. She doesn't know what we're about to face.*

"Hang on," I croaked. "Let me go first."

She gave me an odd look, but she let me step into the lead and round the street corner. My whole body tensed at the blood spattering the pavement. Near a parked car, the changeling had been torn in two. Its top half was sprawled in the road, its pointed teeth hanging from its gaping mouth, while the lower half lay at a twisted angle further down the road.

Isabel swore. "Someone else got here first."

"Nobody friendly." I forced myself to continue walking and confirmed the other two changelings' bodies lay near their brother, their bloodied bodies shredded by sharp teeth. "Something nasty attacked them. Like a—"

Hellhound. A giant furry body appeared, the glamour concealing it melting away. The hellhound's huge head swept to either side, sniffing out for prey. Such as the humans inside the houses a few feet away.

"Oi," I yelled. "Over here, you great hairy bastard."

I had an explosive spell at the ready, but the hellhound moved too fast. I took up my blade instead, slicing across the dog's thick hide before its teeth closed around my arm. Blood spilled out, tinged with the blue of faerie magic. I lunged for the throat next, crimson spattering the road.

"Ivy, run!" yelled Isabel.

Her explosive spell flew past my face towards three other hellhounds which had materialised in the road. When the pencil-shaped spell hit the road, it detonated with the force of a firework. Not only did it send the hellhounds flying back, the impact blew an impressive chunk out of the tarmac, too. I blinked, trying to see through the haze. Bloody hellhound bodies slumped into the road. Had she got them all?

Isabel screamed. I whirled around, and the stinking breath of a hellhound hit my face. Teeth snapped inches from my nose, and I brought the sword up, slicing its forehead open. As I swung my blade a second time, a blast of icy fear froze the breath in my lungs.

My body locked up, my lungs constricting. Isabel made a choked sound and dropped to her knees, shaking all over. She'd never been hit by a fear spell before, but I had, and a burst of rage rose inside me. I was not going to let their magic hurt Isabel. No way in hell.

Blue light flared from my hands, pushing against the wave of fear. I inhaled, tendrils of light swirling around my palms, and felt a renewed strength fill my body.

I flung myself at the hellhound, and my sword plunged into the beast's eye. Crimson spurted, and the hellhound's body went limp. Breathing hard, I yanked the blade free in a shower of blood.

The road lay quiet, but the carnage remained. Clean-up were going to have a situation on their hands.

"I hope Larsen sends the same fuckwit who took out our wards to clear away this mess," I said, hands curling into fists. "I'll introduce them to Irene."

"Ow." Isabel rose upright, wincing. "One of them bit me."

Shit. Given how acidic their drool was, a bite from a faerie dog wasn't good news. "Come on. You need a healing spell."

Why had the changelings been on their way to our house in the first place? Had they been bait for the hellhounds, or had they been running amok around the city of their own accord? It wasn't like I could ask the changelings themselves, but a suspicion that someone had been trying to tidy up loose ends lurked in the back of my mind.

This isn't the end of it. I'd get answers, and I'd start with my soon-to-be-ex-boss.

As we neared home, a green pinprick of light showed me Isabel's tracking spell on the front lawn. She must have left it turned on, and an idea occurred to me. I walked into the garden and crouched down beside the circle's shimmering lines. "This thing's still active. I wonder…"

I held my hand over the circle and let the hellhound's viscous blood dribble onto the lawn. Fresh green tendrils of light fanned out from the spell to my hands, and images drifted into my head. Images of a place I'd seen recently, recognisable even in black and white. A graveyard behind a high fence. A wrought-iron gate. A building with soot-coloured walls.

I lowered my hands, green dust scattering as the circle collapsed. "I don't believe it. The hellhounds came from the necromancers' headquarters."

"What?" Isabel leaned on the fence for balance, blood seeping down her leg, and a spasm of rage shook me.

"Never mind. Let's get you back in the house."

My heart beat a steady rhythm in my ears. *They'll pay for this. I'll kill them.*

16

Isabel looked like living death by the time I'd helped her back into the house and onto the sofa. Worry fluttered in my chest, tempering my growing fury at the necromancers. Not to mention Larsen. My hands shook as I knocked spells everywhere in an attempt to find the first aid kit Isabel kept on the bookshelf behind the sofa. We always kept it well stocked and within easy reach, but I'd never treated a hellhound bite before, and their drool was toxic enough to eat through skin without their teeth making contact.

"This one." Isabel reached over her shoulder to point at a small bottle. Pale veins stood out on her hands. Not good.

I grabbed the bottle and applied the salve to the puncture wounds on the side of her leg. "Why didn't you tell me it bit you?"

"Because another one was trying to eat your face at the time," said Isabel shakily. "Everything's gone blue."

"Oh, shit." That probably wasn't a good sign.

Isabel giggled. "You're blue, Ivy."

"Try to hang on." I set the bottle down on the coffee table. The wounds were an angry red colour, and blood continued to ooze down her shin. I set up a healing circle next and helped her into it, while Isabel snickered to herself.

"Blue everywhere. You look like one of those half-bloods."

I shivered. Some of the colour had come back into her face, but her vague expression sent spikes of alarm through my nerves. Isabel was the healing expert. She'd always been the one to patch up my injuries, not the other way around.

She's fine, I told myself. *She'll be fine.* I made sure she was comfortable on the sofa and then whispered, "I'm going to make sure we haven't left a trail outside. I don't want anything else coming after us."

Isabel didn't respond. Her head lolled against a cushion, but her pulse was steady, so she must have fallen asleep. Leaving felt like a betrayal, but I had to make sure there weren't any more hellhounds sniffing around.

I set up extra wards around the house, both inside and outside, before I walked down the road. At the sight of a gathering crowd, I quickened my pace. Larsen's clean-up crew had already arrived, and none of them looked particularly enthused at the notion of having to pick up hellhound guts.

One of the mercs, a surly-looking guy named Gregor, barred my path. "We got here first."

I raised a brow. "Didn't know you were that desperate to scrub entrails off the pavement." Not that it was overly surprising that a merc wanted to take credit for other people's work. He'd probably brag that he'd slain the hellhounds himself. "Larsen sent you, right? Did he tell you what you'd find?"

"Larsen said you're in league with the faeries."

What? "Larsen's a giant knobhead. Listen, those

changelings are my responsibility, and they died on their way to see me."

"Your responsibility, are they?" He scoffed. "What'd you take them to pieces for?"

"I didn't do that." I gave him a cool look. "I killed the beasts responsible, but I want to know who sent them."

"Who gives a shit?"

"I do." I narrowed my eyes at him. "What *has* Larsen been saying about me? Is there a reason I had a visit from a group of fire imps last night?"

He snorted, then covered his mouth with the back of his hand. "No. What're you talking about?"

"You." I stared at him. "Were you the one who shut down my wards?"

His silence spoke for itself. I pulled out my sword, and the others hastened to clear the space around us. Public brawls were common enough amongst mercs that I wasn't too worried that anyone would intervene. "Larsen told you to do it, did he?"

"Larsen? No." He gave another snort. "Some new client. I thought it was a joke."

"Fucking hilarious." A *client?* Seriously? "Someone paid you to take down my wards?"

"Offered a nice bit of cash for it, too."

He was asking for a chat with Irene. "Who the hell was this client?"

Larsen didn't bother vetting everyone who showed up at the guild, but who'd hire a mercenary to do a job that a witch could have done better? If this client had been trying to kill me by de-warding the property, they ought to have picked someone intelligent enough to finish the job *before* they'd set off the blaring alarm that had alerted us to the attack.

"Shit, I don't know." The merc cringed as my blade pointed at his neck. "Don't you touch me with that."

"You nearly got my friend and me killed," I said. "If you ever come near me again, I'll be carrying a magical tripwire spell that'll make your balls shrivel up and fall off."

The guy winced. "I get it, I get it."

"No, you don't." I didn't lower my sword. "Tell me who the client was, or I swear I'll deliver you back to Larsen in a body bag."

"I don't *know,* all right?" he said. "The guy wore a cloak that hid his face."

"What kind of cloak?" The necromancers came to mind. *They wouldn't hire a mercenary, would they? Or work with the faeries?*

Yet the hellhounds had seemingly come from the cemetery next door to their headquarters. What were they playing at?

"How should I know? Fuck!" He leaned back when my blade's edge nicked the skin of his neck, drawing a bead of blood to the surface. "I'll tell you if I see the guy again, all right?"

"Nah, don't bother." I turned away, disgusted. "And don't come near my house if you want to keep your sensitive anatomy where it's supposed to be."

I walked away, breathing hard. Fucking mercenaries. *Had it been a necromancer who'd hired him?* After Larsen had bitten my head off for bringing necromantic props into the guild, it seemed unlikely, but whoever it was, it was abundantly clear that my time working for the mercs had come to an end.

Fuming, I turned my attention to the image from the last tracking spell. I'd worry about my financial future later. It was time to pay the necromancers a long-overdue visit.

A nagging voice in the back of my head told me that going to see them alone was unwise, but Isabel was injured and Vance had his own issues to deal with. I left before I changed my mind, following the same route Vance and I had driven down on the way to necromancer territory last time.

The squat sooty-bricked building looked the same, except a sign on the door, written in cursive, proclaimed: "Summit in progress. Do not disturb."

If they hadn't been summoning the dead, I might have ignored that sign, but they'd given me an opening to do some snooping. I trod alongside the fence that cut off the area where the people killed in the invasion had been laid to rest. Had someone summoned the hellhounds behind those fences? Not too many people visited that cemetery, since the main public memorial to the invasion lay in a more central location without any bodies buried nearby.

A blue glow drew my attention from somewhere beyond the fence. Faerie magic had been used here recently. *I knew it.*

I approached the wrought-iron gate, drawing my blade. Iron usually kept faeries out, so if any enemy waited, it'd be of the undead variety, like at the station. The gate didn't look to have been opened recently, so I resisted the impulse to employ one of Isabel's explosive spells and pulled a lockpick from my pocket instead.

The gate swung open with little effort on my part. At the front were rows of fancy headstones, designed for rich families and adorned with fresh flowers. An unexpected rush of emotion choked my throat at the reminder of the sheer scale of the deaths the faeries had caused in the invasion. And this was just a single corner of one city.

I wrenched my attention away before I could see if one of the larger headstones bore the name *Colton*. These graves were surely the mages'; nobody else could afford to pay for upkeep, but that didn't mean I wanted to stick my nose where it didn't belong. I'd come here for a reason.

Another flash of blue light caught my gaze, drawing me towards a group of headstones closer to the necromancers' headquarters that were easily the same size as the fancier ones but considerably more neglected. At the end of the row, a grave wreathed in moss drew me to a halt in front.

My own name shone from the stone in vibrant blue, along with the words *"Watch yourself, human."*

"Real original," I said, aloud. "Not to mention disrespecting the dead."

My voice trembled just a little. The blue wasn't ink, but tendrils of coiling faerie magic, semi-transparent as smoke. The person who'd left the message knew I was Sighted.

Beneath the glow, words were carved into the stone, and the name *Swanson* leapt out at me.

Swanson was the family name on the grave.

Was his family more influential than I'd realised? Certainly nobody had visited recently; this whole corner was far from as well-tended despite the proximity of the guild's sooty walls visible on the other side of the fence.

I turned to the next grave, which bore the name *Evander*. Some ancestor of the current guild leader, presumably. But why would Swanson's family grave be next to—

Oh. An ancestor of Swanson's must be a necromancer. Looking at the dates, it'd been around three generations back. He'd denied having any magic in his family, but maybe he didn't know. This place was closed off, and non-supernaturals rarely came to this corner of the city.

I stared around at the carved headstones like the answers lay beneath the ground. Hell, maybe they did, but I wasn't about to start digging. Further along, past the graves belonging to the guild members' ancestors, would be the resting places of the ordinary folk who'd lost their lives. Including my parents.

And me.

We shared a single headstone. I'd seen it, once, on my first visit here, when I'd tried to hire that dickhead of a necromancer to contact my parents. Though my body had never been recovered, I was on the list of the dead, having gone missing at the invasion's start.

I shoved the memories back, shivering at the unnerving thought that I was walking on my own grave.

"Is anyone here?" I called out, not much caring if the necromancers heard me on the other side of the fence. If they were too busy with their summit to notice someone summoning hellhounds next door, they needed a hell of a wakeup call.

A figure materialised out of thin air, above Swanson's grave.

I jerked back, lifting my blade, but iron would be of no use against a ghost. The spirit's features were blurred, but not enough that I couldn't see that his silvery hair glowed, almost transparent, and his angular features left no doubt what he was.

"Who the hell are you?" More like 'who *were* you?' The half-faerie was dead, undeniably. Which brought up a more pertinent question: "Why can I see you?"

"The veil is thin here," whispered the ghost. "You can see what would ordinarily be hidden to your eyes... but I think you already see far more than other humans do, Ivy Lane."

"You wrote my name on that grave?" I gestured behind him. "Or did someone else?"

He eyed me, his eyes an unnaturally vibrant blue even in death. "I've heard your name often from my kin."

"That wasn't an answer." Not that I'd expected one. Ghostly half-faeries would be no more reliable than living ones, though I hadn't even known they *could* turn into ghosts. Had to be an unpleasant experience for someone with immortal blood on one side of their family. "Any particular reason you're hanging around here?"

"To make you an offer."

"Of what?"

"Immortality."

I gave him a blank stare. "Coming from a ghost, that's not a promise I'm inclined to believe."

The ghost's eyes gleamed silvery blue. "There are many of my kin who would give anything to return home, to regain what they lost."

"Well, yeah." True faeries were undying, but half-bloods could die like the rest of us. And, if the Lady of the Tree proved anything, like the pure fae who were also trapped in this realm. "Are you the one making deals with the half-faeries and faeries who've been stranded here since the invasion? Promising them immortality in exchange for looking the other way while you kidnap humans?"

The ghost tilted his head. "You're perceptive, mortal."

"I'm capable of putting two and two together." I narrowed my eyes. "Faerie blood bestows immortality, does it? And you want to give it to *me...* why?"

"The price, I'm sure, is one you're willing to pay."

"I highly doubt it." It was difficult to be afraid of someone who couldn't so much as lay a hand on me, even if the same was true on my end. "Someone sent hellhounds to my house. From here."

Blue tendrils of smoke wrapped around me, and my hand tightened on my blade. The hellhounds might have come from beyond these fences, but this guy couldn't have summoned them, being a ghost himself. Who did he really speak for?

"That wasn't I," he said. "I am no longer part of the world of the living. I'm only an observer. But if you help my master, we will give you everything you desire."

"No, thanks," I said. "You have to be out of your mind if you think I'll ever consider helping your master, whoever it is."

"You won't have a choice," he said. "If you submit willingly, you will be gifted the same immortality all true faeries have when the doors to our realm open again. Once *you* open the doors."

Oh. I gaped at the half-faerie, grasping his plan in one heart-sinking moment. My magic. The power I'd stolen and used to escape Faerie… he and his master wanted to use that same magic to tear open a way back.

"No." I spoke louder. "No. I won't. Tell your master I reject his offer."

"Pity." As he began to fade around the edges, another realisation hit me: as far as I knew, dead people couldn't be cursed by a tongue-tying spell.

"Wait." I stepped forward. "Who is this master? What's his name? Maybe I'll change my mind if I hear it."

Not bloody likely, but my enemy's identity was foremost among the questions nagging at the back of my mind. As was the question of why he needed *my* magic when he could already walk between realms whenever he felt like it.

"The one who waits between, in the place where nothing and nobody truly dies. The Lord of the Grey Vale."

My blood turned as cold as the graves that surrounded me. "Give me the name, or I swear I'll—"

Do what? He was a ghost. Nothing could touch him. With a laugh, the half-faerie's transparent figure vanished in a swirl of blue glamour.

Not a trace remained. The message on the grave had gone, too.

That was when it sank in that I was alone in a cemetery, surrounded by the buried victims of the faerie invasion.

A scratching sound made the hairs rise on the back of my neck. *You've got to be kidding me.*

I stepped towards the noise and spied three pale figures advancing, tattered clothes stained with grave dirt. I held my breath at the stench of decomposing flesh as I swung my sword, decapitating the first one. The undead's hands continued to grab at me even with its head hanging limply from a string of sinew. I struck again, gagging on the smell. Every strike had the effect of hitting a rampaging hydra with a water pistol. I reached into my pocket, scrabbling for the salt canister I kept handy for situations like this and hoping there was enough to take down three of them.

As the thought crossed my mind, several more filed out from behind the row of nearby graves, sunken eyes staring. Ah, shit.

I backed up against the headstone, mentally calculating my odds of escape. Not good. The gate had closed behind me —due, no doubt, to that half-faerie ghost—and the dead moved faster than a decaying person had the right to. The only way to be permanently rid of them would involve a necromancer's binding spell, and with the entire guild tied up in a summit, that was highly unlikely.

Which left me with one person to call.

I threw myself behind the nearest tomb, sprinkling salt in a circle around me. It wouldn't kill the undead, but it would keep them away for long enough to get backup. I grabbed my phone and tapped on the Mage Lord's number.

"There's trouble," I said.

"Of course there is, if you left your house," said Vance.

"Hilarious," I said. "Seriously. I'm trapped in the necromancers' back yard while they're at their summit, and the dead aren't staying put."

"You're joking," he said. "How many?"

"At least a dozen. I don't have enough salt. I need a necromancer, ideally, but you'll have to do."

"How flattering," he said. "I'll be there in a minute."

A gust of wind rose out of nowhere, and in an instant Vance stood beside me.

"Dramatic, much?"

The undead bore down on both of us. Vance's sword appeared at the same time as I swung mine, severing limbs and swamping us in the stench of rotting innards. Yet they kept on coming no matter how much damage we dealt, some missing arms, all bearing deep slashes that didn't bleed.

"They won't stay put," I said unnecessarily. "Unless we cut them into tiny pieces, but–"

Vance's blade sliced out, and an undead fell in three parts, its legs vanishing and leaving its twitching torso to fall onto its front.

"You displaced its legs?"

"I sent them elsewhere within the cemetery," he explained. "We don't want them getting outside."

"Good thinking."

Really good thinking, actually. I wished I'd thought of it.

At least we had a strategy now. I cut the undead, while Vance displaced their body parts so they couldn't pull themselves back together. Within a minute, harmless pieces of zombie surrounded us, bloodless and stinking, but mercifully not trying to gouge our eyes out. I gagged a little when a severed hand attempted to pull itself along the ground, but Vance displaced it before it could grab my ankle.

"Good riddance." I drove the toe of my boot into the mud to dislodge a piece of zombie guts.

"How did you end up here?"

Oh, crap. I didn't want to bring up the ghost, let alone that his master seemingly wanted to use *my* magic to open a way back to Faerie. Instead, I explained the hellhound attack, and that I'd used the tracking spell to come here in search of the summoner and instead found a horde of undead.

"So you called me." The hint of a smirk showed on his face.

"I'm not incapable of admitting I'm in over my head. I did

find another clue, though. The man buried here was Swanson's ancestor. They're part necromancer."

His expression turned serious. "Which is significant... why?"

I shrugged. "No idea. I wish I knew. I mean, faeries rarely take anyone for no reason."

Lying would undeniably come back to bite me, but I refused to let Vance find out I was the cornerstone of the faeries' plan. Vance might be skilled, but he wasn't Sighted. He couldn't see the full extent of the menace we faced.

"I mean, there was that necromantic circle in the Swansons' house," I reminded him. "The Climes family are necromancers, too. It's the only obvious link between the two."

Might Dustin have had some of the gift himself? If so, even necromancer kids just coming into their power wouldn't have had any knowledge of how to set up a summoning circle like the one I'd found in that house. And a changeling would have no gift at all.

Conscious of Vance's assessing eyes watching me, I changed the subject. "Did you find your missing people?"

"I did," he said. "It seems our friend in the train station had an accomplice, and when Bailey went to look, he was ensnared in the same cobwebs that we encountered."

"What? You battled faeries without telling me?"

He tilted his head on one side. "I had the impression you were a tad preoccupied. Also, I wasn't aware you had a monopoly on all faerie killings in town."

"Very funny. What happened?"

"Rod went to help him, and they were able to get out, with some assistance from me."

"Good." One problem down. A million more to go.

"Are you really that bothered you didn't get to kill the faeries yourself?" His eyes gleamed with amusement.

I didn't see anything funny in the situation. I should be home, making sure Isabel was safe.

"Or," he went on, "are you concerned I can't cope with a few spiderwebs without you around?"

Yes. Okay, 'concerned' was a strong word. Like hell I'd let on how relieved I'd felt when he'd come to help me take out those zombies. I'd never live it down. "Don't flatter yourself."

"Not going to thank me for saving your neck again? We ought to keep a tally."

"I'd be more inclined to be polite to you if you didn't make a point of acting like a dick every time you bailed me out."

He raised an eyebrow. "If I hadn't shown up, you might have joined those poor fools in the ground."

"I'm aware."

"Has it ever occurred to you that you need to think before you go off alone?"

"Frequently." If he thought I was a reckless fool, so be it. I couldn't let anyone else end up in as deep shit with the faeries as I had. "I didn't realise I needed to ask for your permission."

He sighed and brushed some of the dirt from my shoulder. "Just think next time. Please."

I froze at the surprisingly intimate gesture. His hand moved slowly, deliberately, down the side of my jaw, leaving a trail of goose bumps. I became aware of the sound of my heartbeat, still racing from the battle, and the same masculine scent I'd picked up on before, underneath the decaying smell of the undead. It drew me to him, one step, then another. His fingertips lingered on the side of my jaw, his gaze deep. Not cool, but the kind of warm that preceded a tropical storm. My breath stopped, like my lungs had decided I didn't need oxygen anymore. Two more steps would close the distance between us. One step.

His hand dropped to his side. "Did you know your clothes are in a state?"

Just like that, the spell was broken. "I can't afford a twenty-four/seven dirt repellent spell like you can. If it's a problem, you don't have to stand within a ten-mile radius of me."

The words snapped out even though I didn't give a shit what he thought of me. I was comfortable in my own skin, dirt, scars and all. But worry for Isabel clawed at my insides, along with a fair helping of guilt that I'd let myself get distracted. I scooted back a few steps, putting a respectable distance between us.

Vance's brows lifted. "I didn't intend to offend you. But you might want to think about replacing those jeans. They're a tad distracting."

I looked down to find that my torn knees had split even further along the seams, revealing entirely too much of my dirt-stained legs. Heat flushed my cheeks. "Bloody zombies."

He smirked at me. "I'm not complaining."

I stepped back. "You're a total arse, you know that? Also, in case you've forgotten, we're trespassing." And there was a half-faerie ghost somewhere in here. Watching us. That thought was a pretty effective way to stop all wayward ideas of him touching me again.

"Yes," said Vance. "We are. And this place... raising the dead here seems like a deliberate shot at the necromancers."

"Unless one of them did it." Had they? Undoubtedly they were more likely to have done so than a faerie, but the necromancers of all people knew the energy levels were unstable near the Ley Line, and I had a hard time believing one of them had been at that train station either. "Or they awakened by themselves."

His expression darkened. "Yes. They might have, but someone sent them after you."

They had, but I couldn't tell him the full truth. However powerful he might be, the weakest faerie would always triumph over the strongest human. Even a predator. Even the Mage Lord.

Only I, a weak human with faerie magic, might be able to stop them.

17

Even outside the gates to the cemetery, the creeping feeling of being watched remained. The autumn chill in the air didn't help, nor did the faint breeze sending tattered leaves skipping past and the stark lines of the building beside us etched against the pale-grey sky. All we needed was darkness and a full moon and we had a serious contender for a horror movie scenario. At least Vance had re-locked the gate, though if he wanted to confront the necromancers about their unwanted zombie infestation, he'd have to admit we'd been trespassing.

I frankly couldn't give a shit what they thought. "Going to knock? Or are they too busy with their summit to hear us?"

"I suspect they are," he replied. "However, we have an audience with them tonight. I already called Lord Evander yesterday."

"Right." My hands itched to hammer on the door and stalk inside, summit be damned. All the curtains—black, of course—were drawn, making it impossible to tell what was going on inside. "When's that?"

"I'll pick you up at seven."

"It's a date." Then I realised what I'd said.

Vance smirked. "I've had worse propositions."

"It's a figure of speech." I turned away, my face heating up. *Nope. Not going there.* "I'm going home to check on Isabel." I'd texted her but hadn't received a response. She was probably still asleep, but I'd taken off right after she'd been injured, and while we'd doubled the wards so no merc would be able to remove them again, I still didn't know who'd actually hired them. *A guy wearing a cloak...* I hadn't seen any actual necromancers lurking in the cemetery, but someone had summoned the changelings, and it certainly hadn't been that half-faerie ghost.

If a necromancer was in on this... well, it was one more reason to demand an explanation from Lord Evander when I did manage to corner him.

Speaking of demanding explanations, part of me was tempted to walk back to Larsen's and tear him a new one for nearly getting me killed, but Isabel was more important. I asked Vance to drop me off at the street corner, where I confirmed the clean-up crew had removed the mangled remains of the changelings and the dead hellhounds and scrubbed all traces of blood from the scene. Didn't change the fact that the faeries knew my address, but the mercs had gone home, and the newly replaced wards on the gate remained intact.

Inside the flat, I found Isabel still passed out on the sofa.

"Isabel?" I walked over to her, waving my hand in front of her face. No response. When I lifted her wrist, her pulse beat fainter than before, and the puncture wounds on her leg had turned an angry red despite the healing remedy I'd used. *An infection?*

I reached for the bookshelf behind the sofa where she

kept her witch handbooks and then clenched my fist. No. I wasn't the expert here, and if Isabel's own home remedies hadn't worked, the only option was an ambulance.

I got out my phone with shaking hands, skipping over Vance's number—she needed medical attention, not a mage —and dialled 999. Once the call was done, I ran to my room and swiftly changed out of my ruined clothes, but I didn't have the time to take a proper shower before the ambulance showed up.

I carried Isabel to the door myself. I didn't dare let anyone inside, not even the emergency services. When they took her into the ambulance, I stood guard outside with Irene clutched in my hand. Probably I looked as unhinged as I felt on the inside, because they didn't ask me how she'd been injured and also let me sit with her in the back of the ambulance without a fuss. I held her hand, one finger on her pulse to reassure myself her heart still beat.

This is on me. It's all my fault.

Once we arrived at the hospital, her hand was wrenched from mine. Time became a blur of sitting in waiting rooms and pouncing on every medical professional who walked past in the hopes of confirming Isabel was all right. She was stable, they said, but nobody here was an expert in hellhound bites, and they could only operate by guesswork. Hellhounds weren't of this realm, after all. They shouldn't be here at all.

I sat in the waiting room chair, traced the hilt of my sword with my fingertips, and imagined driving the tip through the throat of the person responsible for this. When I looked up at the clock and saw it was past six o'clock, I dragged myself to my feet. Isabel had the best care possible here, I knew, and if all else failed, the coven would take care of her. I had their number, so I left them a voicemail message as I left. Walking away from her tore me apart, but this might be my only shot at figuring out how the necromancers were involved in the twisted scheme that had brought hellhounds to our doorstep. And, if the necromancers did turn out to be responsible for the summoning, I'd be more than happy to bury them in their own graves.

Dead on seven o'clock, Vance appeared on the doorstep. I already stood outside, having locked the door and gathered my weapons ready, my body thrumming with nervous energy.

"What happened?" Vance asked. "You're wearing that look."

"What look?"

"The look you get right before you stab someone."

"If this night goes how I expect, I probably will." To my horror, tears pricked at my eyes. "Isabel's in hospital. A hellhound bit her, and the wound… it's bad."

"You could have come to me."

"Have you ever treated a hellhound bite before?" I blinked hard, refusing to cry in front of him. "Being head mage doesn't mean everything is your problem to solve."

His mouth parted in surprise, but all half-formed apologies for snapping died on my tongue as he transported both of us to the sooty-bricked building that housed the necromancer guild.

Lord Evander stood on the doorstep, as grim-faced as ever. The gate to the adjacent cemetery lay open, and I glimpsed more black-robed figures inside. My heart gave a jolt. *Did they find out we were trespassing?*

"Come," said one of the necromancers, beckoning us behind the gate. He was a man of many words, clearly.

I didn't budge. "You want us to walk in there?"

Where we'd trespassed? *And where the half-faerie ghost appeared?* Had the necromancers seen him? Probably not, if they were inviting us in; for all I knew, the ghost had retained his ability to use glamour to hide himself even from those with the spirit sight.

Vance frowned, too. "I thought your summits took place inside the guild."

"There's been a change of plans," Lord Evander said, and offered zero other information. "Come on in."

This better be worth it. Worry for Isabel made my temper fray even thinner than usual, and walking back into the cemetery after dark did nothing to improve my nerves. The graves were shrouded, and while no traces of the undead were visible, the scent of rot lingered in the air.

"What's this?" Vance asked Lord Evander as we followed him through the gate. "I thought you were conducting your summit inside your headquarters."

"We finished several hours ago."

"I was under the impression that you intended to meet us immediately afterwards." Vance's jaw tightened with annoyance. "I did tell you this was urgent, didn't I?"

As the gate closed behind us, I saw the rows of black-robed figures standing between the graves like members of some kind of secret cult. My misgivings intensified, and even Vance didn't look nearly as intimidating as usual. His hands twitched at his sides like he wanted to grab a weapon when Lord Evander gave him an ugly look. "Urgent or not, we have our own business to contend with."

"Did the Mage Lord also tell you the undead attacked us —ah, yesterday?" I assumed he'd mentioned the incident at the train station, even if he'd omitted our more recent act of trespassing and subsequent battle with the dead.

"Yes," said Lord Evander tersely. "Assuming he wasn't mistaken."

"They looked pretty dead to me." I scanned the graves, the hairs lifting on the back of my neck at the certainty that I was being watched by unseen eyes as well as living ones. The image of that half-faerie's face made my hands clench into fists. I wasn't scared of ghosts, whether they'd been human or otherwise.

"And what exactly were you doing in there in the first place?" The necromancer's eyes narrowed. "An old station in the abandoned part of the city seems an odd place for the Mage Lord to spend his time."

"As I told you, we were looking for some missing children who were taken by the faeries," Vance said. "I have reason to believe necromancy was involved, as we found evidence in the bedroom of one of the children who was taken. Given the undead we encountered at the station, I'm inclined to believe my instincts were right."

"And I told you that none of my people broke the law," said Lord Evander. "I will not listen to your accusations in my own home."

"You promised us an audience," I pointed out. "What did you bring us into this creepy place for, anyway?"

"To prove that we had nothing to do with the dead you encountered." He eyed me with disdain. "Perhaps if I show you the veil, you will treat those who use it with respect."

He strode away, leaving me nonplussed. Vance edged closer to me and whispered, "I dropped some hints that there might be trouble within this cemetery, without giving away that you were present here. I believe that's why he brought his people outside, but he won't admit to it."

All right, then. I watched Lord Evander approach his fellow necromancers, who were in the process of laying out candles at intervals on an empty stretch of grass in front of the graves. A summoning circle. Even knowing it was made by professionals didn't make it any less creepy, though with their hoods pulled up, the necromancers looked like they'd just walked out of an audition for the Ringwraiths from the *Lord of the Rings* movies.

Lord Evander, with his hunched, unimpressive countenance, made this scenario considerably less sinister, but I still jumped when the candles lit simultaneously of their own accord. He stepped into the circle, and the candles' white flames rose higher, concealing him from sight.

"Hope that was meant to happen," I murmured. "Is he still in there?"

White light flared around the circle. The necromancer flickered in and out of view, as if he was a ghost himself, but his voice was clear. "There are two spirits stuck on the other side, out of my reach."

Spirits? Did he mean the half-faerie? The necromancers surely had the resources to get rid of a mere ghost, faerie or not, but their leader didn't reappear. Instead, two small faces appeared in the smoke, indistinct, yet unmistakeably human. One male, one female. They couldn't be any older than thirteen. *Are they ghosts?*

Vance hissed between his teeth. I stole a glance at him and saw his pupils had enlarged, and his clenched hands blackened around the edges. He was angry. As if he knew who the people—children—in the circle were.

I looked at the boy, and the familiarity slid into me as surely as the keen edge of a knife. I saw the resemblance to his parents, and the girl, I assumed, must be the necromancers' missing daughter. They were dead. Or *in* Death. Was that the same thing?

"She said they weren't in this realm," I murmured. "The Lady of the Tree… she knew. She never meant they were in Faerie at all."

No. They hadn't been kidnapped. They were on the other side of the veil—inside Death itself—and as far as my limited knowledge told me, there was no way back.

Lord Evander's voice spoke from the circle. "They aren't dead, but their spirits and bodies are trapped."

I sucked in a breath. *Not dead.* "How?"

"They're necromancers," continued his disembodied voice. "They have the gift, but they're stuck on the other side. I can't reach them."

I recoiled. *Necromancers...* they could travel through the veil along with their physical bodies in a way that no other humans could, but new necromancers usually went through intensive training first. Based on what I'd observed, tearing one's physical body loose from the mortal plane was even more damaging than crossing into Faerie.

And someone had done it to those kids.

"Why can't you reach them?" My voice cracked. "I thought you had free run of the spirit realm."

No answer came from Lord Evander. Vance stepped closer to the circle and growled, "Only a necromancer could have taken them. The culprit will be among your own people."

True, but how did the faeries fit in? I'd thought that ghost's master's plan was to open a gateway from their realm into ours. Besides, what necromancer in their right mind would work with the fae? I'd thought they despised one another.

The Lady of the Tree's withered face appeared in my mind's eye, and then the spidery faerie we'd encountered in the station. Both had been desperate, yearning to avoid their inevitable death by any means possible.

Lord Evander flickered back into view. "I believe they operated from somewhere on the Ley Line. That's why I can't find them. Whoever did this could have permanently upset the balance of the realms. There's a reason we don't let anyone cross over the veil without proper training, least of all in that area."

"Because magic's stronger on the Ley Line," I said slowly. "The veil's thinner. And…"

And during the invasion, the veil itself had ripped open along with the doorway to Faerie. Could that be the link? Opening the door to either realm required a tremendous amount of energy concentrated in one place. All three realms ran parallel, but did they also overlap?

Faeries couldn't die, but they *could* be exiled to a place beyond Faerie, beyond life itself. Maybe even beyond Death.

It was entirely possible I was coming up with wild theories nobody in their right mind would believe, yet the longer I watched the swirling fog within the summoning circle, the more memories nudged at the back of my mind, bringing shivers to my arms and making me wish I had Vance's ability to transport myself out of situations at a moment's notice. *I know this. I've seen it before.*

Lord Evander fully reappeared, his expression twisted with anger and shock. "There's someone here who shouldn't be."

As he vanished into the fog again, movement stirred amid the graves, and the stench of rot rolled over us. Blue light gleamed, revealing more undead, standing like waxwork models behind the oblivious necromancers. They'd been hiding here the whole time.

Faerie glamour. They were glamoured.

The undead attacked, as though given a silent command. I ran at the nearest, swinging my blade and severing its wrists. Vance carved another undead in half with a single, deadly swipe of his sword, but another took its place immediately. We were far outnumbered, and the necromancers had broken their formation, running around like frightened kittens. With their leader occupied inside the summoning circle, nobody seemed to know what to do. I'd refilled my salt canister, but I didn't have enough to handle this many at once.

It's a distraction, I thought as I cut down another undead. *Someone wants us occupied with these lackeys instead of helping those kids.*

"A little help, Lord Evander?" I took a startled step back when Vance appeared in front of me, his hands blackened with newly forming scales. He struck an undead so hard he sent it flying halfway across the cemetery, his lips twisted in a snarl, his eyes glazed.

"Real scary," I said, heart thumping, though actually, he *was* pretty fucking scary. Black scales continued to spread up his arms, and he gave no reaction to my words. "Erm… Vance? Are you still in there?"

I gasped as a sudden grey film covered my vision, and the cemetery around me became muted, greyish. Shapes moved underneath, too pale and indistinct to properly make out. Spirits.

No. Not again.

Like a dam had burst, like the sight of grey flooding the world flipped a switch in my mind, the memories came back.

The sky was smothered by thick branches, reaching upward into an eerie twilight. The path slapped against my heels as I ran, like hell itself pursued me. As if I could outrace the power burning in my hands, the blue glow that clung to me no matter how fast I pushed myself.

Spent, I fell to my knees. "Let me go!" I screamed. "Let me out! I'm human. I'm mortal. I'm no Sidhe. I shouldn't have this magic. Please… please let me back home."

The light intensified. I watched myself like a spectator, watched the thickening smoke rise around me until the forest disappeared and became naught but fog.

Within, ghostly figures surrounded me, watching with accusing eyes. Whispering. Their hands reaching for mine.

"You don't belong here," a voice whispered. "You're no spirit."

Wasn't I? Part of me *had* died back then, in a way, when I'd done the impossible and opened a way between our realm and there. Between the living and the dead. But I'd blocked out the memories. Hadn't been willing to face the grim certainty that I'd only got home because I'd come through—

Death.

Something hard and sharp dug into my arm. I blinked, and the fog receded, revealing graves, and a clawed hand wrapped around my arm.

"Hey—what?" Vance had actually drawn blood when he'd grabbed me, but his wide eyes still didn't seem to see me at all. His face was pale, his pupils still dilated. "Vance, quit that." I tugged at his hand, which slowly loosened as he appeared to become aware of his surroundings. Had he seen into the past, too?

"Ivy." He looked down at his hand, horror flashing across his face. "I'm sorry. I didn't hurt you, did I?"

I was spared having to answer when one of the necromancers shouted aloud. Lord Evander had finally emerged from the circle of candles, and the undead that had remained on their feet had ceased to move. I could only assume he'd given them a command, and as the furore died down, his fellow necromancers moved back in to join their leader. Some of their hoods had fallen back, revealing frightened faces. Maybe Vance and I weren't the only ones the spirit world had tricked into seeing some ghastly illusion of the past, but I couldn't believe people who regularly dealt with the dead were such fucking cowards.

Have any of them done what I did? Crossed through Death into—

No. I wouldn't go there. The memories might have come

back, but I didn't need to address them now, not with a more immediate problem at hand.

"You can't fool my spirit sight," Lord Evander spat, addressing two cloaked necromancers who lay prone on the ground in front of him. "I know you're the ones who called the dead and carried those children out of this world."

"Who are they?" Vance's authoritative voice returned as he strode towards the two cowering figures. "The traitors?"

"Cowards," spat the head necromancer. "They always feared death, and it seems they accepted some foolish bargain from the faeries."

Necromancers afraid of dying? I supposed you didn't choose whether you were born with the spirit sight or not, but the notion that we'd finally caught the fuckers who'd taken those kids banished all other thoughts from my mind.

"Where are the children?" I walked forward to join Vance. "If they're in Death, someone must be able to reach them."

"Not from here." Lord Evander's eyes were dull, his posture even more slumped than beforehand. "I'm sure this pair of traitors will explain everything when I have them in an interrogation chamber."

"Leave them to me," said Vance. "I'll loosen their tongues."

"They're my people," said Lord Evander, though his voice sounded a little faint. The candles had died down to embers, but the smoke swirling within remained, wisps of greyness entirely too reminiscent of what I'd seen in the vision. "I shall be the one to question them—"

Abruptly he collapsed, keeling over on the spot. *Well, so much for that idea.*

Another, younger necromancer with bright-red hair crouched beside him. "He's exhausted himself. Can we have help over here?"

"Not from us," I muttered. "Vance—"

The Mage Lord shoved his way through to the pair of

prone bodies, and the other necromancers tripped over the ends of their cloaks in their haste to get out of his path. "I'll deal with these two."

His overly calm tone made shivers run down my back. No trace remained of the fear in his eyes as he'd relived whatever the veil had shown him.

Whatever it was, anything that scared Vance Colton was an adversary I didn't want to meet.

18

Vance must have had backup waiting around a corner, because he had only to bark an order into his phone and a black car pulled up. He threw the prisoners bodily into the back and climbed in after them, leaving me to ride shotgun.

Unfortunately, the driver was none other than Ralph, Vance's faerie guard. He gave me a glare as he started the car. "You're still here?"

"Yes," I said shortly, far from in the mood for another spat.

"I thought the Mage Lord would have kicked you out by now." He spoke in a low voice; from the back, I heard a distinct clicking noise that I suspected was Vance locking all the car's doors from the outside so the prisoners wouldn't be able to make any escape attempts. A glance in the mirror confirmed that he'd bound their hands with some kind of shiny rope and gagged them for good measure. His eyes were narrowed to slits, and a hint of black scales remained on his hands as he surveyed the two captives.

Skin prickling, I dragged my gaze away. "It's my case we're solving."

"Thought you were looking for missing kids, not necromancers."

"It's none of your business, faerie."

His hands tightened on the steering wheel. "Don't call me that."

"It's true, isn't it?" My anger, barely quelled, began to simmer again. "I wouldn't push me. Some of your people are working with necromancers and kidnapping children."

"They aren't *my* people," he said. "Besides, that's total bollocks. All the half-faeries hate the necromancers. They're the reason nobody can get back to Faerie."

I stared at him for a moment, surprise momentarily overtaking my rage. "Because the necromancers closed the way back."

They'd closed the veil, and in the process, they'd also closed the way back to Faerie. All three realms were linked, via the Ley Line. *That's how the fae want to open a way back…* but why take children in order to do so? Because they were easier to manipulate?

"Everyone knows that," Ralph said. "I knew hedge witches were ignorant, but you—"

"That's enough," Vance said irritably from the back. "It might have escaped your attention that there are two dangerous criminals present."

"She accused me of working with the faeries," Ralph muttered.

"I'm not interested," he said. "Save your complaints for later."

"You heard the Mage Lord." In the mirror, I saw the dangerous criminals in question cowering away from Vance on the back seat as the car pulled up outside a squat red-brick building I assumed must be the mages' jail.

I made to open the door, but I hadn't so much as lifted a hand before Vance and the two captives vanished from their seats in the same instant. "Why'd he bother using the car?" I asked nobody in particular.

"Maybe he wanted you to come with him," said Ralph, who didn't look at all surprised at his boss's disappearing act. "Can't imagine why."

I undid my seat belt and opened the door. "I'm the one in charge of this case, faerie boy."

"Stop calling me that!"

His shouts followed me as I marched to the building and followed the sound of thumping through a side door off the reception area. From there, I found Vance in the act of throwing the captives into a cell. The dimly lit corridor cast him into shadow, making him look positively menacing as he conjured up a key and locked the cell door. I shivered, telling myself it was the cold. This place didn't seem to have any central heating to speak of, but the menace in Vance's eyes was pronounced when he turned to me. "Do you have anything you want me to ask before I kill them?"

My mind blanked, the chilling note to his voice chasing away some of my own anger. "I want to know how they took those kids into Death."

"We know how they did it. The children were part necromancer. They had the instinctive ability already." His eyes shone in the dark, as grey as an oncoming raincloud.

"Yeah, but why them?" I wrapped my arms around myself, the shivers intensifying. "And why can't the other necromancers reach them? Lord Evander's far stronger than those two, surely."

"I'll ask." Vance stalked towards the prisoners, who startled upright as though he'd tipped a bucket of icy water on their heads. Even with his back to me, power radiated from him like lightning on water. The hairs rose on my arms, and it took every ounce of willpower I possessed to remain steady at his side.

"I am Lord Vance Colton, leader of the mages, and I have some questions for you," he said. "Did you take two teenagers with you into Death?"

The first man's mouth dropped open, while the second froze like he'd been hit by a hellhound's fear spell. Both replied in whispers, one after the other. "Yes."

"Who gave you the order?"

"A spirit. A—faerie."

"Faeries can't die," said Vance.

"A half-faerie," I said.

Vance barely glanced at me, but something in his stance sharpened. "You took orders from a spirit? Why would you obey a ghost over your own leader?"

"Let me guess," I cut in. "Immortality. That's what he offered you. Right?"

This time, Vance did look at me, but instead of asking what I meant, he addressed the prisoners again. "Is that true?"

Two mumbled yeses followed.

"But it wasn't the spirit who actually wanted the children," I added. "He was working for a faerie—the one who carried the ash blade. Am I right?"

One of the necromancers lifted his gaze, a hint of defiance rising in his eyes. "You shouldn't have interfered."

"Who is this faerie?" Vance interjected. "Did he put a spell on you, too, to stop you from speaking his name?"

"No." The man's lips had turned blue with cold. "He didn't see the need, as we're only human. For now, anyway."

"Tell me." I moved closer, displaying my blade, though hell if Vance hadn't scared the living daylights out of me as well. "What the fuck is this faerie's name? Who's pulling the strings here?"

"Lord Velkas," said the second necromancer, addressing Vance rather than me. "Your time will be over soon, Mage Lord. When the paths between the realms are fully opened, he will come here—and we will be reborn."

Reborn? Whatever *that* meant, I finally had a name. Lord Velkas. The Lord of the Vale. Or *a* lord of the Vale anyway. There might be hundreds for all I knew.

And with the doors between realms open, they would all come here.

I'd wondered, at first, how it had been possible that the children had been taken into Faerie when the paths were closed to almost everyone. Now that I knew they hadn't been taken there at all, my half-formed theory that another Sidhe had somehow figured out how to do what Lord Avalin had proved untrue. Lord Avalin had been the only fae I knew of who could freely pass between the mortal realm and the Vale, and while I'd assumed the person behind this had carried the same gift, that might not be the case at all. If no other exile could leave the Vale, they'd be reliant upon intermediaries— until they found someone who could open the doors to ehm.

"I see." Vance made a gesture as if to swat a fly. The two men fell, blood spurting from their arms and chests as twin blades slashed at them and vanished in the same instant.

"Holy shit!" I'd never get used to the shock of watching a life taken right in front of me, especially when I stood next to the person who pulled the metaphorical trigger. "They might have had more to say."

"They don't now."

That was cold. I stared at the two men, wondering what they'd meant by *reborn.* Had they thought this faerie would make them into one of *them?* Unlikely. Humans and faeries were polar opposites. Regardless, the lie had been enough to trick them into taking those kids and turning on their leader. They deserved their fates, but my unease remained present as Vance tossed the keys to the ground with a disinterested expression.

"So much for an interrogation." I was curious as hell what he might have witnessed in the cemetery, but I'd be a hypocrite if I didn't allow him to keep some secrets of his own. Still, a morbid curiosity persisted. Everyone feared something, but Vance Colton hadn't batted an eyelid at the creepy fae's lair inside the train station. Why should a graveyard be any different? What had he seen that had made him lose the tightly held control he usually kept over himself?

"They were no use to us." Vance surveyed me as if taking note of my presence for the first time. "You're shaking."

"You killed two people in front of me," I spluttered. "You're—you're the leader of the mages. You're supposed to stand for justice, not senseless slaughter." I'd expected him to give them a trial at the very least, however little they deserved it.

"That *was* justice," he said, his voice chillingly low. "This is a dangerous world we live in."

"No shit. I'm the one who told *you* that." I knew I was overreacting. I was a killer. I worked with killers. But I'd never seen a *human* react so casually to taking lives. I'd only seen one person do that. *His* face flashed before my eyes again, fresh from the memories stirred up by the veil.

Vance stepped back. "Regardless, we're done here."

"What did you see?" The words burst out of me, against my will. "In the cemetery? Is that why you—?"

"Does that mean you're going to share what *you* saw?"

I opened my mouth. Closed it. No. I couldn't.

Taking my silence as an answer, he turned his back on the two limp bodies inside the cell. "The necromancers say places that have seen a lot of death carry the memory with them, an imprint usually visible only to those with spirit sight."

I blinked, unsure what he was getting at. "Yeah, but we also saw those kids. They were taken… through the Ley Line, he said."

"Death and Faerie," said the Mage Lord. "Both are tied to the Ley Line."

Damn. I could almost see his mind ticking, his mind heading to the same conclusions as mine. He was too smart to fool for much longer, and at this rate…

"That may be," I said, "but neither of *us* can cross over into Death, and the necromancer leader's out for the count. How're we supposed to get them back?"

"This Lord Velkas…"

I flinched. "If he's a lord of Faerie, he's not here. He *can't* come here."

"The Lady of the Tree implied he did."

"I don't think she said so directly." Had she? "It sounds like he's operating through intermediaries. Via the spirit realm. Since… since they're linked." The implications of *that* set a fresh wave of tremors through my body.

He looked at me sharply. "A half-faerie ghost. Were you planning to mention that to me?"

"We had a run-in at the cemetery earlier, before those zombies showed up. I didn't get anything out of him that I didn't already know." That wasn't the pertinent issue here. "You heard those prisoners. This Lord Velkas plans to open the paths between realms. I didn't think it was possible, but…"

But I can do it.

There was no more running. Not for me. I had to face the faeries head-on, even if it meant going back there. To the Vale. Those kids needed me, regardless of whether the enemy also needed me, too.

"You never asked them why they chose to take children." The question stole into my mind along with a thrill of disconnected dread. "I mean, they had two willing adult necromancers right there. They didn't need kids specifically. They're untrained, which heightens the risk. Unless…"

Unless they'd been bait. For the person whose power they needed to fully open the doors between realms.

"What is it?" said Vance.

I turned away, my spine prickling. "I—I need to check on Isabel."

He knew I wasn't being entirely honest, but now I voiced her name, my worry for Isabel came surging back. She'd been in a bad state when I'd left her, and not only was my address out there among the fae, but Isabel was in hospital rather than safely behind the layers of wards at home.

"You're not leaving alone again." Vance stepped towards me.

"The faeries showed up at my house twice already. Isabel's in hospital, and—I should have stayed with her. She's not safe."

Vance's phone rang. He made an impatient noise, but when I gave him a pleading look, his hand closed on my arm.

The jail vanished. A moment later, so did Vance, and I cursed when I saw he'd left me outside the house and not the hospital. As I broke into a run, a laugh rang out from behind me.

"You're too late, mortal."

I came to a dead stop and then rotated on my heel. A long, spindly faerie uncoiled itself from the window of a parked car, its pointed teeth bared in a grin.

"Who are you?"

"A messenger."

"For Lord Velkas, right?" I raised Irene. "What do you mean, you're too late?"

"Your friend should never have left the house."

"What the hell did you do to her?" *No. Not her. Please.* "I know your master is planning to open the doors to Faerie and the afterlife at the same time. Didn't work out that well the last time, did it? Millions of people were killed, and a bunch of you ended up stuck here in the mortal realm."

"You think we care for mortal lives?" The faerie laughed. "You will help us, Ivy Lane, or else your friend will die."

"No fucking chance." Nobody would die on my account. Especially not Isabel.

Keeping my past quiet wasn't worth her life.

An icy calm settled over me. With a lunge, I stabbed the faerie through the neck. Blood poured out in a fountain, and the faerie choked on a final laugh, causing more blood to bubble from its ruined throat. I withdrew the blade, my hands shaking. That fae was weak, but its master.. damn. I couldn't do this alone.

I dug out my phone and hit the call button. "Vance—"

"They're targeting my family."

I gripped the phone in my bloody hands. "What?"

"They took my cousin."

"Shit." My heart gave a jolt. "They took her, too. Isabel. They—they want to bait us."

Or rather, me. They needed my power, and if I told him *that...* once the truth came out, there was no going back.

I took in a deep breath. "You're going to have to trust me, but I know how to get into Faerie to find the person responsible. I know where he's hiding. I can take us there."

A long pause. Then: "I'm coming."

19

Vance appeared at my side. The storm kicked up by his arrival lifted the hair from my head and tugged at my clothes.

"Where?" he asked, simply.

"Where the invasion started." My voice came out calm, numbed by the iciness in my veins, but it wouldn't last. Either I'd break, or I'd kill whoever stood in my way. I couldn't afford not to bet on the latter.

Vance's fury was a mirror of my own. His eyes were narrowed, his neatly combed hair dishevelled, his mouth an angry line. He didn't even react to the dead faerie lying behind me in the road, and the simmering tension in the air made me wonder what would happen if he lost control of his powers altogether. Would he unleash a wild tornado and tear up everything in sight?

"You might want to tone that down." I shrank away when his eyes, stormy grey, looked into mine.

"You promised me the truth."

I raised my palms. "I'll hide nothing from you, but to be

honest, you're scaring the shit out of me. If you promise you won't kill me without hearing me out, I'll tell you."

Otherwise, I'd mow even the Mage Lord down if it brought me closer to Isabel.

Vance surveyed me for a long, tense moment. I forced my hands to stay at my sides, waiting for him to speak.

"The invasion is the only recorded time the faeries have broken into our realm," he finally said. "That we know of. Is that true?"

I nodded. "I'm no expert. I'm going by guesswork here, I'll freely admit, but I was so certain they took those kids into Faerie that I didn't stop to ask how they pulled it off. Now I know."

"Know what?" Each word was punctuated by a faint breeze that stirred the hairs on the back of my neck and made me certain that Vance's blade was a heartbeat from materialising at my throat.

"That they took the kids into Death because it's linked to Faerie. You can—you can get into their realm through the veil, if you know how." *And if you have their magic.* "I've been there before."

"Show me." It wasn't a question.

I shook my head. "It's not that simple. I can't do it here, and—look, I've never had anyone actually explain to me how it all works, but this is the only explanation that makes sense. There's a part of Faerie that doesn't belong to the Courts, and that's cut off from everywhere else. It's where they send exiles, and during the invasion, that part of Faerie was ripped open and the exiles all came here."

"And so did the veil," he concluded. "Both overlap on the Ley Line."

"Exactly." I pressed on. "This faerie—the one who's behind all this—might have been planning this for years. A second invasion. I don't know exactly what kicked off the first one, but regardless, I'm guessing this Lord Velkas somehow figured out ghosts can freely pass between realms through the veil."

Perhaps some necromancers could, too, though I doubted *they* knew that. Yet another reason to be grateful not to be part of their creepy cult.

"He sent the changelings, didn't he?"

"Changelings are small fae. They don't need as much power to cross between realms." That was my theory, anyway. "The Sidhe, though… it'd take a major event like the invasion to bring *them* here."

"You told me you can get *us* into Faerie."

"Yeah." This was a long shot, but the spiral of memories triggered by what the veil had showed me made me surer than ever. "I think I can."

Cold sweat gathered on my back as a familiar face swam in the forefront of my mind.

He's dead. He's dead, and whoever has taken his place has no claim on me.

Besides, there was a more immediate threat at hand. I looked up into Vance's eyes, that phantom blade's touch against my neck once again.

"You lied," he said. "You don't have faerie blood at all. Where did you get your magic?"

My voice cracked. "I stole it. I stole it from the Sidhe Lord Avalin, after I cut his throat and escaped his prison."

For a long few seconds, I held my breath as he watched me, not speaking, his eyes like dark pits.

Then he lowered his hands, and the tension lifted, the invisible blade no longer pointing at my throat.

"You aren't going to ask for my story?"

"No."

I blinked. "Is that it?"

I'd expected an interrogation at the very least. Unless he wanted to save it until after this was over.

"You've told me what I needed to know."

I'd worry what that meant later. I'd left out the key part... my magic was the crux. The fae needed it to open the way into Faerie. By going to them myself, I'd be giving them exactly what they wanted.

"Except..." He studied me. "You're human. Why would they target you in the first place?"

"I don't know." Not a lie. Faeries didn't need a reason to screw with humans. Avalin had been drunk on power during the invasion. He'd taken dozens of us. Everyone assumed us amongst the dead, and nobody would have ever suspected otherwise.

"Why *your* family?" I asked. "You said your parents were dead."

"They are. My father's brother survived. His daughter, Anabel, is only nine. They took her." A cold breeze arose in the air again, a tempest brewing in his eyes. "That side of the family never got along with my parents. I thought..."

He'd assumed she wouldn't be a target. Perhaps because she was a mage, or because she lived in a fancy house surrounded by protective wards, or—it didn't matter. His dangerous expression alone told me he cared about his cousin enough to tear down Death itself to get her back, just like I would for Isabel.

Why would the faeries have taken the Mage Lord's cousin, too? To ensure he didn't stand in their way? They didn't need *him* to play a part in their plan, unlike me, but I didn't dare say so aloud.

"This is definitely a trap," I said to him. "I'll do my best to get us into Faerie *before* they come here, but I have to level with you... I'm not sure if I can get us out again."

"That's a risk I'm willing to take."

I opened my mouth to speak, but no words came out. *Me, too,* I wanted to say. I knew the risks. Every inch of me knew that I might not return—but I couldn't accept that the same might be true of Vance. I couldn't entertain the thought of them claiming him, too.

"If you're wrong," he said, moving closer, "there's more than our lives on the line."

"I know," I whispered. "God, I know. You aren't going to arrest me or—"

He gave me a grim smile, shaking his head. "No. I'm not. I'll have to order every mage to drive to the Ley Line. I might be sending them to their deaths."

I swallowed. "I know. Believe me."

He looked down at his phone, which had appeared in his hand without my noticing. "I'll put out the word, and the mages will leave right away."

"Guess we have our own transport." My heart skittered as his hand brushed my arm, the skin stinging a little, and he paused at the scratch mark from where he'd grabbed me with his clawed hand and torn through the sleeve. For a moment, we looked at one another. He didn't need to say it aloud—the apology was written on his face. "Vance. What happened back there?"

He shook his head. "If I shift again, stay away from me. Please."

"Can't you control it?" Shifter powers were volatile, I knew, but he seemed to have a handle on them compared to the uncontrolled outbursts that frequently occurred over in shifter territory. I'd never really thought about the level of self-discipline it must take to do that.

"I can," he said. "But only if I'm aware of my own actions. The magic of the veil confused my senses, and I can't guarantee it won't happen again when we're on the Ley Line. Everything is stronger there."

Despite it all, his sincerity warmed the icy sensation inside me a little. Even more so when his hand moved up my arm, brushed against my neck.

"You're quarter-blooded." I found myself inching closer to him, my fear having entirely melted away. "What's your shifter form look like? Might come in handy where we're going."

"Quarter-blooded shifters usually don't have the ability to shift," he said. "What you saw is the furthest I've ever gone. I don't have a full shifter form."

"Still impressive." He stood close, and smelled so good, despite the dangerous aura still hovering above him. The hint of an oncoming storm that might sweep me away into its embrace. Both a warning—and a promise.

"I don't want to harm you." His voice was soft, drawing a shiver to my skin that had nothing to do with the cold.

"I can handle myself, in case you hadn't noticed," I breathed, conscious that his face was close enough that the faint stubble on his chin brushed against my cheek, and his scent overwhelmed my senses.

The spark in his eyes ignited. Then he closed the distance between us, his mouth coming down on mine, and his tongue swept into my mouth in a single possessive motion. All other thoughts left my mind—all thought of the battle ahead, the danger, even the fact that he might have killed me not a minute ago. My heart quickened, my pulse fluttering in my wrists as they twined around the back of his head. His hair was soft as his hands were rough with the hint of the scales he'd worn not long ago.

He stepped away, his forehead resting against mine. "No turning back now."

No kidding. I sucked in a breath, inhaling his scent. His grip on my arms tightened.

A gust of wind swept us up, and a second later, we reappeared in a field I didn't recognise. At least, not at first. Vance released me, and I took a couple of steps, looking around. The grass was mostly burned away, the blackened remains of tree trunks surrounding us. It was only when my eyes found the road running parallel, visible now that there were no trees in the way, that the familiarity slammed into me.

I knew this place.

I'd lived here.

20

This park had once been within walking distance of my own house. The house itself, I knew, now lay in ruins along with the entire neighbourhood. I'd been close, when I'd visited the necromancers' guild, but I'd never directly set foot in here. Never allowed myself to relive the memories of my last day on Earth.

I remembered running down the road to the park, away from the screaming. I remembered a tempest sweeping up the world. Icy blasts interspersed with explosions that rocked the ground underneath my feet. Strange, horrible creatures materialised in the streets, ripping open any human unfortunate enough to get in their way. I pressed my hands to my eyes, trying to stem the flow of images.

Roads buckled as giants pulled themselves out of the earth. Fire-throwing imps ran down the streets, hurling balls of flame at houses. Crawling, spindly faeries smashed windows, long fingers gouging at eyes and tearing at throats. Kelpies crawled from lakes and ponds and trampled people beneath iron-hard hooves. A gaping-mouthed creature perched on the roof of a building, a child's limp body dangling from its hand. A giant rampaged past, leaving a trail of gore in its wake. A hellhound—not that I'd known the term at the time—had its mouth buried in a man's chest, its teeth stained crimson.

I'd been at school at the time, and the blaring of a fire alarm had sent us fleeing outside. None of us had known we'd find the streets outside torn up, the sky flaming red and monsters spawning in the streets.

The sight had flipped on the survival instinct buried deep inside me. I ran, so fast my feet might have grown wings, following the desperate impulse of a child certain that if I got home, everything would somehow make sense again.

Then *he'd* appeared. A knight in shining armour. A hand in the dark, reaching to save me.

"Ivy." Vance's voice brought me back to reality. His mouth had pulled into a thin line, his eyes cold and sharp. Had he seen the invasion, too? He'd lost most of his family in it, though given the warped way time passed in Faerie, he'd been younger than I had at the time. God, this was so fucked-up.

I took a steadying breath. *I'm not that girl anymore. And this time, I don't have to face them alone.* "Where are we?"

"The Ley Line." He gestured to an overgrown stretch of grass bordering the park's boundary. It extended downhill, and when we approached, glowing lights shone from the grass. Candles, spaced out at intervals.

Shit. It was a giant summoning circle. Within lay a woman, slumped on the grass. *Isabel.* Next to her, a smaller figure. Vance's cousin. I heard his sharp intake of breath and turned to him. "Can you displace them out of the circle?"

He shook his head. "We're on the Ley Line, right on top of a key point. If we aren't careful, we might alert whatever that circle's intended to summon."

Damn. He had a point. Booby-trapping a summoning

circle was the sort of underhanded shit I'd expect from the faeries. "We can't leave them in there."

"I can try to break the circle." He stepped forward.

I made to follow, and a pair of ice-cold hands closed around my throat. I shoved my elbows back, hitting something solid. Human or not, it didn't matter. My sword swung around and would have decapitated the guy behind me had it not passed right through his transparent neck as though he didn't exist.

What the hell?

The ghost offered a smile. From his pointed ears, he was another half-faerie, but how had he been able to touch me?

A second ghostly hand grabbed at my arm. Once again, I stabbed, and once again, the faerie's body turned transparent.

"Shit. The walls between realms are breaking down." I lifted my blade, but I'd have to wait for my target to become solid again before I could strike. "They're ghosts, but they're being fuelled by the energy of the Ley Line."

Just like in the invasion. I slashed with my blade and met only air. Magic swirled around me in a blue cloud but left no impact upon the dead. Vance moved in, his hands faintly darkening when his shifter blood reacted to his rage, but even he couldn't land a hit on a creature without a solid body. His attacks would have torn apart a solid opponent, but he soon tried a different tactic. He held out both hands, and the spirits reeled back, pushed by a sudden torrent of air. The hairs lifted from my head, and I dug my heels into the ground to keep from being blown sideways. The spirits tried to advance, but the air pushed them back until they faded from sight.

"I displaced the air," Vance said. "Thought it was worth a try."

"Good thinking." They'd be back, but we'd won some time. I moved towards the circle, and the ground gave a sudden shudder. A ripple ran through the grass, snaking downhill to where the circle lay. "What's going on this time?"

"I'm trying to move the earth," said Vance from my side. Clever idea. If he collapsed the ground and knocked the candles askew, it'd break the spell holding the summoning circle together. "Can you?"

"No…" I gave him a questioning look. "I told you my magic only works defensively."

"Does it?" he pressed. "You also told me you didn't know much about how it worked."

"Well, no." I watched cracks spread over the earth at his command. "You might've noticed the fae aren't overly keen to share their secrets with humans."

"We work on defensive magic first when training new mages," Vance said, "but I find that offence and defence are usually two sides of the same coin."

"Is this really the time for a magic lesson?"

He lifted a hand, and the air rippled around his palm. "I'm shielding. Now I'm going to attack." He flipped his palm outward, and air rushed into me, causing me to stagger back a few steps. "Now you try."

"I'm not a mage, am I?" Despite the blue glow highlighting my skin, which he couldn't even see, I was a hundred percent human. "I don't know how to—"

I jumped back when a ghost popped out of nowhere and punched me in the face. I reeled, surprised how much getting hit by a dead person hurt. Vance moved in and stabbed at the half-faerie, but since the enemy had turned transparent again, his weapon had no effect.

I swiped and stabbed, my sword useless against the dead. "Too much of a coward to fight fair, are you?"

The spirit's teeth pulled back in a snarl. "You're her, aren't you? The girl who crawled out of Faerie alive."

A trickle of fear ran down my spine. "How do you know who I am?"

"Everyone does," said the spirit. "Now Lord Velkas is after you."

"Is *he* too much of a coward to show himself?" I knew otherwise. Despite the energy stirring in the air, the doors between realms remained closed—for now. I tapped into my own magic, which surrounded me in tendrils of swirling blue. "You're dead. You'll never be alive again, let alone immortal. Give it up."

The faerie lunged for my throat, hands turning solid. I caught its wrist and twisted hard. The half-faerie screamed in pain, the rest of his body solidifying, and I took the opportunity to stab him through the neck. He reeled, clawing at his throat, though no blood spilled from the wound. When I lunged again, the faerie ghost retreated into the fog.

Vance kicked his own opponent so hard that the ghost went flying past the summoning circle.

Within, Isabel stirred, lifting her head. "Ivy?"

"Shit. Don't move." I began to walk towards the circle again. "I'll get you out."

A quiet laugh sounded at my ear. "Do you truly think you can best Lord Velkas using magic that doesn't belong to you?"

A blast of icy air slammed into me, sending me staggering back. Instinct alone kept me on my feet, and I didn't see the speaker until he appeared in a ghostly haze, his hands alight with magic as blue as my own. Winter magic. In fact, he was the same half-faerie I'd encountered in the cemetery, but he sure as hell hadn't been able to use magic back then.

Twin ice crystals sprang up at my feet. I leaped out of range as they grew into stalagmite-like formations and swung my blade. Bits of ice flew everywhere, but the spirit vanished with another laugh. I turned, swearing, and a flurry of ice shot at my face, forming into daggers as it did so.

Damn. Tapping into my faerie magic, I dodged the icy shards brushing against my body, impatience rising within me. "Lord Velkas, if you're out there, I'm done playing with your stooges. I want a real challenge."

Another blast of air struck me in the back, sending me pitching forward. I clenched my teeth together as I fell onto my knees onto ground that had frozen into rock-hard ice. My hands numbed and the air turned so cold my lungs ached. The spirits were drawing on the strength of Winter itself. No exile should have access to such power, but here on the Ley Line, *all* the realms overlapped. Did that mean Winter and Summer were reachable, too?

A blast of heat shot over my head, igniting the dead husk of an old tree. Vines exploded into life, tendrils creeping over the ground, while the sound of a thousand birds singing crashed into my ears. *And now Summer's joined in.* Surely somebody in Summer or Winter must have noticed their magic being stolen, but that didn't mean they'd intervene to save a bunch of humans. In the invasion, they'd only shown up after the Vale's exiles had already killed half the planet.

An icy hand grabbed at my arm. I whirled and snatched at the air as the hand went transparent and so did the creature it belonged to. A tall, long-fingered half-faerie grinned at me. "I remember you," crooned the faerie. "The little girl with the big mouth."

I remembered him, too. He'd been one of Avalin's few half-faerie guards, who'd taken a particular delight in tormenting me—right up until Avalin himself had got mad at him for some minor infraction and decapitated him.

I forced my mind to focus on the here and now. The spirits had no power over me. I was stronger than they were, and as my anger climbed, I let every particle of rage in my body flow to the magic in my hand. Blue energy surged, and I leapt to my feet.

The spirit hissed between his teeth. "That power is not for you."

"Are you still loyal to the shithead who cut your head off?" I asked. "Or are you supporting this new guy instead?"

Lord Velkas couldn't have promised *all* these ghosts immortality, could he? Someone was talking bullshit. and it wasn't me.

He smiled again. "You know you're too late to save those children, don't you?"

"Fuck you." I swung my blade, but a dozen or more other spirits rose to join him on each side, forming a barrier that pushed me backwards. Away from the circle.

A torrent of icy energy roared at me as I swiped at every target I could reach, but even with my magically enhanced instincts, there were a thousand of them and only one of me. When another shard of ice flew at my face, I dropped to the ground to avoid it. Ice formed cuffs around my hands, around my ankles, and prevented me from rising.

"Get off me." My gaze sought Vance, but he'd disappeared amid the flurry of magic wielded by the dead.

I won't die here. I can't die.

Fire burst into life, crashing straight into the ghostly army and sending them scattering even further. Not Summer magic, but real flames that left a singed pattern on the grass and melted the icy cuffs around my ankles.

"Need a hand?" asked Drake, walking out of the fire with his cloak swirling around him.

21

With the arrival of the other mages, the ghosts were distracted enough to take their eyes off me. I kicked off the remnants of the cuffs and jumped to my feet, while Drake threw another handful of fire, dispersing the ice crystals lingering in the air.

"You picked a fight with the wrong mage," he said to the ghosts, a wicked grin on his face. "I wonder… if you can turn solid, does that mean can I light you on fire?"

The spirits scattered when he flung more fire into their midst. Flashes of green and blue lit up the air as Summer and Winter magic flew at the mages, but the ghosts' unexpected solidity meant a fair few of their attacks hit their own allies instead.

The ongoing blaze of fiery light made it easy to keep an eye on Drake, but I'd lost track of Vance again somewhere in the crush. I drew on my own magic and pushed my way forward until I spied a familiar tall figure among the dead. "Vance?"

He kicked a half-faerie aside, his blade slicing at thin air. "The necromancers should be here."

"I doubt they'll show their faces." Drake strode over, vibrant flames streaming from his hands. "More of the mages are coming, though. Some had to take an alternate route after a car, erm, crashed into a tree."

"Were you the one at the wheel, by any chance?" I asked.

"Such accusations." Drake let out a gasp of mock horror. "Maybe it was Bailey."

"He's okay, then? After the station incident?" I hadn't thought to ask. Hadn't had time.

"Oh, he's fine." Drake snorted. "Better than fine. If you ask me, the reason it took him and Rod so long to get out of that cobwebbed hellscape is because they finally had an excuse to spend time together. It's painful watching two people flirt but not *do* anything about it."

"Not that you're capable of such a feat," Vance said, knocking another ghost aside. "Can you try to focus on the issue at hand?"

"I can multitask." Drake grinned, flinging more fireballs into the mass of ghosts. "Please tell me you two finally made a move on each other, too."

I gaped at him. "Excuse me?"

Vance shot him a scowl. "Drake, you'd matchmake between a lamp post and a fire hydrant if you had no other options available."

"But it's true, right?"

I didn't dignify that with an answer. More mages had joined the fray, and I glimpsed Bailey among them, surrounded by a circle of churned-up earth. Unfortunately for him, earth magic had little effect on opponents that could turn incorporeal in the blink of an eye, and the same went for water and lightning magic, too. The air mages fared better, sending great gusts of wind into the fray that further added to the melee, while the fire mages soon had the upper hand. Drake used his hands to direct his flames to separate into two paths, forming a protective barrier around our group to keep the ghosts at bay, but it seemed impossible to get rid of them altogether. No matter how hard we hit them, they came flying straight back at us.

"We do need the necromancers," Vance said through gritted teeth. "They'll be able to put out the candles without triggering whatever wards are stopping us from reaching them. Look, even the ghosts can't get into that circle."

He was right. Now that I looked closer, the circle's boundary kept even the dead out.

"What about your magic?" I asked Vance. "You can't displace the candles?"

A muscle ticked in his jaw. "No. They wanted to ensure nobody could reach them."

I hadn't seen the missing kids either, which meant they must still be somewhere on the other side of the veil, where none but a necromancer could reach them. "Pity the Ley Line doesn't give you a boost."

"Nope." Drake hurled a fireball, knocking three ghosts flying backwards. "Even I can tell there's a shit-ton of energy stirred up here, though."

"From that circle, do you think?" Had to be. The summoning circle kept the power contained within its boundaries, and the person responsible had stuck Isabel and Vance's cousin in there to lure us inside. Or rather, to lure *me* inside.

Grey smoke swirled around the fiery barrier, swamping even Drake's flames. Then a grey film smothered my vision and everyone—half-faeries and mages alike—disappeared beyond the haze. In the background, the faint sound of music arose, as quiet as a whisper yet somehow loud enough to pierce through the clamour of the fight. Dread coiled around my heart at a familiar sense of icy cold trailed down the back of my neck.

I pressed my hands to my ears and moved into the dense grey fog. Ghostly faces stared at me, but these spirits didn't attack, didn't do anything except watch me. They were human, young, mostly. Their frail bodies were dressed in ragged clothing, their accusing eyes following my path.

No. God, no.

"I tried to save you." My voice cracked. "I tried."

I knew them all. Had seen them fleeing when Avalin's castle had come crashing down on our heads. The magic I'd taken had shielded me, protected me from the carnage, and ultimately opened a way home. One that had closed behind me, forever trapping the other survivors in the Vale.

For years, their faces had haunted my dreams. Helena, my closest friend, the one I'd trusted above all the others. I'd found her body on my way out. Gerry, the man who'd trained me, who'd given his life so I'd have a fighting chance to escape. A hundred other faces, some of whom had stayed for years, others mere weeks. Had they lingered here on the other side of the veil for all this time? Or was this a simple faerie trick, like the music that continued to brush against my ears, a melody played for me alone?

I didn't know, but whether they were real or not, so too were the living, breathing people who needed my help. I might have failed to save Avalin's other prisoners, but I wouldn't let the same fate befall those children. Or Isabel.

"I'm sorry I left you behind," I said, "but I can't help what I did in the past, and I have a job to do. If you're real, you'll understand."

"We're as real as you are," Helena whispered, her eyes round and beseeching. "You can help us. All you have to do is surrender and you'll be free of the guilt. I promise."

"You aren't her." It might sound like her, but Helena would never say that. "Sorry, but there are living people who need me more than you do."

I closed my eyes and walked past the ghosts, my cheeks wet from tears I hadn't felt fall. The grief was still there. I'd had to lock it away or I'd never have been able to move on, and I had to do the same now.

My eyes flew open when I bumped into someone solid and tall. "Vance?" Fog surrounded both of us, but it was definitely him, though he wore the same blanked-out expression as he had in the cemetery.

"Sarah," he said, looking right through me, as pale as a ghost himself. "Sarah, what are you doing here? Get back in the house. It's not safe."

"I'm Ivy, and we need to go." I tugged on his arm, but it was like trying to shift a metal post. "Vance, you're more than a match for faerie trickery. You can snap out of this."

He continued to look right past me, and his hands were icy cold. I looked down to see black scales covering his fingertips. Oh, shit. He'd told me to back off if he shifted, but he was the only solid thing in this forest of smoke. I shoved him in the side, bruising my elbow.

"Vance, snap the hell out of it! You're the Mage Lord, for crying out loud."

No response. The faeries had him, and I never figured out how to get around their mind tricks. If I hadn't known better, I'd still be pleading with Helena's ghost.

I slapped him across the face and sent him stumbling back a few steps. My hand stung, but relief flooded me when the blankness in his eyes turned to puzzlement.

"Ivy?" Vance shook his head, wearing a dazed expression. "What...?"

"Faerie tricks," I said. "Whatever you saw, it wasn't real."

Anger flickered across his face. "Blasted creatures. Did you hit me?"

"Didn't know what else to do." I spun on my heel, but the fog surrounded us in a thick haze. "I can't see the others."

"I'll find them."

"Who's Sarah?"

A pause. "My sister. She was supposed to hide the night of the invasion, but she got scared and ran out of the safe house. I didn't get to her in time. The... the dead took her."

Oh. "I'm sorry."

There was no time to comfort him, nor to address the vision I'd seen myself. Vance faced the wall of fog and brought down his sword in a slash that would have easily cut an opponent in two, but the grey was unrelenting, as if we were in Death itself.

The realms were colliding, merging, and there wasn't a damn thing I could do to stop them.

The sound of a car's engine cut through, as did a stream of piercing light. The fog parted, and Vance and I both spun around to see hooded figures—necromancers—walking towards us, the fog dispersing around them. *Finally.*

22

"About bloody time." I watched two robed figures approach, making for the summoning circle, and ignoring Vance and me altogether.

Wait. Isabel was still trapped in there, and I didn't trust them not to accidentally hurt her in their attempts to take out the circle.

"Hold on," I called out. "Be careful with that."

"It's only a summoning circle," said one of the hooded figures without looking back.

"Only?" How clueless could you get? "There are dozens of half-faerie spirits around here. I don't know why they've gone quiet now, but they're intending to use the veil to open a way back to their own world."

"She's right," said Vance. "Don't dismantle that circle unless you're certain you can deal with whatever it might unleash."

"You have no right to tell us how to do our jobs, Mage Lord," said the hooded figure. "We were ordered to abandon our *own* territory when the undead are rising on our doorstep, because apparently helping your incompetent colleagues is more important."

"It might have escaped your attention," said Vance, in his most dangerous voice, "that the Ley Line is unstable, and that we're at risk of the veil tearing open. I assume this summoning circle is the work of *your* colleagues."

"How *dare* you—"

A ghostly half-faerie appeared and thrust its hand through the necromancer's chest. A dozen more ghosts appeared in the same instant, and ice-cold flooded the air as the fog crept in again, around the necromancers.

The one the ghost had punched had gone completely still. I didn't see the spirit any longer, but when the necromancer raised his head, a high-pitched laugh issued from his throat and an inhuman smirk twisted his lips. Lifting a hand, he sent a blast of cold blue light from his fingertips.

I dodged on instinct, my heart plunging. That was *faerie* magic. "Fuck. He's possessed."

Ghostly faeries possessing human bodies. What the hell next? My own magic flooded my veins, but the necromancer matched my speed, driven by the spirit inside him. As he aimed another attack, Vance swung a clawed fist, now covered in shiny black scales. The necromancer flew back several feet and landed at a twisted angle on the grass.

"Whoa, Vance." I flinched in surprise. His eyes had narrowed to dark slits, which combined with the claws and scales, gave him a positively demonic appearance. "Er... Vance?"

Fear squeezed my chest. At precisely the wrong moment, I remembered Vance had said he'd become the mages' leader by killing his predecessor after the last head mage had lost control of his power.

Oh god. What if he's losing it, too?

The second necromancer moved towards us with the unnatural speed of a faerie. My sword swung, blood spurted, and the necromancer crumpled into a heap. I stared transfixed for a moment, until another growl from Vance drew my attention back to the oncoming ghosts. He didn't seem to care that most of his attacks missed; he'd gone into full shifter mode and no longer seemed conscious of my presence.

"Vance!" I shouted, but he didn't react to his name. I considered slapping him again, but his furious shifted form might take my head off with those claws. The Ley Line's surging power would likely have the same effect on any other shifter who stepped within range, except most shifters didn't also have mage powers.

Around us, spirits—too many to count—thickened the air. This fight wasn't going to end until the veil cracked open. Or until I stopped the person responsible.

A glow caught my gaze. The candles. We'd moved closer to the circle than I'd realised, and a thrill of dread chased through me when a shadow passed over the other side. A large, furred shadow, far more solid than the ghosts. Hellhounds. My heart stuttered. *Isabel.* Dammit, I had to get her out of there, but how to do that without breaking the barrier and giving the faeries exactly what they wanted?

That doesn't matter now. I ran, magic quickening my steps, and Vance barred my way. I ran straight into him and flew back onto my rear. "Ow!"

Some of the haze in his eyes faded, for a moment. "Ivy... your magic..."

Then the darkness was back, the shifter in full control, and he flew back into the fray. I rose upright, wincing. My magic? What had he meant?

Vance's words from earlier filtered into my mind. *Offence and defence are two sides of the same coin.* He'd thought I could use my magic to attack as well as shield. I'd never tried, but the blue light around my skin was more noticeable than ever as I approached the circle. A candle's glow greeted me at the edge. Magical or not, candles weren't unbreakable, and removing a single one would break the circle.

I flipped my hands outward, like Vance had done in his demonstration. The blue light clouding the air shone around my palms, resembling the power those ghosts had flung at me.

Their power came from Winter, originally. I pictured one of the ghostly figures lifting a palm to send a wave of ice at me and drew my fingers inward, forming a fist. Then I took aim at the flame raging upward from one of the candles at the circle's edge and plunged my fist into its midst.

Blue light flared brighter, mingling with the pure white flame rising from the candle. I drove my fist downward, and the candle tilted sideways. The flame sputtered.

Gotcha. I called more power into my palm and took aim again. This time, the candle flew sideways, and the pillar of white light vanished altogether.

On the other side lay Isabel, next to a young girl who I could only hope was unconscious and not worse, and a pair of hellhounds loomed over them both. One lifted its head, and my body froze, muscles locking in place. *No you fucking don't.*

I called the faerie magic again. Energy flooded my veins, and I leaped into the circle, slicing the hellhound's throat in the same move. The second swung its paw, but I brought my sword in a slashing motion across its nose. Then I thrust the blade upward through its chin, its mouth, straight through the roof into the monster's brain.

I dropped to a crouch beside Isabel. She stirred, and relief seeped through me, though tempered by the concerning stillness of her companion. The girl, even younger than those missing teenagers, wasn't lying down as I'd initially thought but had drawn her knees up to her chest and pressed her forehead to the ground as though to wish the nightmares away. *Good. She's alive.*

"Hey!" I saw more hellhounds lurking in the mist and rose upright, brandishing my sword. "Come and get me, you fuckers. Leave them alone."

Three hellhounds stalked towards me, jaws slavering, but a torrent of fire knocked one of them into the other. I glimpsed Drake running towards what was left of the circle. The third hellhound tried to bite me, but I brought up my blade to slice open its throat, and Drake moved in with another blast of fire to finish it off. Confident that he had this taken care of, I crouched beside Isabel again.

"Don't worry," I said, slipping my arm around her. "I'll get you out of here."

"I'm okay." She lifted her head a little. "The coven showed up at the hospital and loaded me up on healing spells. I can walk."

I had my doubts. "I'll help, and then I'll stop the fucker who did this."

"It's too late." She groaned. "I—I'm sorry, Ivy. I couldn't stop him."

"Couldn't stop who?" Dread punched a hole in my chest. I followed her gaze past the bodies of fallen hellhounds, and my vision doubled as my eyes tried to show me two scenes at once. The remnants of the summoning circle on the grass, wreathed in fog… and a twilight path leached of colour and life.

She groaned again. "He wants… he wants you dead, Ivy. Don't go after him."

What? "I thought he needed my magic."

He'd already opened a door. With the surge of energy on the Ley Line growing strong enough to solidify a thousand spirits, of course there'd been enough to open the veil without my magic being necessary at all. Yet… why go to the trouble of luring me here if he didn't need me?

"Huh?" She lifted her head blearily. "Ivy, what are you doing?"

"I'm going after him. I have to." If I couldn't stop the Sidhe lord from opening a path between realms, I'd make damn sure he never set foot here himself before I slit his throat. "It's the only way to get those kids back."

Isabel sucked in a breath. "Ivy…"

I blinked hard, took in a shaky breath. "Isabel… stay here. Drake will keep those bastards away from you."

Vance would help, too, once he'd come to his senses again. Nobody could do this but me.

"All right." She spoke quietly. "Please… please come back."

"I will. I did it once before." I'd never told her. Why hadn't I told her? I'd wasted so much time. So many years, shutting out the past. And for all that, I might not get lucky a second time.

I gave one brief look over my shoulder, but I couldn't bring myself to meet Vance's eyes. I had to do this alone. I wasn't strong enough to stop and say goodbye, in the end.

I rose to my feet, magic swirling around me in tendrils and extending outward, almost as though the magic itself was being drawn towards the place it had come from. The place I should have breathed my last.

"Welcome to your new home," whispered Avalin's ghostly voice. *"I've made it comfortable for you."*

My teeth chattered. With each step I took, my legs became more and more like lead weights beneath me. The grey path awaited, the realm of nightmares that had become my prison, and the piano music returned with a vengeance. Along with the voice. *His* voice. When he'd spoken, every one of my senses had been ensnared. I'd gone with him into the faerie realm without a second's thought.

Now, I was doing the same, but for different reasons entirely. I gripped Irene and advanced. The dead grass beneath my feet vanished, turning to grey leaves tinged with silver. A carpet of leaves fallen from dead trees, covering a winding path that extended into the distance without end.

The Grey Vale.

23

"**W**elcome to your new home," Avalin's voice whispered. "I've made it comfortable for you."

I tried to close my eyes, tried to shut off the scene I'd relived a thousand times, but to no avail. I stood on the same path, silvery leaves cushioning my feet, shadows blanketing the trees on either side.

Behind lay death and confusion. Ahead lay uncertainty. But Avalin stood at my side, smiled at me with perfect white teeth, and reached for my hand. His pointed ears, porcelain-pale skin and glistening dark hair painted him as far from human. He was too perfect to be anything but a prince from a storybook. The armour he wore was an image from a book, too, silver and black, a sword sheathed at his waist.

I'd never thought I'd ever need a fairytale prince to rescue me. Not before the world outside had turned into a horror story.

His smile widened as I took his hand. His skin was surprisingly soft, and up close the armour didn't appear to be made of metal at all. The texture was wrong. Like bark, maybe. But I was too captivated by his eerily handsome face to think, to do anything more than follow his lead.

Was the veil showing me the past again, or some faerie illusion? Whatever the cause, why did I always relive *that* memory, my first sight of Faerie, instead of the last? The one where I'd escaped?

As though prompted by my thoughts, my vision flickered, and another scene unfolded before me.

This time, I stood before Avalin, no longer in the forest but inside a high-ceilinged entrance hall. He wore the same armour, but his true face shone through, a delighted smile twisting his mouth at the prospect of tormenting a helpless human.

"Avalin," I'd said. "I challenge you."

He'd laughed when he'd seen the dagger I'd chosen, a fraction of the size of his fae-forged sword. "You challenge me with that pathetic excuse for a weapon?"

I nodded, my head bowed. I'd played my part well for three years. Meek. Obedient. Helpless.

But I'd lived.

Iron was the only way to kill a faerie. It went without saying that Avalin didn't allow one single fragment of iron to enter his home, and whenever he brought in new humans, he stripped them of everything they owned and threw their belongings into the dust.

A single, rusty nail was my salvation. The boy it belonged to was long dead. Why he'd been carrying it, I hadn't known at the time. Now, of course, I knew it was because the faeries had taken over our world, and the survivors had swiftly figured out the best way to defend themselves.

That small piece of metal became my lifeline. I'd been nothing more than a human, without a drop of magic to my name. All I'd had, aside from the iron, were my wits and a hell of a lot of luck.

I concentrated on the memory, pushing all others aside,

and savoured the taste of the triumph as I held Lord Avalin's own sword in my hands.

And brought the blade across his throat in a crimson smile.

When he'd died, more than blood had spilled from the wound. Magic had, too, the energy he'd drawn from all those tortured souls for the past three years and who knew how much longer.

The magic wrapped around me, and I cried out, hands outstretched, as if to push it away. I pushed the memory away, too, not wanting to relive the last part. Not wanting to see the castle collapse on its helpless human prisoners, crushing everyone except for me.

But I saw them all the same. Saw myself running, my bare feet pounding on the leaf-strewn path. Magic, twining around my wrists like bonds of rope. All I'd known about the magic was that it was fuelled by suffering. *Our* suffering. Avalin's magic fed on pain, on fear, on anger. And when I'd called upon those emotions within myself, when I'd begged to go home…

Home. That had been my goal, and when I'd found myself lying on real grass with true sunlight shining on my face, I'd believed for a shining instant that the world was as I'd left it. That I'd walk home and find my parents waiting for me.

I'd been wrong, horribly wrong. My parents were dead. Everyone in my life had gone, and I'd had no home to return to.

This time, I did.

My eyes flew open, this time for real. My feet rested on silvery leaves, shadowed by trees on either side of the path. All was silent. I shoved the last threads of memory aside and addressed the facts. Avalin was gone. Dead. *That* hadn't changed in the decade since my absence. This Lord Velkas was an unknown.

I was no expert on Faerie, but I'd picked up a few things in my time in the castle. Here in the Grey Vale, the territory was divided between exiles based on whoever commanded the most power and not in an organised way like Summer and Winter. Avalin, exiled for murdering another Sidhe, had been stripped of his original magic upon his banishment and had somehow gathered the strength to steal from another.

And, thanks to the vow I'd made when we'd duelled, his magic was mine. The Vale, I'd learned, adapted itself depending on who controlled that territory. Avalin had turned the paths into a maze that ensured nobody ever got away from the castle.

If this Lord Velkas had claimed the territory in his place, he'd know I was here, but *he* didn't hold Lord Avalin's magic. I did.

I walked onward, head held high, Irene in my hands. The path ended at a clearing, where someone waited. Tall, jet-black hair at shoulder length, piercing green eyes. Obsidian armour edged in gleaming silver.

I knew that armour. He must have stolen it from Avalin's corpse.

The Sidhe lord smiled. "Ivy Lane," he said, his voice light, melodic. "What kind of creature are you?"

"Human. You know that." I glared at him. "Why didn't you look for me yourself rather than waiting for me to come to you?"

The faerie laughed. The sound tinkled like the gentle pressure of fingertips on piano keys, and my magic blazed brightly in response. "This is my territory. I'd rather have the advantage. Wouldn't you?"

Not when you're at the mercy of my iron blade. He must know that iron had killed Avalin, and I'd only possessed a small sliver at the time. Now, I held Irene, and she would cut him to pieces.

"Out of interest," I said, "why'd you promise all your followers you'd make them immortal? Couldn't think of a more convincing way to trick them into working for you?"

He laughed again. "You're bold. I can see how you survived Lord Avalin."

"And killed him." I hefted my blade. "Same as I'll kill you, too."

"I don't think so. Avalin might have let a mortal get the better of him, but I'm not as ignorant of your kind, and I know your allies are losing the fight. Even that Mage Lord of yours has succumbed to his animal side."

"You were watching. Too scared to join in?" I paced around him, knowing that as soon as I struck, he'd counter with all the speed a true Sidhe possessed. "You didn't need to trap those two children in Death. Didn't need children at all, in fact. Why take them?"

"As a changeling taken by the fae yourself, I would have expected you to have realised sooner."

"You wanted me," I confirmed. "But you don't need my magic. The veil is already opening."

"Yes." Velkas smirked. "Did you believe I wanted your magic to open a door between our realms? I intended to take Avalin's magic for myself long before you were born, human. You aren't worthy to wield the power of a Sidhe lord."

"What, you want to rule his territory? That's all you want?" My heart thudded. *He wants my magic.* That was the prize. If I hadn't killed Avalin myself, Velkas might have challenged him directly, but I'd put a wedge in that plan when I'd claimed the other Sidhe lord's magic with my own hands.

I'd never intended to, but Avalin and I had sworn a vow before we fought. If I won, I'd be allowed to go back home. That was all I'd wanted, but the vow had endured beyond Avalin's death, and when he'd died, it had sought to fulfil the promise by any means possible. His magic, in the end, had been my only way home.

I would never let Lord Velkas claim it.

"You think too small, human," Velkas said. "Your fragile mortal plane has left you weak-minded. My desires are far grander. Even Summer and Winter will surrender to the power I wield."

"Seriously?" He wanted to conquer Summer *and* Winter? "Seems a bit much for one person. What about those half-faerie ghosts? You promised them all immortality, and they'll be pissed off at you when they find out you lied."

"Oh, I didn't," he said. "A lord of faerie needs an army, does he not?"

"You're deluded." He wasn't Avalin. Oh, Avalin himself had possessed the same sense of melodramatic entitlement, but he'd spent three years tormenting me, and I'd still prevailed. This faerie might have stolen Avalin's armour, but he wasn't the same Sidhe. Not even a pale imitation.

Velkas hissed between his teeth. "Do you challenge me, then, mortal? We shall make a vow, to ensure no more trickery."

"Isn't trickery more your thing than mine?" No, he wanted my magic as a prize, and a binding agreement would guarantee that Avalin's power didn't escape this time.

Except it also meant I could demand something from him, too.

"Yes," I said, my voice ringing through the clearing. "When I win, I get to escape and take any mortals you have imprisoned here with me. And you leave our realm the fuck alone."

"No," he said. "If you defeat me, you can take those two children home with you. No more."

"Fine." If he was dead, he'd no longer be a threat to

anyone, and I could deal with the rest. "If you win, you get my magic. That's what you want, isn't it?"

"Yes." His eyes gleamed. "You will beg me for death, Ivy Lane."

"No chance." I lifted my chin. "I'm not in the habit of begging for anything."

"Then let's begin." His lips pulled back from his teeth in a feral manner, eliciting a shudder that ran through my very bones.

Then he transformed. Fangs sprouted and claws lengthened, biting into the earthen ground. Fur grew all over his head, which hunched over as his body expanded into the monstrous form of a hellhound.

Shapeshifter, is he? That would explain the question nagging at the back of my mind—the descriptions I'd initially heard had told me he had silver hair, not black, and his green eyes painted him as a Summer Sidhe and not Winter—but faeries were capable of shifting their appearance at will. That he'd willingly turn into a hellhound might have been a surprise, but he was certainly fearsome. Its four giant paws padded towards me, its jaws slavering.

I jumped, dodging its sharp teeth with ease, and drove my blade across the hellhound's throat. Or I would have, if the hellhound hadn't vanished.

Glamour. That, too, was a classic faerie trick. Either he was holding back, or I'd been dead right when I'd thought he was no match for Avalin. Defeating *him* had almost destroyed me. Hellhounds were nothing. I kept quiet, listening out for the tell-tale sound of its footsteps.

Magic crashed over me like a fountain, smothering my body and trapping the breath in my lungs. I gasped, arms flailing, a sudden green haze obscuring my vision. *What the hell is this?* For a heartbeat I wondered if I was drowning, but my breath still came, albeit painfully. An unseen pressure squeezed my chest, but the pain wasn't physical. More like I was being deprived of something other than air.

Like magic.

Oh, shit.

I reached for my power and found nothing but suffocating blankness. The green haze dimmed, but the sense of being squeezed around my chest remained, and not a trace remained of the magic that always came to my defence when I fought against the faeries.

Calm down, Ivy. My sword remained in my hands, a reassuring weight. As well as Irene, I had other spells in my pockets that the faeries would never have encountered before. I still had a chance of beating him.

I sucked in air and inched my hand into my pocket for an explosive spell.

My fingers closed on empty air. My pockets felt suspiciously light, and when I withdrew my hand, black and grey fragments scattered between my fingertips. Had he disintegrated *all* my spells? If his power affected witch magic, too, I was left with only my sword. Irene was my best asset, admittedly, but this was a wrench I hadn't anticipated. I'd expected to fight with magic. The same magic I'd barely begun to learn to use. It should be stronger than ever here, in the place where I'd claimed it. Where I'd taken it from Avalin's corpse.

"Show yourself!" I shouted at thin air. "Or are you too cowardly to face Avalin's magic directly?"

A cascade of leaves swept up and pushed me backwards. I grimaced, struggling to stay upright as the wind hit me with a force that bent the trees backwards, and the leaves began spinning in a dervish of sharp edges. I screamed for real this time, my blood mingling with the swirling leaves in a whirlwind of red and silver. Drawing my arms tight to myself, blood soaking into my shirt, I thought, *Come on, magic. I need you.*

The wind kicked up again, and another scream tore from my throat. I'd have fallen, but the wind held me in place, suspended in the air. My clothes whipped around me, and even the daggers sheathed all over my body were torn free. Only the sword in my hands remained solid, and it took every remaining ounce of strength I possessed to hang onto the hilt as the leaves ripped at my skin. My face was wet with blood and tears. *Come on. I can't have lost the use of my magic altogether.*

It was stronger than ever here. I *knew* it was. I reached for the power again, focusing on the dormant glow that I knew was always present.

The pain faded a fraction as sudden blue light burned my vision, and the suffocating sensation lifted. As the wind ceased, I opened my eyes properly to see the blueness formed a shimmering barrier between me and the slicing torrent of leaves. Bright glyphs swirled to life on my arms and hands, and the pain faded to nothing but tingling. Blood still dampened my arms, but the wounds had gone, like they'd never existed.

The whirling leaves dropped to the ground, and the hellhound reappeared. Its paws slammed on the ground, and a deafening roar cut through the air. *Now I've made him mad.*

My blade flashed out as I leaped, fuelled by the boost from the magic. From *my* magic. The hellhound fell with a pained noise as blood poured from its neck.

As I dug the sword in deeper, sudden resistance pushed me back. A shimmering greenness arose around the open wound, and the blood from its neck stopped flowing. *Shit. He can heal, too.*

The hellhound vanished, and the Sidhe appeared in his place. His teeth were still bared, his furious silver eyes ablaze. "How dare you strike me with iron, mortal."

"I'm surprised you're still standing." Avalin had been

felled by a mere sliver of iron, but Lord Velkas had healed too fast for the metal to leave an impact. Not good.

He drew his own sword from a sheath. It gleamed in the light filtering through the canopy. Not real sunlight, or moonlight, but the Vale's imitation, and a reminder that I had to finish this fast. Or else I might lose ten years again.

He swung the blade. I blocked, the impact shaking my whole body. While an ordinary sword would have snapped in two, his was as solid as the blade with which Avalin had fought, and even the iron didn't leave a mark on its gleaming edge. Fae-forged blades were far stronger than any human-made weapon.

Avalin's magic gave me speed to match the faerie's own, locking us in a deadly dance of metal on wood, blade on blade. The faerie's eyes went wide as I gained ground, driving him back, step by step.

"You don't have the right to use our magic," he snarled. "You're nothing more than a simple human."

"No one ever said life was fair." I fought to push back against his blade, but I was tiring, and he wasn't. My knees trembled. Blue tendrils swirled around me, intertwining with the green haze that seemed to come from both the blade and Velkas himself. My weapon hand faltered, my body bowing with exhaustion that shouldn't have set in so fast.

What is he doing to me? Sidhe or not, my magic ought to be enough for me to match his speed. His own power was more noticeable now, forming green tendrils that caressed the blade in his hands.

When they pulsed brighter, a fresh wave of exhaustion swept over me, and my blade grew leaden in my grip.

Holy shit. He's draining my energy. His blade's vibrant green glow was as bright as the blue luminescence in my own hands. His magic, equal to mine—but he knew how to control his, and I didn't, and every moment stole more strength from me.

"Give up, human."

I glared at him, sweat dripping down my face. My legs bent at the knees, and the blue glow around my blade dimmed. His power was from Summer, given its bright-green sheen. Mine was from Winter, and didn't feed on life, but on death. There was no shortage of the latter here and Avalin's own power had been fuelled by the pain and agony of his captives, but the blue glow was fading while the green light became stronger.

Regret seized me for not learning to control my own magic while I'd had the chance. I'd grudgingly accepted its presence in my life out of necessity, but I'd never learned to master it the way Avalin had. I'd suppressed the memory of my victory, just as I'd suppressed that of my escape.

Velkas's blade gained ground. I clung to my weapon, pushing back, but it was like trying to move a car with my bare hands. Inch by inch, my death loomed closer. In seconds, he'd push me aside and cut my throat, as I had Avalin's.

And he'd take the former Winter Lord's magic for himself.

The power remained, blueness swirling around me in tendrils that reached upward as though searching for something to feed on. Winter magic, by design, gained strength from death, but Avalin's had had an even more twisted source. Up until today, my memory had been a blank from the moment I'd fled the castle to the second I tumbled out into the mortal world, but now I knew how I'd escaped. I'd drawn upon the pain and suffering—my own, and that of all my fellow captives—and that endless well of misery had given me enough power to tear open a way through the realms. Through Death itself.

Death was still reachable here. That was how Velkas had sent his ghostly messengers into our realm in the first place, after all. Somehow...

With a sudden lunge, Velkas kicked Irene out of my hands so hard that the momentum sent me crashing onto my back. Magic swirled before my eyes, blue and green intertwined, locking together. Fighting for dominance.

His blade stabbed downward. I rolled over, drawing on what little strength I had left. Streams of green light continued to reach for me, to drain my energy, but I pushed back, envisioning my own magic forming a shield to block his. Despite my exhaustion, the blue haze solidified, strengthened, and a renewed rush of energy surged into my veins. My sword lay discarded nearby, and comprehension dawned. The iron... might it have been affecting my magic? If iron was deadly to faeries, it made sense that it had a dampening effect on faerie magic, too. Yes, Irene was the best weapon I had, but ultimately it was magic that shielded me from Velkas's attacks, giving me a chance to catch my breath.

I might not be its master, but I was no stranger to improvising. Recalling Vance's brief instruction, I splayed my hands outward and willed the magic to turn into a blue stream. Triumph rushed over me as a bolt of icy energy shot towards Velkas and sent him staggering back. I'd watched faeries use Winter magic enough times to know how it worked, and now I'd faced those memories, I knew where Avalin's magic gained its strength. From pain, and suffering. Including my own.

My own pain was still there, even after all these years. After my return, I'd moved on, but here it lingered, in the place where nothing and nobody truly died. Not just my own pain, but everyone who'd suffered here, everyone who no longer had a voice of their own.

I drew on every screaming second of misery spent in

Lord Avalin's castle. Every life snuffed out before my eyes. And I fed them all into the glowing ball of light forming in my hands.

The past couldn't hurt me anymore. It only gave me strength.

I remembered every second of misery and made it my weapon.

Magic overflowed from my fingertips, struck the Sidhe full in the chest and knocked him flat onto his back. His weapon went spinning from his hand, his mouth slack, shocked. He tried to rise and I hit him again, my veins humming with energy. Was this how Lord Avalin had felt all the time, whenever he'd enlisted the same power to inflict torment upon some helpless human?

Was that what the magic wanted? To hurt and to destroy, to wield me like a tool instead of the other way around?

Oh, no. I'm not playing that game.

I knelt and picked up Irene. The bright glow around my hands faded notably, and the wild rush of energy quietened. Velkas lifted his head, but I was already lunging forward, driving the iron blade through the Sidhe lord's neck.

Blood spurted in a blue-red fountain. I lifted the blade, breathing hard, watching the last of his immortal life bleed out. Lord Velkas was no more.

And yet despite the iron, the blue haze of magic remained around me, pulsing with the lingering pain and anger that I'd never truly reckoned with. I knew better than to think I'd ever forget what I'd experienced here, but that didn't mean I'd let that pain rule me forever. Nor would I become its weapon.

"I won," I whispered. "I want those children back."

Were they here in the Vale? Or were they still in Death after all? I turned away from the dead Sidhe, and the clearing greyed out, fog rolling in. I squinted around and then recoiled when a semi-transparent face appeared out of the grey. Definitely *not* a child, but an adult, dressed in what might have been a smart suit, once. He spoke with a masculine voice. "You shouldn't be here."

"I'm looking for two children." Who the hell was this guy? "Are they in here?"

They must be, but the man before me blocked my line of sight, blurred and indistinct yet with enough presence to make me wonder if he was a necromancer. If so, who was he? Definitely not Lord Evander.

"You got lucky once," said the stranger. "I shouldn't allow it to happen again."

"I'm not here for my sake." I tried to catch his eye, but his face all but blended in with the surrounding grey. "Listen, mate, I don't want another fight. I want to take those mortal children back home. I won a bargain with a Sidhe lord. This is my prize."

"Yes… there are two children here," said the strange man. "You were a child, last time."

"You were here." I remembered now. He'd seized my hands, pulled me away from the ghosts trying to drag me into their midst. "You helped me get back home."

"I did." A moment passed, and I had the distinct sense he was looking me up and down, as if to get the measure of me. "You intrigue me. A human with faerie magic… I cannot say I've encountered anything of the sort before."

"I don't care." I gave him a pointed stare. "The children. They're innocent. Send them home."

"Yes." He moved aside, and I glimpsed two shorter figures behind him, hidden in the smoke. "You may take them with you."

"I *may?*" I echoed. "What are you, a necromancer? Is that why you're still here?"

"I was a necromancer in life, yes," said the man.

He's dead, then. No shit, Ivy. I peered over his shoulder as the two small figures moved closer. Their faces came into focus, both terrified, as they clung to one another amid the grey.

"Hey." I extended my hands towards them. "I'm Ivy. You must be Dustin and Melanie. I'll get you out of here."

Slowly they let go of one another. Reached back, until two small hands folded around mine, holding tight. As the greyness began to fade, the necromancer moved to my side, close enough for me to hear his whisper. "I expect I'll see you again soon, Ivy Lane."

"Not on your life. Or death. Whatever." I was done here, and my own voice sounded distant as the last of the grey bled out of the world. "I'm going home."

"Ivy."

I knew that voice.

"Vance." My eyes opened slowly.

"You're alive." There were worse sights to wake up to than Vance Colton leaning over me, his usually immaculate suit covered in dirt and debris. Small cuts marked his face, but he appeared otherwise unhurt. "And… you brought them back."

I twitched my hands, felt two steady pulses against my fingertips. Both children lay on their backs with their eyes closed, but they were undeniably alive.

"That's right." I released their hands, launched to my feet and threw myself at Vance. I could tell I'd taken him by surprise when he went still, and then his arms wrapped around me.

"You saved her. My cousin, Anabel. She's with the others."

I sagged with relief, my arms still around him. "Isabel?"

"Also alive. Once you disappeared, so did the hellhounds, and the ghosts didn't last much longer either."

"Thank god." I leaned my forehead against his chest. He

was warm and solid, his heart racing as fast as mine. "The Ley Line…?"

"Is back to normal, more or less," he said. "The turbulence stopped shortly after you took out that summoning circle."

"Good." Velkas hadn't gathered enough power to rip the way between realms open, in the end. I'd stopped him first.

Vance pried my arms free. "I told you not to stand next to me when I shifted. I might have killed you."

"Think I was more concerned with the oncoming apocalypse." Now I'd stopped using magic, I ached all over like I'd been hurled into the middle of a tornado, and my legs threatened to give out.

"I knew I made the right choice in recruiting you."

I snorted. "In your dreams. In case you've forgotten, you coerced me by threatening my job."

His mouth curved in a frown. "That wasn't my intention. I think the two of us work well together."

The heated spark in his eyes somewhat restored my flagging energy. Was he remembering the kiss, before we'd teleported here? When we'd both thought we wouldn't live to see another day?

He leaned closer. Someone screamed my name. *Isabel.* I lifted my gaze and saw her sitting on the grass next to some of the mages, who were picking apart what remained of the summoning circle.

I turned my back on Vance and ran over to her, all exhaustion forgotten. Crouching, I hugged Isabel, taking care not to jostle her wounded leg. "I thought—"

"You were dead," she finished. "You're the one who walked into the afterlife, Ivy."

"Technically, I walked into Faerie."

"That's even worse." She reached into her pocket. "Do those kids need a healing spell?"

"Maybe." I glanced over at the teenagers, who Vance was

checking on. "I guess being stuck in the afterlife will have had some side effects. The other necromancers… where'd they go?"

"Oh, *they* took off as soon as they dismantled that circle," said Drake, scowling. "Stole the candles, too."

"I mean, they were probably stolen from the guild in the first place." I looked back at the two teenagers, my hands curling into fists. "They didn't even stick around to help those kids. Arseholes."

"They claimed they needed to see to their dead. Two of their people got killed by those ghosts."

Ah, shit. Technically, Vance and I had killed them when they'd been possessed, and while it had been in self-defence, I somehow doubted the necromancers would see it that way. Maybe it was for the best that the other necromancers hadn't stuck around.

Luckily, the two kids soon woke up when Drake started a small fire on the grass to warm them. They were freezing cold but not injured, and the same was true of Vance's cousin. The younger girl wouldn't speak to anyone except him, and all I saw of Anabel Colton was a pair of big grey eyes half-hidden behind a sweep of dark hair.

Some of the mages bore minor injuries, but according to Bailey, the worst had come from Drake crashing the car on the way there.

"I knew you were the one who did that," I said to the fire mage, who pretended not to hear me. "How much damage do you have to pay for?"

"None whatsoever." Drake grinned at Bailey. "Did you and Rod agree on a date yet, or…?"

Bailey went scarlet. "Stop playing matchmaker."

"You didn't answer the question." He swivelled to me next. "What about you and Vance?"

I felt my own face heat up, too. "No comment."

I did notice Bailey and one of the air mages holding hands as they left the scene. While the other mages dispersed, Vance approached me. "You'll need to give a report to the other Mage Lords, I'm afraid. As I was a witness, too, your account doesn't need to be in-depth, but I do need to know what you did in Faerie today. In detail."

"Take those kids back to their parents first," I said. "Please. I'll explain later."

He nodded, to my surprise, and led us to a car waiting at the park's edge. Drake was given the duty of watching the kids in the back while Vance and I sat in front, and he applied himself to entertaining them by conjuring up fireballs.

I'd had an emotionally exhausting day already, and delivering the kids back to their parents damn near finished me off. I had to wipe a couple of tears away when we parted with Swanson's son outside his family home.

Afterwards, we dropped Isabel off at home on the way to the manor. I wanted to go with her, but I'd promised to talk to Vance. Seeing my dilemma, Drake hopped out of the car and volunteered to keep watch outside the house.

"That's not necessary," Isabel protested weakly as she climbed out of the other side. "And please don't throw any fireballs near the garden."

"Drake won't set your remaining flowerbeds on fire, don't worry." I gave Drake himself a warning look, and he grinned and offered a thumbs-up in exchange.

Leaning back against my seat, I glanced over at Vance, but his attention was on his cousin's reflection in the mirror. With Drake gone, she sat alone in the back, her head down. *I hope she's okay.* The poor kid had been through a lot, but Vance would take care of her.

When we reached the manor, Vance instructed the driver

to take his cousin to join the other mages until her parents could come and pick her up.

Then we were alone. *Here we go.*

I took in a breath. "You never asked how I ended up in Faerie."

"I can put two and two together," Vance said. "I looked at your records. You're listed as amongst those killed in the invasion. Your name is on a grave in necromancer territory, along with your parents."

His words pierced me unexpectedly, and I reached for the door handle. "You know, I don't think I want to have this conversation with you. I'll tell the Mage Lords what you need to know, then I'll go."

His hand barred the way. "Wait."

My eyes stung. "I'm not in the mood, Vance. I kept my name because I didn't want the faeries to take away my identity, if that's what you want to know. I've told you everything else."

"I wasn't condemning you," he said. "Or any of the choices you made."

"Sure sounded that way to me." I blinked angry tears from my eyes. "You can find anything else you want to know from the records you took from Larsen. Even *he* wasn't nosy and interfering enough to go looking for my grave."

"You can't work for him anymore." A deep frown formed on his face.

"That's my choice, too." This wasn't how I'd imagined this conversation going. I'd imagined a lot *less* talking, for a start. "Now our arrangement is over, I'm in the clear. I can go back to the guild, or work alone, without having to report to you."

"If that's what you want," he said, "but you have an offer open to work here with the mages, as a freelancer."

"You mean, work for you," I said.

"No, for the mages," he said. "We pay far above the

minimal rates that Larsen does. You'd be compensated for the risks you take, and you'd be allowed to choose which jobs you wanted to pursue."

His offer was exactly what I needed. Which was precisely the problem. I'd cut all ties with the mercenaries, and while I could find my own clients, there'd be a rough transition period, made tougher by the damage those fire imps had inflicted on our house. Working for the mages would take some of the burden off, but there were a hundred and one reasons that interacting with Vance Colton on a daily basis was a *really* bad idea. Even if the mages' protection would come in useful after all the enemies I'd added to my list over the last few days.

"I still haven't officially quit my last job yet," I evaded. "I need to tell Larsen to go fuck himself."

"I'd like to see that." A gleam entered his eyes. His smile invited me to ask, to push this further. To pick up where we'd left off before the fight.

"You haven't won this," I informed him. "I don't take kindly to people snooping into my life."

"Not even if they're curious?" He tilted his head.

"You could have just asked me."

"Could I really? Up until recently, I wasn't sure you weren't a dangerous enemy to the mages. I had to be certain. You're... a difficult woman to read." The gleam in his eyes turned deeper, more intense.

"I'm choosing to take that as a compliment."

He tucked a strand of hair behind my ear. I was too startled to react as his lips lightly brushed against mine. My heart rate kicked up again, and all sensible thoughts melted away. This wasn't a *we might die in five minutes* kiss. This was a tease, a promise of more, and damn, was I along for the ride.

"Lord Colton!" someone called from the manor.

I let go of Vance's shoulders, and he gave me a look that said quite clearly, *We'll pick this up later.*

We'd better, I thought, climbing out of the car.

———

I woke up the following morning after a surprisingly refreshing night's sleep to the sound of Erwin the piskie flying around the living room, shrieking at full volume. "I'm home!"

"Erwin." I jumped out of the bed and opened the door, just as the piskie flew full-tilt into the ceiling light and nearly knocked himself out cold. "I thought those imps killed you."

"Not dead!" He flew downward, cross-eyed. "Hiding!"

Would you believe I was glad to see the little bugger alive? Isabel was back on her feet, too, and already baking cookies. As much as I wanted to stay and share in the deliciousness, I had an ex-boss to see.

I dragged myself to the guild straight after breakfast. The red-brick building looked the same as ever, though I'd been told the majority of the mercs had hidden inside there when shit hit the fan the previous day. The necromancers had managed to keep the undead from leaving the cemetery and flooding the town, but everyone had felt the disturbance when the realms had briefly collided. The faeries certainly knew, and I didn't know how many of them Velkas had interacted with. How many he'd swayed with empty promises of immortality.

As for me, being alive was more than enough.

I pushed open the door to the mercenary guild with my head high and my sword at my waist.

"You." Larsen greeted me in the doorway. Nobody else was in the lobby. I'd heard a few mercs had quit overnight, as the rumours began to spread about the guild's involvement with yesterday's attacks. Rumours I suspected Vance had encouraged, if not started.

"Surprised to see me alive?"

"No," he said. "Why would you think that?"

"Let's not waste time," I said. "You nearly got me killed. Your people damaged my property, put my flatmates in danger, and lured the faeries to my home. I'll certainly never be working for you again."

Larsen's mouth twisted. "You're a fool. There are no other jobs for people like you."

"I beg to differ," I said. "I've just received a generous offer from the Mage Lord himself to start a full-time freelance position, and I'm considering accepting."

He gaped at me. "What?"

"You heard me." I removed my hand from my sword long enough to display the blue light igniting in my palm. "And just in case you were thinking of ever coming near me again, I have faerie magic, and I know how to use it."

I turned on my heel and left, the door swinging shut behind me. I doubted I'd seen the last of him, but a pissed-off human was the least of my problems.

Besides, I wasn't alone. When my phone buzzed, I hit the 'accept call' button. "Good timing. I just left the guild."

"How'd it go?" asked Vance.

"As of today, I'm temporarily unemployed."

"Temporarily means you're considering my offer?"

"Yes," I answered. "But with conditions. I'll tell you about them later."

"Done," he said. "Are you free tomorrow?"

"Of course. No job, remember?"

"How about we continue our conversation from yesterday?"

By 'conversation', I imagined one of the non-verbal variety. That, I could get on board with. "That seems adequate."

His chuckle vibrated through the phone. "I'll pick you up at seven."

Well, that was something. Or possibly a lot more than something. I grinned to myself as the call ended.

This wasn't over. Now I'd drawn their attention, the faeries wouldn't so easily forget my name. I still owed the Lady of the Tree a favour, for a start, and Velkas's death would have a ripple effect, both here and on the other side of the veil.

But for now, the day was mine. And it was about damn time I told Isabel what had really happened to me in Faerie.

ABOUT THE AUTHOR

Emma is the New York Times and USA Today Bestselling author of the Changeling Chronicles urban fantasy series.

Emma spent her childhood creating imaginary worlds to compensate for a disappointingly average reality, so it was probably inevitable that she ended up writing fantasy novels. When she's not immersed in her own fictional universes, Emma can be found with her head in a book or wandering around the world in search of adventure.

Find out more about Emma's books at www. emmaladams.com.

"Ivy."

I knew that voice.

"Vance." My eyes opened slowly.

"You're alive." There were worse sights to wake up to than Vance Colton leaning over me, his usually immaculate suit covered in dirt and debris. Small cuts marked his face, but he appeared otherwise unhurt. "And… you brought them back."

I twitched my hands, felt two steady pulses against my fingertips. Both children lay on their backs with their eyes closed, but they were undeniably alive.

"That's right." I released their hands, launched to my feet and threw myself at Vance. I could tell I'd taken him by surprise when he went still, and then his arms wrapped around me.

"You saved her. My cousin, Anabel. She's with the others."

I sagged with relief, my arms still around him. "Isabel?"

"Also alive. Once you disappeared, so did the hellhounds, and the ghosts didn't last much longer either."

"Thank god." I leaned my forehead against his chest. He

He's dead, then. No shit, Ivy. I peered over his shoulder as the two small figures moved closer. Their faces came into focus, both terrified, as they clung to one another amid the grey.

"Hey." I extended my hands towards them. "I'm Ivy. You must be Dustin and Melanie. I'll get you out of here."

Slowly they let go of one another. Reached back, until two small hands folded around mine, holding tight. As the greyness began to fade, the necromancer moved to my side, close enough for me to hear his whisper. "I expect I'll see you again soon, Ivy Lane."

"Not on your life. Or death. Whatever." I was done here, and my own voice sounded distant as the last of the grey bled out of the world. "I'm going home."

9 781915 250513